THE FORGOTTEN TEMPLE

The Lost Riders

Book 3

JASPER ALDEN

D.K. HOLMBERG

ASH
PUBLISHING

Chapter One

SOARING HIGH IN THE SKIES ABOVE THE TOWN OF Mysteria, Hal Norath wondered who invited the circus to town.

The late winter air bit his exposed cheeks as he watched the large convoy of wagons making its way up the Desolate Tops. The newcomers had been reported by scouts a couple of hours ago. They weren't nomads – their route was too direct.

Hal was worried that they could be Malarsan mages in disguise. The war against Queen Bariwa's forces had grown worse over the past two months, and Hal wouldn't put anything past her.

There were four wagons drawn by strange creatures that looked like a combination of elephants and goats. He also counted twenty people, though there could be more sheltering inside the carriages.

The wagons themselves were decked in pastel colors: blue, pink, and white. The men directing them had brightly colored hair and wore expressive costumes that made them stand out like a bloodstain on a white bed sheet. The men who walked on either side of the caravans had swords sheathed at their sides, their armor glinting with deep metallic reds and blues.

Wow, said a familiar voice in Hal's head. *Those guys make even your royalty's clothing look modest.*

Hal looked down at the dragon he rode upon. The yellow dragon, closer in size to a large horse rather than a normal dragon, flapped his wings furiously to keep them both afloat. His dragonic eyes also gazed at the caravan below as they circled the clouds above, close enough to keep the caravan in sight but far enough to make sure that the travelers couldn't see *them.*

Unlike the travelers below, Hal felt perfectly warm sitting on his dragon's back, thanks to the natural heat which dragons' bodies produced. Especially in cold weather like today, although Hal still made sure to put on the warm pelts that his mentor and friend Old Snow had made for him not long ago.

Hal smirked. *Says the gold dragon.*

Keershan grunted. *I'm not even complaining. We've been away from human civilization for so long that I've forgotten just how extravagant your people can get. Anija would probably look good in the pastel pink.*

Hal rolled his eyes. *Please take this mission seriously.*

Hal felt a sense of disapproval rumble through Keershan's mind. *I still don't think it's a good idea, unless getting killed is the plan.*

Hal sighed. He and Keershan had had this argument about a dozen times already over the last two months and still hadn't made any headway. In Hal's experience, bonding with a dragon didn't make them any less stubborn. *Never mind. We have bigger fish to fry. Like the caravan below.*

A flapping of wings filled Hal's ears, and two more pairs of Dragon Riders and Steeds entered the clouds with him.

Anija, dressed in pelts similar to himself, sat on the back of a black dragon that was massive even by dragon standards. The red-haired woman had a bow-and-arrow slung over her back, her relic necklace glinting in the dim light.

"Hey, dear leader," Anija said as her dragon hovered nearby, flapping her wings with even more power than Keershan. She gestured at the caravan below. "What's the plan? Do we incinerate them all now and dig through the ashes for clues later or introduce ourselves like civilized beings and ask them to identify themselves?"

Hal grimaced. "Very funny, Anija. Keershan and I were just debating that."

"You mean you *still* haven't made a decision?" Anija said. She shook her head. "So indecisive."

"Keershan has always been indecisive," the black dragon replied in a deep but distinctly feminine voice. "I am not surprised that his Rider shares that nature."

"It's not about indecision," Hal said, "but prudence. We can't just attack every group of people that comes within ten miles of our territory without first making sure they are enemies."

"In case you forgot, we're in the middle of a war for

survival. Every second we let them get closer to the town is another second we put our own people in danger."

Hal scowled. "I know that, Anija, but—"

"Can't we please get along? I hate seeing you guys argue."

Hal turned his attention to the other Dragon Rider who had accompanied them. He was younger than Hal and Anija by a good five years or so, but he looked older, thanks in part to his short, black beard and sideburns. A shiny golden bracelet tied tightly around his left wrist had the symbol of a dragon on it while a broadsword was strapped to his back. His dark eyes were intense but sincere, matching the eyes of the gray dragon he rode upon.

"Sorry, Cav," Hal said. "You're right. Arguing will get us nowhere."

"I don't know," Anija said with a shrug, "I kind of like it. Lot more interesting than everyone getting along and having a nice time."

Cavrieo Solaki, the Dragon Rider in question, frowned at Anija. "Maybe, but it also won't help us determine if the people below are friends or enemies. Right, Onito?"

Onito, which was the name of his gray dragon Steed, nodded and rumbled in a voice that was high for a dragon, "Aye. I sense no hostile intentions from the people below. But humans are very good at concealing their true thoughts, I've noticed."

Hal frowned and glanced down at the caravan. Though he, too, did not think the caravan was a threat, he agreed with Onito that it was suspicious nonetheless.

That was one of the things that Hal appreciated about Cav and Onito. Though Cav may have been young—having just graduated from the Malarsan Military Academy a year ago—he had a surprisingly solid, down-to-earth head on his shoulders. And Onito, an elderly dragon who had been a close friend of the previous Clawfoot Clan chief, had turned out to be the perfect match for him during the bonding shortly after the Battle of Dragon Valley, hence why Hal had brought those two with him on this mission.

Hal said, "The only way to know for sure is to go down and ask them."

"Excellent," Anija said, a vicious smile crossing her features as she looked down at the caravan. "I can't wait to see the looks on their faces when they see three dragons—"

"I'm going down. Alone."

Anija's eyes darted back to Hal so fast it was like some sort of magnet drew them to him. "Alone? But what if they attack you? Do you really want to put your own safety in the hands of a bunch of strange-looking foreigners?"

"Anija has a point," said Rialo. "Though I do not doubt your competence, Hal, there are at least twenty of them versus two of you. They may even have magic we do not know about, as they do not appear to be from Malarsan."

"That's why you guys need to stay close," Hal said, gesturing at the skies around them. "If they attack me, you guys can swoop in and protect me."

Anija chuckled. "Yeah. Like *anyone* would want to

form an alliance with those 'brigands' who 'murdered' General Omaros and pose—what was the phrasing?—an 'existential threat' to the kingdom's existence."

Hal frowned at Anija. "I thought you only read Queen Bariwa's announcement of the end of the Dragon War once."

"Point is," Anija continued, "that I think 'attack first and ask questions later' is a perfectly valid wartime tactic."

"Says the woman who didn't join the army and has zero military training," Hal shot back. "You do know there is more to war than fighting and killing, right?"

Anija rolled her eyes. "Fine. Do what you want. But if I see them do *anything* suspicious, our dragons will be having fried foreigner tonight."

Hal nodded and then urged Keershan toward the ground. Keershan immediately obeyed, heading toward the path directly before the caravan.

As they flew, Hal looked over his shoulder. Anija and Cav's forms, along with those of their dragons, soon disappeared into the clouds behind them, vanishing from view entirely, though Hal knew they were still there.

You do know that Anija cares about you, right? Keershan said, his voice in Hal's mind suddenly.

Hal looked down at Keershan. *What?*

She cares, Keershan repeated. *Plus, her bond with Rialo is probably amplifying it.*

Hal groaned. *We don't have time for this.*

Fair enough, Keershan said. *But if you ever want relationship advice, I can give it to you. I read lots of romantic myths and legends during my studies. Most end tragically, but maybe yours won't.*

Hal didn't even bother to respond to that one.

When Hal and Keershan landed before the caravan, the response was immediate. The wagons came to abrupt stops, nearly running into each other or going into ditches on either side of the rough path. The odd elephant-like mounts reared up and made hissing noises, their large hooves stomping on the ground. The drivers cursed in a strange language that certainly wasn't Malarsan.

The guards immediately formed a tight wall in front of Hal and Keershan, drawing notched swords from their belts which glowed with an odd light.

"Halt!" Hal said, holding up a hand. "We do not mean you any harm. I am Halar Norath, leader of the Dragon Riders of Mysteria. State your names and business."

The guards, who did not seem impressed by Hal's boasting, immediately started chattering among themselves. Their tone was far from hostile or terrified.

In fact, it sounded excited.

One of the guards broke off from the rest and ran back to the nearest wagon. Its driver nodded and pulled on some kind of rope. A small set of wooden steps fell out of the wagon's entrance and landed on the road with a *thud*, and a second later, a figure stepped out from under the wagon's protective covering.

The figure was odd-looking even by the standards of his fellow travelers. He was covered from head to toe in a mixture of thick winter coats and bundled robes that made him look more like a walking pile of cloth than a human being. A broad-brimmed hat covered his head, and his face was wrapped with some sort of scarf. The only exposed parts were his striking yellow eyes.

The figure moved with relative grace, however, walking down the steps without issue. He spoke with the guard, who once again gestured at Hal, then said something that sounded like a dismissal, before walking over to the guard wall with the guard.

While the guard took his position with the rest of his fellow guards, the robed figure kept walking until he was approximately ten feet in front of the wall. That seemed odd to Hal, as he did not see any weapons on the robed figure. Perhaps the figure wasn't afraid of them.

A strong perfume, like roses in full bloom, wafted off the figure so much that Hal had to wrinkle his nose. He was so used to the stench of Mysteria that smelling something good made him feel a little sick.

"Hello," said the robed figure in an unfamiliar accent. "You are Halar Norath, leader of the legendary Dragon Riders, yes? That is what my bodyguards tell me, though their lack of understanding of your language means I needed to verify it for myself."

Hal frowned. The robed figure's accent made his words sound strange, but his Malarsan was surprisingly good. "Your bodyguards heard correctly. You can trust them."

"Good to know," said the robed figure. "Of course, I trust them with my life, but as we say up north, never believe a child's imagination, yes?"

Before Hal could respond to that, the robed figure's

gaze shifted to Keershan, and he made a whistling noise. "You really *do* ride a dragon, and a rather handsome dragon it is. Seems like our reports did no justice to the majesty of the Malarsan dragons."

"Uh, thanks for the compliments," Keershan said, who sounded as off-balance as Hal was. "Though I am rather small for a dragon."

"And they even have manners and humility!" said the robed figure. He clapped his hands together excitedly. "Oh, His Iciness will be so pleased to hear this, to know that we are not chasing a myth or legend, but real flesh-and-blood beings."

"That's nice," Hal said, "but in Malarsan, it is typically considered polite to introduce oneself *first* before you start celebrating."

The robed figure brought his gloved hands close to what Hal assumed was the man's mouth. "Excuse my rudeness! We have simply traveled such a far way and through such difficult circumstances that we were starting to lose faith. Thus, seeing you is proof that we did not waste our time, resources, and, in some cases, our very lives, to travel all the way out here."

Hal raised an eyebrow. "Sounds like you had quite the journey. Where are you from?"

With a sweeping bow, the robed figure said, "I am Inquirer Dedeket, close confidant and adviser to Glaci Emperor Kryo Kardia Himself, God-Emperor of the Glaci Empire and Defender of the Seven Realms. And I am here on a diplomatic mission to offer the Dragon Riders of Malarsan our support."

Chapter Two

Now it made sense. Hal had thought that Dedeket and his men looked familiar but, until this moment, had not been able to place exactly where they were from.

And now he was almost wishing that he'd followed Anija's initial advice of torching them.

It might have been less trouble than talking to them.

Keershan, on the other hand, did not appear to know who they were, because he said, "Glaci Empire. That name sounds vaguely familiar to me, though I can't place it."

Dedeket rose to his full height again with surprising grace and fluidity. "Why, everyone, human and dragon alike, has heard of the Glaci Empire! When you feel the north wind closing in, when the sun shines weaker and a chill settles in the air, when the waters start to freeze over, know that the boots of the Glacian Imperial Army are marching across your land, all for the glory of the God-Emperor Kryo Kardia Himself!"

Keershan blinked. "Impressive speech, though I still do not quite know who you are."

"The Glaci Empire is an empire from the far north," Hal said, causing Keershan to glance up at him. "They are one of the largest human empires in the world and a veritable force to be reckoned with. Malarsan has often come into conflict with them over various territories because the kingdom's borders go up against Glacian territory."

"You speak true knowledge about my people, Dragon Rider Halar Norath," said Dedeket in an impressed voice. "Someone has done their homework."

"Before becoming a Dragon Rider, I worked as a Relic Hunter in the Malarsan Army," Hal replied. "Never dealt with any Glacians myself, but I heard lots of stories from my superior officers about how ruthless your own soldiers can be. The slaughter at Blood Ridge still gives me nightmares sometimes."

Dedeket chuckled. "Yes, Glacians do have a reputation for our strength and efficiency. If your empire had been born in the heart of the least hospitable terrain to human life in all the world, then I'd imagine your people would have turned out the same."

Keershan tilted his head to the side. "Did you say that your ruler is named God-Emperor Kryo Kardia?"

"I've heard of him as well," Hal said with a nod. "He's the founder of the Glaci Empire. Some say he's immortal and others that he is a god, hence the title, though I understand that he doesn't usually make public appearances."

"Indeed, he does not," Dedeket agreed. "After all, the

gods themselves rarely put in appearances, so why should His Iciness ever lower himself to our level? His ways are greater than ours."

"I also heard that he has personally killed thousands of people," Hal said. He locked eyes with Dedeket. "But, of course, that is just rumor."

Dedeket did not look taken aback by Hal's comment. "His Iciness has never taken a life unjustly. All who live in His domain live only because He wills it. Should He ever will otherwise, the glorious Glaci Empire will exist no more. Even the dragons within our borders exist only at His pleasure."

Hal nodded, though more out of politeness than agreement. He knew from listening to his fellow soldiers that the Glaci Empire's cruelty was beyond even that of the dragons. Though Dedeket had yet to threaten them, Hal still didn't trust the oddly dressed Glacian.

"What brings you all the way from the Glaci Empire?" Keershan asked. "It sounds like you traveled a long way."

Dedeket nodded. "Indeed we did! We came to see if the rumors that the wintry winds had brought into the ears of His Majesty were true, that a group of humans and dragons had banded together to form the legendary Dragon Riders, and that said group was fomenting a rebellion against the Malarsan royal family."

Hal raised an eyebrow. "We haven't sent news up north, or anywhere, actually, about the Dragon Riders. We've been a bit too busy with that rebellion you mentioned to do that."

Dedeket folded his arms in front of his chest. "So it

would appear that the rumors are true. His Majesty will be more than pleased to hear this, for He has always had His eyes on Malarsan, which has been a persistent thorn in His side for over a hundred years."

Hal narrowed his eyes. "If you are planning to invade the kingdom to add it to your empire, then perhaps you should turn around now while you still can."

Dedeket laughed, a shrill sound like ice breaking. "Apologies for the misunderstanding! Though part of my inquirer education involved learning how to speak over a hundred different foreign languages fluently, I still find foreign phrasing a bit hard to remember. I did not mean to imply that His Iciness planned to invade your country or add it to the empire, even though that would indeed be a good thing. I simply meant that His Iciness is sympathetic to your struggles and wishes to offer you support."

"Support?" Keershan questioned. "What kind of support?"

Dedeket gestured at the wagons behind him. "Why, the riches of the Glaci Empire, of course! Hundreds of pounds of gold, some choice weapons and armor for your men, even some spell books that your mages would no doubt wish to study, along with many other priceless items that you cannot find anywhere else in the world. A veritable kingdom's treasure, all for you."

Hal looked at the wagons himself with surprise and skepticism. "You mean you're just going to *give* us this stuff? Because Kryo Kardia likes us?"

"Because His Iciness is benevolent and sympathetic to your struggles," Dedeket added. "His Majesty has always known that the Malarsan royal family dabbled in the darkest arts, but the rumors we've heard—of demons stalking the lands, men selling their souls for blasphemous power, the queen attempting to resurrect a long-dead demonic god—have troubled His heart more so than it already was."

Now Hal was even more suspicious. Despite Dedeket's description that those were just 'rumors,' they were too accurate to be mere hearsay.

Are there Glacian spies in the kingdom, sending news back to Kryo Kardia? Captain claimed those were just rumors, but maybe there's more truth to them than I thought.

"And, of course, we have heard of your personal struggles," Dedeket continued. "How you have been forced to hide in the Desolate Tops, almost totally isolated from human civilization, with access to resources very limited. Should you accept this gift, then we'd be happy to continue to fund and support your efforts to topple the Malarsan royal family, and even aid you in reconstructing your land after this terrible conflict is finished. It would be a wonderful opportunity to establish close and peaceful relations with the Kingdom of Malarsan. Wouldn't you agree, Hal?"

Hal noticed Dedeket use his name like they were old friends, even though he had never seen Dedeket until today.

And he had to admit that Dedeket's offer was tempting.

Over the last two months since the Battle of Dragon Valley, acquiring resources to support their little group of Dragon Riders had been taxing. Though Old Snow knew the Desolate Tops well, it was still a struggle to survive out in the wilderness.

Even Keershan seemed tempted by Dedeket's offer. His green eyes darted toward the wagons. "That's a rather generous offer from your leader. And we sure could use those resources."

"But what's the catch?" Hal said. "What does Kryo Kardia want, in other words?"

Dedeket put a hand on his chest, seemingly in surprise. "His Iciness wants nothing except to see the Kingdom of Malarsan restored to its original glory and to be ruled justly and fairly. As I said, his heart aches at the knowledge that a ragtag band of rebels like you—no offense intended—is having to struggle to survive in the wilderness while your enemies live in luxury and with near-limitless resources."

Hal eyed Dedeket carefully. "I suppose it would also benefit Kryo Kardia if we were to successfully overthrow Queen Bariwa and establish our own government. Perhaps it would even give Kryo Kardia another kingdom to add to his empire."

Keershan looked up at Hal in surprise. "Hal, what are you talking about? These people are promising to give us their support in exchange for badly needed resources. This may be a gift from the gods themselves, for all we know."

"I know, Keershan," Hal said, though he didn't take his eyes off of Dedeket. "But I also know that in politics, things are rarely as they seem, especially with the Glaci Empire. How many nations and kingdoms have lost their indepen-

dence because Kryo Kardia offered them seemingly uncon-
ditional support in their time of need? There's a reason the
Glaci Empire's name is feared throughout the world."

Dedeket kept very still, though his eyes seemed to
glow. "Please, Halar. If His Iciness wished to add
Malarsan to His empire, then we wouldn't even be
having this discussion right now. Or perhaps we would,
but in the Glacian language, which I find to be a more
elegant tongue than the clumsy words of Malarsan."

Hal nodded, but before he could respond to that, a
commotion rose up from among the guards behind
Dedeket.

A young girl—who couldn't have been older than six
or seven—had somehow sneaked past the guards and
was running toward Dedeket. Dressed in colorful, thick
robes, the girl had long, snow-white hair that flew out
freely behind her. Her face was partially hidden under a
hood, though Hal caught a glimpse of skin as white as
snow and big, childish eyes that were the same colors as
Dedeket's.

The girl ran into Dedeket's legs hard enough to
nearly make the inquirer fall. She hugged him fiercely.

"Jinka?" said Dedeket. He pulled her off him and,
hands on her shoulders, glared at her. "I thought I told
you to stay put in the wagon."

"I just wanted to see the dragon."

As Jinka spoke, she glanced shyly at Keershan, who
just blinked back at her in puzzlement. Hal didn't quite
know what to make of the little girl, either, as he wasn't
good with kids.

Dedeket, on the other hand, let out a long-suffering

sigh. He looked at the guard who had been chasing Jinka. "Take her back to the wagon. And next time, don't let her leave unless I give her permission."

The guard nodded apologetically and, taking Jinka's hand, led her back toward the wagons. Jinka kept glancing over her shoulder at Keershan, at least until she nearly stumbled a few times. When the guard helped her back into the wagon, she gave one last look toward Hal and Keershan before disappearing inside.

Dedeket sighed again and turned to face Hal and Keershan. "Apologies. There aren't many dragons up north, so my daughter has never seen one before. She can be very troublesome, even if she is as cute as a snow rabbit."

Hal pursed his lips. He had not expected to see a fatherly side of Dedeket, but it did make him feel a little bad about being so harsh with him before. Though Hal was not a father himself, he missed his late father terribly and found himself appreciating that Dedeket, though a bit stern, seemed to love his daughter nonetheless.

Even so, Hal said, "Thanks for the offer, but can we have time to think about it? I want to discuss this with the other council members first before making any decisions."

Dedeket tilted his head to the side. "You mean you are not the sole leader of the Dragon Riders?"

Hal grunted. "It's complicated. How do we stay in touch?"

Dedeket held up what looked like a notecard and threw it at Hal, who looked at it closely.

It was made with the sort of thick stationery only

used by royalty, and showed a snowflake crossed with a heart in icy blue paint.

Hal looked up at Dedeket. "This is—?"

"A Calling Card," said Dedeket. "Throw it into any fire and you will be granted automatic access to His Iciness Himself."

Hal raised an eyebrow. "Never heard of magic like that."

Dedeket's eyes gleamed from within his hooded face. "Because Glacian magic is far more advanced than your Malarsan kind. In any case, keep it safe. His Iciness doesn't like it when we hand these out willy-nilly."

Hal put the Calling Card into a pocket in his leather shirt for safekeeping. "Fair enough. Will you guys be nearby, should we need to contact you?"

"Aye," said Dedeket. He gestured at the wagon. "We can stay as long as necessary for you to make a decision."

"You could stay within the walls of Mysteria with us," Keershan offered. "We have plenty of room for your people and it's much safer than being out in the Desolate Tops."

Dedeket shook his head. "Thank you for your generosity, but we can take care of ourselves."

Hal glanced up at the snow clouds overhead but decided to take Dedeket's words at face value.

"All right," Hal said at last. "But if you need help, we aren't too much farther up the mountains."

Dedeket chuckled. "Trust me, Halar Norath, if even half the rumors I've heard about your group are true, we aren't the ones who are in need of help."

Hal nodded. "Perhaps."

Dedeket hesitated. "By the way, what does the term 'Mysteria' mean? My research failed to come up with a proper etymology for that word."

"It's the town's original name before it was abandoned," Keershan explained. "We wanted to honor the original Dragon Riders who came before us."

"Fascinating," said Dedeket. Then he bowed deeply again, the tips of his scarves touching the ground. "May His cold wind strike freezing fear in the hearts of your enemies."

With that, Dedeket turned and walked back toward the caravan, humming some tune under his breath that Hal had never heard before.

As Dedeket walked away, Hal felt the Calling Card in his pocket. Although he wasn't entirely sure that the Glacians would be fine out here on their own, one thing Dedeket said *was* true: They needed help.

Badly.

Chapter Three

"LET ME GET THIS STRAIGHT," SURRELS SAID A COUPLE of hours later. Sitting at the main table, with his arms folded in front of his chest, he squinted his weaselly eyes. "These Glacians were sent by God-Emperor Kryo Kardia himself to offer us the Glaci Empire's support and resources in exchange for establishing peaceful diplomatic relations between Malarsan and the Glaci Empire. As an upfront payment of sorts, they offered you four wagons full of gold, weapons, equipment, and enough money to fund an entire army."

Hal, sitting in his stone seat across from Surrels, nodded. "That's about it, yes."

Surrels leaned forward across the table, a glint of greed in his eyes. "Then I say we take it! Though I'm not exactly a fan of the Glacians myself, if Kryo Kardia himself is willing to support us, then that will solve most of our resource issues in one go."

Anija, who sat on the right side of the table, shook

her head. "I don't trust those bastards. Knew a few rogue Glacians in the Dark Tigers. Those guys are very persuasive, especially when they're stabbing you in the back."

Surrels glared at Anija. "You didn't talk to them, did you? So how do you know if they were genuine or not?"

Hal said, "Their offer, I think, *was* genuine, but I have to admit I am hesitant, which is why I am bringing it to you guys."

Seated around the old stone table were what the other Dragon Riders had come to refer to as the 'council,' which was largely made up of Hal's close friends and allies.

They were meeting in the Forgotten Temple, an ancient building that had been dedicated to the Dragon Riders of the previous age. Though unfit for human habitation, it served as an excellent meeting place, as it was centrally located in the town and had enough room not just for humans, but dragons as well.

Rialo and Keershan sat several feet away from the table—an object which Hal and the others had discovered in a hidden storage room in the temple—their heads down and their tails flicking back and forth. Neither of them had said much since the meeting started, though Hal knew they were both listening closely.

"I'm glad you did, Hal," Fralia said. She brushed her long dark hair out of her face. "My father once told me that Glacians had freezing fingers."

Hal looked at Fralia in confusion. "What does that mean?"

She raised her fingers and placed them against the cold, smooth surface of the table. "It's an expression meaning that if you make a deal with them, the Glacians won't let you out of it. Even if it ends up not working out the way you expect it to."

Surrels snorted. "Why don't we ask what Old Snow thinks? Surely he's had experience with the Glacians. Right, Old Snow?"

Surrels's words were directed to the elderly looking man who sat at the other end of the table. With a short, snow-white beard and brown traveling robes and a hood, the old man did not look much different from your typical mountain hunter.

The old man nodded. "Back when I was king, I spoke with Kryo Kardia occasionally. Usually whenever there was some sort of territorial dispute between the kingdom and his empire or when negotiating trade deals and relations. And most of the time, I'd be speaking with one of his diplomats, rather than the God-Emperor himself."

Hal looked at Old Snow in surprise. This was the first time he'd heard Old Snow talk in detail about his time as King Rikas Bariwa, former king of Malarsan. Though Hal had known that fact about Old Snow for several months now, Old Snow had refused to speak much about his time as king except in the most general and vague of terms.

The Glaci Empire must be serious if Old Snow is willing to talk about them, Keershan said in Hal's mind.

Hal glanced at Keershan. *I know. And I'm not sure I like it.*

"So what's he like?" Anija said. "Is he *really* a god, or is that just propaganda?"

"I am not sure. Kryo Kardia has ruled the Glaci Empire since its founding five hundred years ago."

"How old *is* this bloke?" Anija said in disbelief.

A thoughtful look crossed Fralia's face. "It's not quite as impossible as it sounds. Magical theorists have suggested that there are certain spells and magical techniques to extend one's lifespan. Granted, it's an area that Malarsan mages haven't studied in depth due to our ongoing war with the dragons, but it's possible that mages outside of Malarsan *have* figured that out."

"Regardless, this is a typical Glacian move," Old Snow noted. "Reach out to dissident or rebel groups in an enemy country, offer them support in exchange for peaceful relations when the rebel group is in charge. And then, once the rebellion is successful and a new government is established, take over said country from its new government, and annex it to the Glaci Empire."

Anija snorted. "While I can appreciate a good deception as much as anyone, that still seems like too much work to me. If I were in charge of the world's biggest empire, I don't see why I'd bother politicking when I could just crush any country myself."

Old Snow shook his head. "Kryo Kardia dislikes wasting his resources. Think of it from his point of view. He could either attempt a full-scale invasion of Malarsan —which would involve considerable sacrifice of time, resources, and manpower even if the invasion is successful—or weaken the country from within. It is cheaper to fund rebel groups than it is to use your own soldiers. And even if the rebellion fails, it often weakens a country enough to make it easier for a normal invasion anyway."

Hal grimaced. "I knew that Kryo Kardia was very politically savvy, but I didn't realize he was *that* good."

Old Snow nodded. "Yes. Why else would the Glaci Empire be so powerful? Empires are not created accidentally, after all. I should know. I was the one who reached out to Kryo Kardia first."

Everyone looked at Old Snow in shock.

Anija said, "What the hell, old man?"

Hal gave Old Snow a hard look. "I don't remember you telling us you were going to reach out to the Glaci Empire."

Old Snow did not look very ashamed of his decision. "I didn't know if Kryo would listen to me or not. He usually doesn't have time for former royalty like me."

"Still, you should have at least warned us," Hal said. "Anija here was this close to blowing them to bits."

"Perhaps I *should* have, if they're as sneaky as Old Snow says they are," Anija said. She looked at Hal. "Where did the Glacians say they were making camp?"

Old Snow held up his hands. "I know, but I was just trying to find help. As Surrels pointed out, we are in a very fragile position, and we need all the resources we can get."

Hal frowned, but he could not disagree with that statement.

Two months ago, Hal had managed to convince several dragons, along with a small chunk of the Malarsan Army, to join them in their battle against Queen Marial

Bariwa. They'd even managed to acquire a large number of relics, which they had used to bond several new pairs of Dragon Riders and Steeds together. That brought the total number of Dragon Riders to twelve, which was impressive because there had only been two Dragon Riders—himself and Anija—only a couple of months ago.

Unfortunately, their overall numbers were still quite small. Last Hal counted, they had maybe a couple thousand soldiers, versus the tens of thousands that served Queen Bariwa. The queen's forces had managed to enslave a good chunk of dragons, and their number of mages was considerably greater.

And that doesn't take into account the demons, either, which we still don't know how many they have.

Feeding and watering over a thousand humans, plus about three dozen dragons, was not an easy task under ordinary circumstances. But up in the Desolate Tops—the largest mountain range in Malarsan that was inhospitable to human and dragon life alike—it was damn near impossible. The only reason they'd survived at all was because of the mages, whose magical skills had been useful in finding water sources and other resources that the new camp needed to survive.

But we all know just how precarious our situation is. Hal looked around the table at the council. *Every one of us.*

"If it helps, I reached out to other neighboring kingdoms for help, but no one has responded yet."

"Probably because they don't want to piss off your ex-wife," Surrels said with a chuckle.

"I can't be the only one wondering how we got to the

point where we feel the need to ask one of the most brutal dictators in the world for help."

Old Snow nodded. "I understand your concern, but if there is one thing I learned in politics, it is that sometimes you have to work with bad people to stop *worse* people."

"Let's table this for now," Hal said. He looked around the table. "Progress reports. Who wants to go first?"

Anija raised a hand. "Our spies in the capital say that celebrations all over the kingdom have cropped up since Queen Bariwa declared the end of the Dragon War. Tons of people are apparently naming their newborn children after Marial or one of the generals, and some cities and villages have even made 'Dragon's Day' a new holiday to celebrate."

Hal grimaced. "What about our public perception?"

Anija laughed. "Still in the mud. Apparently, we're 'dangerous rebels' who have been 'seduced' by the few dragons that were not enslaved by Queen Bariwa's relic-wearers, and citizens are being urged to report any sightings of us to the authorities. Oh, and apparently we all have really big bounties on our heads."

"On the other hand," Fralia said, raising her hand, "magical training has gone well. I've been able to take some of the less able mages and raise their skill to the point where they're almost as good as me. Plus, we just discovered another water source near the town, which we're constructing a well around." Then Fralia frowned. "On the other hand, without the proper books, learning and teaching new spells is difficult."

Hal didn't know how to address that without stealing the books from the mage schools.

And that would be a really good way to make ourselves look even worse *in the public eye.*

Hal then turned his attention to Surrels. "Report on defense?"

Surrels sat up a little straighter. "Not much to report. The scouts have not reported seeing any demonic forces near the town, nor have our sky scouts reported on any dragon activity. We've been going through basic drills and tactics, but trying to make a cohesive army out of humans and dragons that hated each other's guts before recently has been challenging, to say the least."

Hal knew what Surrels meant. For the last five thousand years, humans and dragons had hated and warred with each other all over the world. It wasn't until recently that Hal himself had learned about the Dragon Riders and how humanity and dragonkind were meant to be one, but that truth was easier said than put into practice.

"Plus, the rate of bonding has dropped," Surrels added. "Actually, it's fallen through the floor."

"Are we out of relics already?" asked Hal worriedly.

"We still have about two dozen relics left, but not too many volunteers. Both humans and dragons seem to be happy with staying separate. Our newest bonded pair was two weeks ago, and I haven't gotten a peep from anyone, human or dragon, since."

Hal's hands balled into fists under the table. He'd hoped that the humans and dragons would be willing to put aside their prejudices long enough to at least try to bond, but it seemed like their prejudice was running even deeper than he thought.

How do we convince them to keep bonding? We need as many Dragon Riders as we can get. Those relics aren't going to be around forever.

"What about the Dragon Riders we already have?" asked Old Snow.

Hal pursed his lips. "It's been hard. Though I've managed to form the Dragon Riders into a fairly cohesive team, it's difficult because I haven't been a Dragon Rider long myself. Keershan has been doing more research on how the Dragon Riders of old did things, which has helped, but so much of their old practices and traditions have been lost to history that we really don't know much."

Old Snow raised an eyebrow. "Lost to history or defaced?"

Hal looked up at the massive faded painting on the wall behind them. It depicted over a dozen Dragon Riders flying into battle against a demonic enemy who Hal assumed was the Nameless One. He could still smell the acrid ashes of the Defacer that Queen Bariwa had sent to destroy this painting in his nostrils, although that had been over three months ago, and the ashes had long since dissipated.

That was the hardest part about restoring the Dragon Riders. Over the last five thousand years—but particularly within the last ten—a group of demons known only as the Defacers had made it their mission to destroy every last shred of evidence of the Dragon Riders from the world. They'd burned books, defaced paintings, smashed statues, tore down entire buildings, and killed anyone who might have knowledge about the Dragon Riders.

They'd been very thorough, which, in addition to the natural decaying effect that time itself inflicted on things, meant precious few historical materials on the Dragon Riders still existed. What was left was barely comprehensible to the average person, and it was near impossible to distinguish between myth and fact. Heck, Hal and Keershan had discovered a lot of Dragon Rider powers on their own that none of the legends had even bothered to mention, such as the Rider gaining the ability to read the written form of the dragons' language.

As a result, Hal found it hard to train his fellow Dragon Riders well. He was able to teach them the basics—such as how to draw upon dragonfire through their bond, telepathically speak to their dragons, and so on—but anything more advanced was still out of his reach.

Surrels sighed heavily and rested his chin on his hand. "Sounds like this whole rebellion thing really isn't working out the way we thought. Maybe we need the Glaci Empire's help, after all."

Before anyone could respond to that, however, the screams of a young girl could be heard outside, followed by a man shouting and a dragon snarling.

The council jumped and bolted out of the door, Hal following. Perhaps the attack had come already.

Chapter Four

Fralia emerged from the temple first.

A large, green dragon with gold-lined wings stood not far from the entrance, its golden eyes fixed on the man before it. The man in question was completely bald and more muscular than average. He was clad in black furs and greenish-silver armor that looked quite beaten and had a long black beard going down his chest. A shiny golden ring stood out against his dark skin on his right hand, glowing softly with power.

The man looked even bigger compared to the color-fully robed little girl he held with one hand.

"Let me go!" the young girl wailed, swinging her arms and legs like windmills. "Let me go now, or I'm telling!"

"Telling?" said the man in a deep, booming voice that fit his large self quite well. He held the girl at arm's length as if she was some kind of wild animal. "I, too, am going to tell. I am going to *tell* the council that a

Glacian spy was caught trying to sneak up on them, perhaps with intent to steal vital information."

The young girl paused her struggles to look at the man. "What? No. I just want to see the dragons."

"She may have a point, Ragnol," said the green dragon in a slightly dry voice. "I cannot imagine something as small as she is being much of a threat to anyone."

"That is because you lack imagination, Dinne!" said Ragnol. "Back when I was in the Malarsan Army, I studied Glacian spy techniques. They aren't above using young children or even elderly women to accomplish their vile ends."

"I don't care!" the young girl cried. "I just want to see the dragons!"

"What is going on here?" asked Hal sharply as their group walked up to Ragnol and Dinne. "Ragnol, what is this?"

Ragnol glanced at Hal and started. "Captain Norath! Glad to see you. As you can see, I have successfully apprehended a Glacian spy. She claims she *only* wants to see the dragons, but there is always more than meets the eye with Glacians."

Fralia sighed. Though she didn't recognize the girl, she knew Lieutenant Frik Ragnol quite well at this point.

Lieutenant Ragnol was the fourth Dragon Rider after Cav and was also the chief of security in Mysteria. His job was to essentially enforce laws and make sure that the town was safe. He was a good security guard, but he was also a bit too enthusiastic at times, or so Fralia felt.

She liked Dinne a fair bit more. The green dragon

was more down-to-earth than Ragnol and often kept his imagination from getting too wild.

That was probably why Dinne said, "And I was telling Ragnol that maybe we shouldn't be accusing little girls of being spies and assassins."

"Dinne is correct," Hal said. He gestured at the girl. "You recognize that girl, right, Keershan?"

Keershan, who stood to Hal's right, squinted his eyes before recognition dawned in them. "Oh, yeah! Isn't she Dedeket's daughter? The one who tried to pet me? Jinka, I think her name was?"

The little girl, apparently named Jinka, waved happily at Keershan. "Hi, dragon! I came to see you, but this mean old man caught me and says I'm a bad girl."

"Old—?" Ragnol sputtered. "I will have you know, young lady, that I am only thirty-four, which hardly makes me *old*—"

"How did you even get here?" Hal asked Jinka, apparently ignoring Ragnol's sputtering. "I thought you were still with your father."

Jinka suddenly looked away from Hal, a clear tell of her guilt. "Um, I might have sneaked out of our wagon to see the dragon when father wasn't looking."

Fralia blinked. She had no idea where the Glacians had encamped, but based on what Hal and Anija had described of their encounter with the Glacians, it wasn't very close to the town. She noticed that Jinka's robes were dirty and even torn in a couple of places, though that was the only sign of her no-doubt arduous journey through the Tops's rocky clime to reach them.

How did she even know where to find us? It's not like you can find us on a map.

"Wonderful," Surrels said sardonically. "We have a wayward child that wants to 'see the dragons.' I can't wait until her father accuses us of kidnapping her and we make ourselves another powerful enemy we don't need."

Hal scratched the back of his neck. "We'll just have to take her back to her father. Jinka, do you know where your father's caravan has camped?"

Jinka nodded. "Yeah! I can take the dragon there if you want."

"Sorry, but we're not sticking around your daddy's camp," Anija said. She gestured at herself and the others. "See, we're also adults who have adult things to do. None of us have time to babysit a squirt like you."

Jinka pouted. "But I wanted to see the *dragons*."

Old Snow laughed. "You know, I think I like her. She's someone who knows what she wants and won't be satisfied until she gets it."

"Maybe," Hal said, "but as Anija pointed out, she's not ours to keep. If we don't return her to her father right away, I doubt that will make the Glacians like us very much."

"I agree with Captain Norath," Ragnol said. He gestured at Dinne. "Dinne and I will deliver the girl back to where she comes from. If we fly, it shouldn't take us very long to do."

Jinka looked at Ragnol again, her mouth hanging open. "Fly? I want to fly on a dragon! Flying sounds fun."

Fralia chuckled. Like Old Snow, she could not help but find Jinka's enthusiasm infectious. It almost made her want a child of her own, even though she knew that she probably wasn't going to be getting married anytime soon.

Though who knows? Fralia glanced at Hal. *Maybe once this rebellion is all done and over with, we can start thinking about our future.*

"I don't think it would be wise to send Jinka back with you guys," Hal said. He glanced at the sky. "Especially given what the weather looks like."

Fralia also looked up at the sky and noticed how white the clouds had gotten. "It looks like it's going to snow."

"Not just snow," Surrels said when a strong gust of cold wind blew through. "Blizzard."

"Exactly," Old Snow said. "That leaves us with two options: Either we keep Jinka with us overnight and return her in the morning once the storm has settled, or return her now and hopefully get back to town before the blizzard gets too bad."

Another cold gust of wind blew through at that moment, making Fralia shiver slightly. Over the last couple of months, Fralia had learned from experience how miserable blizzards and snowstorms could get up here.

And according to Old Snow—who has lived here much longer than the rest of us—we haven't even hit the worst part of storm season yet. Fralia rubbed her hands together to warm them.

"I can stay," said Jinka brightly. She looked at Keershan anxiously. "I want to stay with dragons."

"Sorry," Hal said, "but your daddy wouldn't be

happy if you disappeared right before a snowstorm hits. He'll be worried sick about you. Do you want to worry your father?"

Jinka's bright smile faded slightly at the question. "No, but I want to see the dragons, too."

"What an annoying brat," Anija said. She tapped the side of her head. "One-track mind and all that."

Give her a break," Fralia said, glaring at Anija. She looked at Jinka. "She's only, what, five?"

"Actually, I'm five-and-a-half," Jinka corrected. She folded her arms in front of her chest. "I'm a big girl now."

"Of course," Fralia said, flashing Jinka a sweet smile. She looked at the others. "Since we probably don't want the Glacians mounting a siege on Mysteria, I'll take Jinka back to her father."

Hal gave her a skeptical look. "Not by yourself, surely?"

Fralia frowned slightly in annoyance. "I never said I would go by myself. I can take some of my fire and earth apprentices, or maybe rope one of your Dragon Riders into escorting us."

"I would accompany you, Miss Jeniq," said Ragnol, standing up straight. He gestured at Dinne. "Dinne and I know the Tops like the backs of our hands now after all the patrols we've been on. Finding the Glacian campsite should be a piece of cake."

"I don't want you and Dinne leaving the town when you're head of security," Hal replied. Hal looked at Fralia. "Take Cav and Onito instead. They've seen the Glacians before. They know where we saw them last."

Fralia sighed. However much she may have found Ragnol's gung-ho personality a bit tiresome, she liked him a good deal more than Cav, who was simply *too* reserved for her tastes.

Nonetheless, she nodded. "All right. Where is Cav?"

"I'll tell him to meet you and Jinka at the south gates," Hal said.

Jinka sighed. "Okay."

"You'll get to ride on a dragon with me when we take you back to your father," Fralia told Jinka. "Doesn't that sound exciting?"

Jinka's eyes widened. "A *big* dragon? Or a *small* one?"

Fralia frowned. "Um, I think Onito is pretty average for a dragon in terms of size."

Jinka clapped her hands together. "Yay! I like all dragons. All dragons are good."

Fralia chuckled at that. She really did like the little girl, who reminded her of herself at that age. She hadn't been nearly as hyper-focused on dragons as Jinka, but she recalled getting excited about magic with similar enthusiasm.

Yep, I think we're going to get along just fine, Fralia thought as Ragnol set Jinka down on the ground with surprising gentleness. She still landed on her bottom somewhat roughly, but she jumped to her feet anyway. *Again, wouldn't mind having a child of my own. If Father were alive—*

Fralia shivered as another powerful gust of wind passed through. The clouds looked rather ominous.

Even magic can't stop everything. *Especially a storm that looks as big as this one.*

Chapter Five

ONCE FRALIA AND JINKA WENT DOWN TO THE SOUTH gates, the council split up, agreeing to revisit the Glacians' offer as soon as Fralia returned.

To Anija, it seemed like a waste to send Fralia to the Glacians before deciding on whether to accept their help.

Surrels had gone to check on the town's military forces and reports from Mysteria's scouts while Hal and Keershan had returned to the Forgotten Temple with Old Snow.

As for Anija, she decided that she needed to check on the town itself more than anything. Her spies in the kingdom had already made their report this week, and she could not expect another report from them for at least another week. That left her with little to do until later in the afternoon, when Hal would call the council together for another meeting, likely to discuss the Glacians' offer in further detail.

As Anija couldn't think of anything more boring than

a meeting, she and Rialo had taken off into the air to fly over the town.

Before Anija had become a Dragon Rider, she hadn't realized how much *fun* flying was. Feeling the wind flying through her hair, clutching tightly onto Rialo's back, being close to—or sometimes among—the clouds was the most exhilarating feeling in her life, and she had no idea how she had lived this far without it.

She wasn't even sure she *could* live without it, at least not anymore.

Anija especially liked getting the bird's eye view of Mysteria below. Peering over the side of Rialo, Anija saw Mysteria as if it was little more than a very realistic diorama.

The town itself was decently sized, about a mile across. One would think that would make it hard to hide, but because it was nestled deep within the largely unexplored Desolate Tops itself, Mysteria had thus far avoided invasion from the Malarsan Army.

In fact, that was why it had been chosen as their base of operations after the Battle of Dragon Valley. The high peaks and cliffs acted as natural protective walls. Granted, most of the buildings had been abandoned for years, but the former Dancing Army had managed to fix up most of the houses and make them somewhat livable, though there were still many collapsed structures everywhere.

Another good thing about the Tops was that it had plenty of nearby caves for the dragons to make into their nests. Rialo headed to hers now.

I want to check on the hatchlings, Rialo told Anija. *I told them to return should they sense a blizzard coming.*

Anija nodded. Even though it wasn't snowing yet, it felt incredibly cold in the air. Anija likely would have frozen to death if not for the fact that Rialo's body was constantly generating heat that made Anija feel as if she was wrapped up in a comfy blanket in front of a warm fire.

Soon, over a dozen caves could be seen below. Some of them were full of dragons and their hatchlings while others were empty or appeared so. As Anija had discovered from personal experience, the caves within the Tops were quite deep.

Nor did it escape Anija's notice that the dragons in their caves all looked up at Anija and Rialo as they passed. That was because Rialo was the chief of the Clawfoot Clan, the largest dragon clan in the kingdom, as well as the one with which the Dragon Riders had allied. That made Rialo the leader of the dragons, who hung on her every word like gospel truth.

They definitely respect her. Anija felt the respectful gazes from the dragons focusing on them as they flew. *Which I can't disagree with. She's certainly a respectable dragon.*

If there was one thing that Anija did not like about dragons, however, it was the smell. Dragons generally didn't believe in bathing, and while they did not *deliberately* make themselves smell bad, they didn't bother trying to clean themselves, either. Though Anija's nose had adapted to the stench of dragon droppings and scales over the past two months, every now and then she received a strong reminder of it.

Such as when they landed in Rialo's cave and she got a big whiff of the rotting mountain goat carcass and dragon droppings within,.

Covering her nose, Anija said, "Ugh. I love you, Rialo, I really do, and your little ones, but would it really kill you to learn how to clean up after yourselves? Would make things a bit more pleasant."

Rialo rolled her eyes. "I noticed that you humans do not bathe very regularly, either."

Anija ran her hand through her red hair, wincing slightly at how dirty it felt. "That's because we really don't have any baths, and what water we do have is needed to make sure that no one dies of thirst."

Rialo just snorted before walking into the cavern. She growled a few times, and a second later, half a dozen dragon hatchlings in a variety of different colors came running toward her. The hatchlings mobbed their mother's legs while Rialo did her best to look at each one and rub her snout against their faces.

Anija climbed down and stepped back. Though she liked the hatchlings well enough, she knew how enthusiastic they could get when seeing their mother and she didn't want to accidentally get caught in the middle of it.

A brown-and-black-scaled hatchling broke off from the rest. Skidding to a halt before Anija, the hatchling made a happy growling sound, prompting Anija to pat her on the head.

"Hey, Yiko," Anija said. "How are you doing?"

Yiko made another happy growling sound.

Yiko was Anija's favorite hatchling from Rialo's group. She and Yiko had saved each other's lives several times over the last couple of months. Of course, Anija felt rather maternal toward most of the hatchlings, thanks to her bond with Rialo. Even now, she could feel maternal warmth and happiness flowing through Rialo as she checked each hatchling to make sure they were okay.

Once Rialo was satisfied with the health of her hatchlings, she made a series of roars and growls, their meaning quite clear: A storm was coming and the hatchlings needed to go deeper into the cave and huddle together to stay warm. The hatchlings immediately ran away from their mother toward the back of the cave, where they began to play and wrestle with each other.

"You really love them, don't you?" asked Anija, continuing to pet Yiko, who had not yet gone to play with the others.

Rialo nodded, looking at the playing hatchlings. "Of course. I gave birth to each one of them. While we dragons do not coddle our children like you humans do, we do try to make sure they are safe and healthy. Otherwise, the clan would not last very long."

Anija nodded in response, but then a question occurred to her and she asked, "What about their father? I don't think I've heard you mention him even once."

Rialo grunted. "Fathers. I've had multiple mates."

Anija stared at Rialo in amazement. "Really? Don't you dragons have any sort of marriage or anything like that?"

"No. Whereas humans tend to pair-bond with one mate for their whole life, it is very common for dragons to have multiple mates. Generally speaking, dragons only mate during the season when our mating instincts peak. Once a male impregnates a female, it is up to the female to birth, hatch, protect, and raise the children. It is rare for male dragons to have much say in or control over how the children are raised, mostly because they usually want nothing to do with the hatchlings."

Anija furrowed her brow. "So the men just leave the women and children to fend for themselves?"

"No," Rialo replied. "Males will protect women and children from threats, as well as lead the clan and defend it from external threats. But generally, males have little interest in protecting individual women or children. In fact, most male dragons can't even identify their own children most of the time."

"Now *that's* weird," Anija said. She scratched her chin. "And whilst I am far from a proper housewife and mother myself, it sounds like a pretty raw deal. Women have to deal with all the childrearing while the men can do whatever?"

Rialo snorted. "It's not quite as bad as you make it out to be. Without our brave men on the front lines, we females and our children would have been killed long ago. Mother dragons are very much capable of protecting our own, but that makes it harder for us to protect others' children without abandoning our own. The men, therefore, play the important role of protecting and providing for *all* of us, even those they did not mate with."

"What about your dad? You seemed close to him."

Rialo stiffened. "Father was unusual for a male dragon. Not only did he pick one mate—my mother—

but he also formed relationships with each of his children. I think that is probably what blinded him to Jaspus's traitorous nature."

Anija nodded. She was still learning more and more about dragon culture all the time.

They were surprisingly similar to humans in the way they treated their dead. Dragons would often bury the dead and perform funeral rites on them to mark their passing and remember their lives. They would even give the friends and family members of the deceased a chance to speak in honor of the dead dragon, which could cause dragon funerals to go for a long time.

Anija had found *that* out the hard way when they held a funeral for Chief Bronda outside of Mysteria about two weeks after the Battle of Dragon Valley. Both Rialo and Keershan had insisted on it. They had unfortunately failed to retrieve Chief Bronda's body, but they used one of his scales instead.

It seemed like every member of the Clawfoot Clan had something to say about their departed leader. The funeral had started in the morning and didn't end until late that night, by which time most of the humans had fallen asleep.

But it had also been a very beautiful funeral. Anija had been affected more deeply than she thought she would, primarily because of her bond with Rialo, allowing her to share Rialo's feelings. The overwhelming grief had been almost too much for Anija at times, especially when Rialo gave her speech and went into detail on her memories of her father.

Rialo glanced at Anija. "What about your parents?"

Anija stiffened. "What about them?"

"Are they still with us?"

Anija frowned. "I don't know. They might be. They might not be. I was raised by Shadow Mask, so he was my 'father' for all intents and purposes."

"Was he a good father?"

Anija shot Rialo an annoyed glare. "Given how he tried to kill me because someone offered him enough money, no. Glad he's dead."

Rialo nodded. "As am I, although I do wonder if the Dark Tigers will come after us or not. They seem to have been very quiet since their leader's death."

That was something Anija had noticed as well. Shadow Mask had been the leader of the Dark Tiger Guild, a criminal organization that specialized in theft and assassination.

Without Shadow Mask randomly threatening to kill people who don't obey him, how will they survive? Maybe they'll kill each other and that will be the end of it.

Of course, Anija knew that was a little too optimistic. Many Guild members would likely see Shadow Mask's death as an opportunity to seize power or enrich them-selves. She'd known many such members growing up in the Guild and shuddered at the thought of any one of them taking control, as some of them were even *worse* than Shadow Mask, if that could be believed. She doubted it would be long before the Dark Tigers showed up again.

Let them. Anija glanced at Rialo. *If they wanna try to kill me, they'll have to go through her first.*

Rialo seemed to catch Anija's thoughts or at least

sense her triumphant attitude, because she glanced at Anija and gave her a sly smile.

The moment was broken when Anija heard the flapping of wings outside the cave mouth. A large red dragon was soaring toward them, a woman with shockingly blonde hair sitting atop her back.

The dragon landed and walked inside, each step making the ground shake a little due to her weight.

"Kikow," said Rialo. "What is the matter?"

Kikow stopped several feet away and knelt. "Apologies for the interruption, Chief Rialo, but I have urgent news from the scouts on the eastern front."

Anija raised an eyebrow. "What sort of news?"

The blonde woman sitting on Kikow's back, who wore a shiny gold earring that partially resembled a dragon head, looked at Anija grimly. "A dragon was spotted to the east. And not a friendly one, either. A slave."

Anija and Rialo exchanged worried looks. The slaves were the dragons that had been forcibly conquered by the Malarsan Army during the Battle of Dragon Valley. Whereas Dragon Riders and Steeds used relics to form voluntary bonds with each other, slaves were dragons forcibly brainwashed by Malarsan soldiers using relics. This gave the soldier in question complete control over the dragon, thereby giving them a powerful weapon at their disposal.

The exact number of slaves was not known, but Hal had once estimated that the Malarsan Army had to have about 300 or so slaves under their control. Anija had heard rumors over the past month of dragons from other parts of Malarsan getting enslaved as well.

If even one slave was nearby, then that likely meant that there were many more.

"Are the other council members aware of this?" asked Rialo.

Soma nodded. "We've reported the sighting to the town. Commander Surrels is marshaling the defense forces even as we speak, but Rider Hal and Keershan are currently in the middle of an important meeting with Councilman Old Snow and are therefore unavailable for battle."

"Unavailable?" Anija repeated incredulously. "What could be more important than defending the town from a slave?"

"Probably Keershan getting distracted by a fragment from an ancient history book," said Rialo dismissively. She spread her wings. "Did you say that the slave was spotted to the east of town?"

Kikow bowed her head. "Yes. About a mile out."

Anija sighed, but said, "Then let's go."

Chapter Six

HAL HAD INTENDED TO CALL A MEETING OF THE DRAGON Riders after sending Fralia off to return Jinka to her father. Before he could do that, Old Snow tapped him on the shoulder and asked him to come with him back into the Forgotten Temple. Old Snow apparently had something important he wanted to show Hal and Keershan but would not say what it was.

That was how Hal and Keershan found themselves back in the Forgotten Temple, standing at the foot of the familiar ancient painting of the Dragon Riders. Every time Hal looked at the painting, he was reminded of his fight with the Defacer that had started this whole adventure in the first place.

Back then, I couldn't even imagine *myself being friends with a dragon, much less bonding with one. Now look at me. I'm trying to not merely lead the Riders, but am in the process of reviving them and opposing Queen Bariwa's rule.*

Hal glanced at Keershan. The golden dragon was

also staring at the painting with even more interest than Hal. Keershan was more of a scholar than he was and an expert in all things Dragon Rider. Knowledge that had once gotten Keershan exiled from his own clan had now put him in a position of prominence among his people.

Guess we've both come a long way, haven't we, friend? Hal said to Keershan mentally.

Keershan looked at Hal and nodded. *Yeah. I remember when you tried to kill me right here because you thought I was going to eat you. Fun times.*

In my defense, you looked very *scary,* Hal replied. *But yes, times have certainly changed. Though I wonder what Old Snow is going to show us.*

Old Snow currently stood in front of the Dragon Rider painting, running his hands along the rough, chipped stone wall. He seemed to be looking for something, though what, Hal couldn't say. Nor had Old Snow offered to explain, either. He just told Hal and Keershan to be patient while he 'searched.'

Hal was used to that. Although he trusted Old Snow with his life, he had to admit that Old Snow could be very enigmatic and even secretive. Hell, Old Snow hadn't even told Hal and the others that he was actually the former king of Malarsan until they were almost put to death by Old Snow's ex-wife.

Even so, Hal had come to learn that Old Snow often had good reasons for doing the things that he did. He was the original protector of the Forgotten Temple and Mysteria and it had been his suggestion that the Dragon Riders return here and make it into their base of operations.

Even so, I kind of wish he'd be a bit more straightforward sometimes, Hal thought.

Agreed, Keershan replied in his mind. *He reminds me a bit of my mother. She could also be mysterious sometimes, though not as much as Old Snow, for sure.*

"Tell me, Hal, Keershan," Old Snow said suddenly, without looking at either of them. "What was Mysteria's original purpose?"

Hal blinked. "You mean before or after we settled it?"

"Let me rephrase that question," Old Snow said, still not looking at them. "Who originally founded Mysteria and why?"

"The Dragon Riders," Keershan said without hesitation. "As you once told us, Mysteria is the birthplace of the Dragon Riders. It is where humans and dragons first bonded and where the last of the Dragon Riders fell, where the Dragon Riders learned how to use powers like mind-jumping, dragonfire, and similar powers."

"Wrong," Old Snow said even before Keershan finished speaking. "The Dragon Riders did not found Mysteria. The town existed long before the Dragon Riders, though the original corps was founded here, and this is the place where the first Dragon Riders were born."

Hal raised an eyebrow. "So if the Dragon Riders didn't originally found Mysteria, then who did?"

"Good question," Old Snow said. He bent down briefly as if to pick up a shiny coin on the ground before rising to his feet again, tapping the stones on the wall in an odd, almost rhythmic pattern. "And my answer is another question: Who created the relics?"

Keershan looked stumped by that question, which was impressive.

But Hal, drawing upon his old Relic Hunter training, said, "I was taught that humans created relics from metal, dragon bones, and magic to create weapons to help us protect us from the dragons."

Keershan gave Hal an odd look. "What a weird story. The legends I read said that the first relics were designed by dragons as a way for them to communicate with and learn from humans. It was our dragonfire that made the relics special."

"Fascinating stories," Old Snow said. He stopped tapping the stones and turned to face Hal and Keershan. "Unfortunately, both of them are hilariously wrong."

With that, Old Snow turned and tapped a single stone sticking out of the wall at eye height. There was a grinding sound. The wall shuddered slightly under the strain. Hal was afraid that the whole temple might collapse.

But then a portion of the wall slid down with a loud *boom*, revealing an empty doorway and staircase that descended into what looked like endless darkness. A musty, dust-like scent rolled out of the doorway, reminding Hal of his relic hunting days.

Old Snow pulled out a torch and smacked it against the wall to his left, lighting it. Old Snow raised it above his head to illuminate his path as he walked.

Hal hesitated for only a second before following with Keershan close behind him.

The hidden passageway was big enough for a dragon of Keershan's size to fit through, but it still felt rather tight to Hal. Perhaps that had to do with the fact that the staircase had clearly not been used in years. Though his bond with Keershan gave him limited night vision, Hal still felt wary.

The stone steps were covered in a thin layer of dust. They seemed quite well preserved, despite the lack of use. The staircase spiraled to the left, leading them down deeper and deeper into the earth. The air became dustier and harder to breathe, but Hal did not complain. He just remained hyper-aware of their surroundings, listening closely to their footsteps, his own breathing, and the sounds Keershan made as he walked. Keershan, too, felt rather tense, though Hal sensed a hint of excitement in the runt dragon as well.

Old Snow, per usual, seemed perfectly at ease in the mysterious underground tunnel. He walked in the lead, holding his torch high, which let Hal see the carvings and paintings along the walls.

Unlike the ones on the surface, these ones were much more well preserved, like they had been painted yesterday. Unfortunately, they were also coated in rather thick layers of dust.

From what Hal could see, the paintings appeared to depict beings—he didn't want to say humans, despite their humanoid shape—working in forges and on anvils, crafting objects that he couldn't make out.

"Wow," Keershan said as they walked.

"They depict the Relic Crafters," Old Snow said, not even glancing up as he walked. "They are the people who originally made the relics, and the founders of the original town of Mysteria. They are no longer with us."

Hal frowned. "When you say people, do you mean they were humans? Or dragons?"

Old Snow looked over his shoulder at Hal with an odd look on his face. "Neither."

Hal furrowed his brow. "Then I don't understand."

"I don't expect you to," Old Snow said, turning his attention back to the staircase before them. "Mostly because I do not entirely understand them, either. Ah, here we are."

Hal felt the stairs stop and the ground level out at their feet. They stood in a doorway. Old Snow tilted his stick into the top of a torch in front of him. Without warning, the fire jumped from torch to torch across the room, gradually illuminating until soon Hal could see it as clear as day.

With the various ancient equipment scattered about, the chamber reminded him of the local blacksmith's workshop in Lamb's Hand, his hometown.

There was some sort of forge filled with coal in the center of the room, its piping connected to the ceiling. A worktable sat a few feet away, covered with tongs and hammers. Half-finished pieces of armor and weapons were scattered everywhere, and the whole room was rather cold. There was a hint of lingering smoke in the air, as if the smell had been sealed in the room for years.

All in all, the room was both very familiar and yet oddly strange to Hal. Although it was about the size of a human blacksmith workshop, something about the tools and equipment scattered here and there made him think that whoever had used this forge likely *hadn't* been human.

"What is this place?" Keershan said, his green eyes darting about as he took in everything.

"I call it the crafters' workshop," Old Snow said, folding his arms in front of his chest. "And I believe this is where the relics—or at least some of them—were forged."

Hal looked at Old Snow with new understanding. "By the Relic Crafters, you mean."

Old Snow nodded once. "Yes."

"How did you even find this place?" asked Keershan. He sniffed the air. "It was really well hidden back there. Heck, even my nose didn't pick up anything and I have a good sense of smell."

Old Snow cast his gaze about the workshop. "When I wasn't dissuading potential relic thieves or foolhardy adventurers from going into the Tops in search of treasure, I spent a good deal of time exploring the ruins of this ancient town myself. Honestly, I found the workshop almost by accident, as I'd noticed a stone out of place on the mural and I felt an urge to push it back in."

"Amazing," Keershan said. He furrowed his brow. "But in all my years of studying the Dragon Rider legends, I've never heard of the Relic Crafters."

"That, I believe, may be intentional," Old Snow said, glancing around the empty workshop.

Hal scowled, thinking about the Defacer they'd faced up in the main room of the temple what seemed like a lifetime ago now. "Because of the Defacers, right?"

Old Snow, surprisingly enough, shook his head. "No. The Relic Crafters, I believe, *wanted* to be forgotten.

Hence why they sealed up their workshop, abandoned their town, and have since disappeared."

Hal stared at Old Snow in shock. "Wait, you mean that you think that the Relic Crafters are still around? Why would they hide from the rest of the world?"

Old Snow tapped his chin in thought. "If I had to hazard a guess, I'd say it's because of that thing on your head."

Hal instinctively grabbed his helmet. "My relic? What do you mean?"

"Not yours in particular," Old Snow said, lowering his hand. "I have reason to believe that the Crafters regretted making the relics and decided to take their knowledge with them."

Keershan tilted his head to the side. "But why would they *regret* making the relics? Relics are amazing things. They let humans and dragons form bonds that we couldn't otherwise form on our own."

"Not quite," Old Snow corrected Keershan. "Remember, Dragon Riders and Steeds can form bonds without relics. The relics simply make it easier."

"Even so, Keershan's point still stands," Hal said. He glanced at the ceiling. "And given how puny our forces are, I wouldn't mind a few more relics."

Old Snow shrugged. "From what I have gathered, the Crafters were a peaceful people who disliked any sort of armed conflict. They likely saw their relics being used as weapons of war."

Hal could understand disliking conflict. The gods knew that Hal wasn't exactly a warmonger himself.

But he also wasn't naive enough to believe that war itself was always bad.

Or that simply taking your toys and running away *ever* solved your problems.

"Then why are you showing us this place at all?" asked Hal. He gestured at the forge. "If the Relic Crafters are long gone and they didn't even leave instructions on how to make more relics, then this room is an idle curiosity, at best."

"I brought you and Keershan down here for a reason. I was hoping you would figure it out yourselves, as you two are quite intelligent young individuals."

Hal looked around but saw nothing in particular that stood out to him. "I see nothing. Keershan?"

Keershan squinted his eyes and sniffed the air. "I'm with you. While I'm sure this place is chock-full of history and secrets, I don't see why this place is relevant to *us*."

Old Snow folded his hands in front of his body. "Keep looking. I'm sure you will see it."

Hal scowled again. He knew that Old Snow meant well with his cryptic way of speaking and testing them, but that did not stop Hal from occasionally feeling short with him or wishing that Old Snow would speak plainly for once in his life. He wondered if Old Snow had always spoken this cryptically, even when he'd been king, or if it was a habit he picked up from being an isolated mountain hermit for the past decade.

But all frustration faded when he noticed something on the other side of the room. It was another painting, appearing to depict a figure riding on a dragon, though that wasn't what caught his attention.

As if in a trance, Hal crossed the room. He heard Keershan walking right behind him.

Standing before the mural, Hal brushed the dust off its surface. He kept brushing and brushing, clearing away layer after layer of dust, until he could finally see the mural clearly enough to know that he hadn't needed to clear it away at all, because he'd already seen it accurately from across the room.

An exact replica of himself and Keershan painted on the wall before them, in almost perfect condition.

Chapter Seven

"I'm hungry."

Fralia stopped and looked over her shoulder. Jinka sat right behind her on Onito's back, clutching the back of Fralia's robes for support.

Fralia frowned. "Didn't we give you some bread before we left town?"

"Yes, but I'm still hungry."

Cav grunted. "Dig through my bag. Should have some extra rations that you can share with her."

Fralia fished out some more bread and, breaking off a chunk, handed it to Jinka. "Here you go."

Jinka took the bread and, to Fralia's surprise, ate the entire thing in one gulp. She looked at Fralia expectantly. "More?"

Fralia sighed as she put the remainder of Cav's bread back into his bag. "Sorry, but we need to preserve our rations in case we need them later."

"But I'm hungry *now*," said Jinka in a whiny voice.

Fralia rubbed her forehead, starting to question her earlier desire to have children of her own.

They had only been flying through the Desolate Tops for about five, maybe ten minutes, but Jinka had already gotten bored of the flight and seemed to be a never-ending fountain of questions. That surprised Fralia, as she'd expected the little girl to be too fascinated by flying on a dragon's back to care much about anything else.

Of course, Jinka had to go ahead and prove me wrong. I hope I wasn't this *bratty when I was her age. If so, I wish I could have apologized to Father before he died.*

Fralia asked, "Have you spotted the Glacians yet?"

"Nope!" Cav replied. He glanced at the ground. "Just more mountains. Right, Onito?"

Onito nodded. "Aye. I haven't even smelled them yet."

Fralia frowned. Jinka had informed them that she had entered Mysteria from the east, which, being the least-defended part of the town, explained how she had managed to sneak into the settlement without anyone noticing. Thus, Fralia and Cav had decided to head east, flying low enough to the mountaintops to see any signs of people below but not high enough to deal with the huge winds that they would have had to struggle with at higher altitudes.

Not that their carefulness had done them much good so far, however. The Desolate Tops were a big place. There was a reason they had been mostly abandoned by humans for thousands of years and it was due to the massive size of the place, along with a lack of ready resources to exploit. Fralia herself marveled at how a girl

Jinka's age had managed to find their town at all on her own when even the Glacians themselves did not know exactly where it was.

And the storm is getting worse, Fralia noted.

Fralia had been keeping a careful eye on the sky during their search for the Glacians. Though it wasn't snowing yet, the clouds were now a very bright white, and the temperature of the winds had dropped sharply even just within the five or ten minutes they'd been flying. Granted, part of that was due to their altitude, but Fralia doubted it was much warmer on the ground. It made her grateful for Onito's body heat, which made her feel warm even with the cold wind whipping about them.

Still, we need to get Jinka to her father before the blizzard really *gets going.* Fralia shuddered slightly at a particularly sharp gust of wind that stung her exposed cheeks. *Once it starts up, even Onito will struggle to return to town.*

That pleasant thought was interrupted by a sudden growl from Onito's throat, which Fralia felt shake through his whole body. She looked at the back of Cav's head and said, "Cav, what's the problem?"

"Danger," Onito answered for him.

Cav gripped Onito's reins more tightly than before. "We're not alone."

Fralia saw nothing except the peaks of the Tops and the large sky overhead. Even so, her own instincts were kicking into high gear.

Jinka, on the other hand, just giggled. "Dragon go *vrr* again! Dragon go *vrr* again!"

"Trust me, Jinka, you don't want Onito to go 'vrr' again," Fralia said. "Going 'vrr' is not a good thing."

"But it's fun," said Jinka.

Fralia was just about to tell Jinka that there was nothing 'fun' about danger when she heard the loud flapping of wings nearby. She looked at the sky overhead but did not see anything at first.

That was, until a large purplish-black dragon shot through the clouds toward them. It was close in size to Rialo but infinitely less friendly. Its massive wings flapped rapidly, its green eyes glaring down on Fralia and the others, a deafening roar escaping its lips as it drew closer and closer to them.

"Another dragon!" Jinka yelled. "Yay!"

"Not a friendly one," said Cav. "Hold on!"

Cav pulled back on Onito's reins, and the elder dragon dove forward, forcing Fralia to hold onto Cav's waist even more tightly. She felt the wind displaced by the enemy dragon as it passed by overhead.

Righting himself, Onito shouted, "I think that is one of the queen's slaves!"

It was already turning back toward them, a deep growl emitting from its throat that made Onito's sound like a hatchling's.

Oddly enough, the slave kept its distance, glaring at them with its unnaturally green eyes.

"Why isn't it attacking us?" Fralia shouted, raising her voice to be heard over the flapping of Onito's wings and the roaring wind around them.

"No idea!" Cav replied. "Maybe it's—"

"Incoming!" Onito shouted.

Creatures straight out of Fralia's worst nightmares plunged through the clouds overhead.

They looked like giant, vaguely humanoid bats. Half a dozen in all, they hurtled toward Fralia and the others. It took all of Onito's agility to dodge them as they flew past like fired cannonballs.

But the bats banked sharply and formed a loose ring around Onito. Fralia could see their long, sharp fangs far too clearly.

"Ugly," said Jinka, staring at the bat-like creatures with disgust.

One of them swooped in toward her, fangs bared, but Fralia blasted it with an airburst that sent it spiraling out of control toward the ground below. The bat managed to regain control of its trajectory quickly, and flew back up to rejoin its brethren, but did not attack again.

"What *are* those things?" said Cav.

"Demons," Fralia said.

Cav shuddered. "They don't look like General Omaros very much."

"Demons come in all sorts of shapes and sizes," Fralia said.

As if to prove her point, the bat-like demons started screeching at the tops of their lungs before launching at them. Fralia used her air blasts to keep them at bay while Onito spat fireballs at them.

Unfortunately, the demons were too swift to get hit. They ducked or veered off their chosen path at the last second.

Jinka made oohing sounds whenever Onito shot a fireball and giggled like crazy when one of Fralia's air blasts either knocked a demon out or sent it off-course.

Fralia was glad that Jinka was enjoying herself,

because she certainly wasn't. And Cav and Onito did not seem to be having a good time, either.

Fralia considered creating some sort of localized storm around the four of them, which might knock the demons out of the sky, but she was worried about the effect it might have on Onito.

That was when Fralia felt a single snowflake land on her cheek. The clouds were starting to snow slightly. It wasn't very much, but Fralia could tell it was starting to pick up, and once it did, they'd all be trapped in a blizzard with little visibility and no way to get home.

Visibility …

Fralia leaned into Cav's ear and shouted, "Have Onito take us into the clouds."

"The clouds?" Cav repeated uncertainly. "But they look very—"

"Just do it!" Fralia snapped. "I have a plan."

The gray dragon abruptly shot up into the sky toward the clouds. In their wake, a couple of demons accidentally crashed into each other.

Fralia clung on tightly to Cav's back while wrapping one arm around Jinka's waist, holding the young girl close to her chest. Jinka cried in delight as they flew faster and faster until they entered the clouds themselves. Glancing over her shoulder, Fralia spotted the bat-like demons flying after them, which was exactly what she wanted.

But Fralia had forgotten just how *cold* the snow clouds were. And wet. A chill set in her bones, her clothes became heavy with moisture, and the exposed parts of her skin began to sting with ice.

"What now?" Cav yelled, his teeth chattering slightly.

"Stay in the clouds!" Fralia replied. "Wait until you can see every demon!"

The shrieking became louder. The thick white clouds made it damn near impossible to see anything, but Fralia caught glimpses of dark wings. More importantly, the *demons* couldn't see them, either, which was exactly what Fralia had been hoping for.

"Cav!" Fralia yelled. "Turn us around and get ready to burn up some demons!"

Onito wheeled in midair in the direction of the demons' shrieks and screams. Fralia started moving her free hand, which glowed with soft green moulash, attempting to make Onito as silent as possible.

The spell seemed to be working, because the flapping of Onito's wings became softer and softer. Fralia mentally counted down the seconds until they reached the demons, which sounded like they were all congregated in roughly the same area.

Five, four, three, two, one!

Onito burst out of the snow clouds into a medium-sized clearing. Just as Fralia thought, the demons had largely congregated among themselves in a tight group, perhaps wary of hunting a dragon among the mists.

Too bad the *dragon* was hunting *them*.

White-hot heat shot up Onito's back and then a stream of burning fire erupted from his mouth. The stream slammed into the assembled group of demons. The firebreath carved a hole through the chest of one demon while setting the rest of them aflame. The dead demons dropped like rocks while the survivors desperately tried to scatter.

Fralia had no intention of letting them leave. She spun her hand, focusing on creating whirlwinds around the demons that would hinder their progress. She felt powerful rushing winds swoop past her ears and encircle the burning demons, tossing them about like paper.

That did not kill the demons. Onito's claws and teeth, however, did.

The dragon tore through the remaining demons with gleeful abandon. Limbs were ripped off, chests were caved in or torn open entirely, heads went flying, black blood shot into the air. Fralia bent over Jinka in an attempt to protect her from the worst of it.

In seconds, the slaughter was over with all of the dead demons gone. Their remains disappeared into the clouds below, and Fralia got the impression that whoever was on the ground below was *not* getting snow from the clouds.

"Whew!" said Cav. He looked over his shoulder at Fralia and smiled. "Good plan, Fralia!"

Jinka threw her arms up into the air, nearly hitting Fralia in the face. "Whee! That was fun. Can we do it again?"

"Not unless you want to get attacked by more of those demonic abominations," Onito grunted. He spat something out of his mouth. "They don't even taste all that good. Disappointing."

Fralia grimaced. "Well, at least we got rid of them. That means we can resume our search for your father, Jinka."

Jinka wrinkled her nose. "Okay. But can I keep that dragon?"

Fralia frowned. "What dragon?"

Without warning, the slave burst through the clouds overhead. It slashed at Onito's wings, its sharp claws cutting through them with ease.

Onito cried out in pain and instantly plunged toward the ground below. They passed through the clouds and back into the cold winter air, the wind racing past Fralia's ears, her hair flying out behind her. Everyone was screaming, especially Jinka, her small hands grasping Fralia's robes with an iron grip.

Onito spread his wings to try to level them out somewhat, but he was too late.

The last thing Fralia saw was the ground coming up toward them like a meteor.

And then they smashed into the earth and Fralia did not know anything else.

Chapter Eight

ANIJA DID NOT QUITE KNOW WHAT TO EXPECT AFTER Kikow's description of the slave. She'd come prepared with a sword and armor. Rialo had also clearly prepped herself for a fight, chomping her teeth and swiping her claws through the air as they flew.

But as it turned out, a fight was the last thing they would get. If, indeed, they would get it at all.

Their flight took them out about a mile east of Mysteria, per Kikow's report. They were above a particularly rocky part of the mountains with boulders and steep cliffs scattered everywhere. Already, it was starting to snow, but Anija estimated that it wouldn't really pick up for at least another half hour.

That was why she was surprised to find a slave sitting, seemingly by itself, at the top of a nearby cliff.

The slave in question was a dragon she recognized all too well. Though his face was covered in scars and his silver scales were damaged and chipped in several places,

Jaspus looked surprisingly good for a dragon who was dead.

Anija felt hostility rising within Rialo at the sight of her traitorous older brother, a feeling Anija could relate to all too well. Jaspus, after all, was the one responsible for the fall of Dragon Valley in the first place.

Last I saw, Jaspus was dead, Anija thought as they flew. *He doesn't look very dead right now.*

Appearances can be deceiving, Rialo replied. *Particularly when dealing with demons.*

Anija knew that all too well at this point. Demons were inherently tricky beings, capable of casting sophisticated illusions and tricks to ensnare the unwary. She wouldn't put it past them to do something like that here, though she didn't quite see the point in conjuring an illusion of Jaspus.

Fortunately, Anija had brought Soma and Kikow too.

Jaspus appeared to take notice of them once they were within his range. He lifted his head and shot them a rather wicked grin that Anija did not particularly appreciate. His teeth had black stains on them now that they did not have before.

"My, my, my," said Jaspus, raising his voice to be heard over the howling winds. "What a treat. I didn't expect my own sister to be part of the delegation sent to meet me."

Rialo landed on an opposing cliff not too far from Jaspus. Kikow landed beside her a moment later and let out a thick grumble.

Jaspus tutted. "Growling like a mindless beast. And

here I thought that Dragon Riders were supposed to *civilize* their Steeds."

"Growling is the *least* we can do to you, traitor," Rialo snapped. "It is currently taking all of my willpower not to finish the job our father started."

Jaspus shook his head. "How rude. You must understand that the dark magic of the demons can perform many feats considered, ah, unnatural by those who are not initiated in their ways. Including, of course, saving from death those who were at death's door."

Anija took note of Jaspus's neck. It was not torn out anymore, like it had been when Chief Bronda killed Jaspus. There was, however, a series of strange black lines running along it that definitely did not look natural.

"So what are you, then?" said Rialo. "A puppet? Not the real Jaspus?"

Jaspus chuckled. "I am *very* real, sister, as real as you or the human you let ride your back like some sort of horse. But you are correct to assume that I am different."

As Jaspus spoke, the black lines in his neck seemed to wriggle and shift, though that may have just been Anija's eyes playing tricks on her.

"In any case, I don't know why you came out here alone," said Rialo. "Unless you want to die again, that is, which I would be more than happy to help you with."

Jaspus snorted. "Per usual, Rialo, you are so focused on what you can see that you don't notice what is creeping up behind you."

Anija did not see anything, but had the strongest gut feeling—instinct honed over years of training with the Dark Tigers—that Jaspus may not be lying.

"I want to talk."

"Talk?" Anija repeated, turning her gaze back to Jaspus. "About what? How you're an absolutely awful dragon and make my old boss look like a moral paragon of virtue and righteousness?"

"I only did what I did because I *had* to," said Jaspus. "Not that I would expect a former professional thief to understand."

"I've changed," Anija replied. "You, on the other hand, I am less sure about."

"I agree with Anija," said Rialo. She glared at Jaspus. "Whatever you want to talk about, we do not want to listen. Because we're not currently in a murderous mood today, we will let you leave unharmed."

Jaspus smirked. "You may not *want* to listen, but only because you don't know what I want to talk about."

"Who cares?" Anija said dismissively. She raised her sword, a thin rapier, and wagged it at Jaspus threateningly. "Personally, I think we should just carve out one of your eyeballs and send it back to the queen with best regards. Just to make a point."

"So barbaric," said Jaspus. He shrugged his large shoulders. "But so be it. If you don't want to learn about the upcoming Day of Shadows, then I won't tell you about it."

Jaspus turned to leave, but Anija, puzzled by what he said, said, "Wait a second. Day of Shadows? What is that?"

Jaspus cast a rather passive-aggressive look over his shoulder at them. "I thought you didn't *want* to talk."

"We shouldn't," Rialo said to Anija. "Whatever

Jaspus tells us will just be lies. Or at best, lies mixed in with truth, which is almost worse."

"No need to be so harsh, dear sister," said Jaspus as he turned around to face them again. "I'm more than happy to share what I know about the coming Resurrection Day with you and your Rider. Even though there's probably nothing you can do about it."

Anija bit her lower lip. Though she understood Rialo's distrust toward Jaspus quite well and even sympathized with it, she also sensed that this 'Resurrection Day' thing that Jaspus mentioned was important. "Talk. We'll listen, but no guarantee we'll believe."

Jaspus smiled. "Thank you for being so reasonable, human. I appreciate it."

Anija scowled. "Just talk."

Jaspus nodded. "Resurrection Day is the day on which the Nameless One will finish his revival process. Also known as the Day of Shadows, it is the day in which the Nameless One will return to this world and spread darkness over the land that will last for an eternity. It is also the darkest day of the year."

Anija froze. "And you say it's going to happen soon."

"Within the next month, in fact," said Jaspus. He glanced at the sky. "It will happen on the first night of the new moon. Once you can no longer see the moon, despite the lack of clouds in the sky, you will know that the Nameless One is risen and all is doomed."

Brushing snow off her shoulders, Anija said, "How do we know you aren't lying?"

"Ask Keershan," said Jaspus snidely. "He knows all the old legends, does he not? Though I imagine the real thing will be quite different, at least if Queen Bariwa's plans go well."

"Even if you are telling the truth, why are you warning us about it?" asked Rialo. "Do you want us to try to stop it?"

Jaspus laughed. "Stop it? At this point, no one can *stop* it. Haven't you wondered why there have been so few attacks on your settlement, even though the Malarsan Army now has hundreds of dragons under its control?"

Anija pursed her lips.

"Besides," Jaspus went on, "I remember hearing that dragon energy is supposedly needed to resurrect the Nameless One. Queen Bariwa obtained more than enough dragon energy at the Battle of Dragon Valley that she's no longer quite so concerned about you Riders anymore," said Jaspus. He shuddered. "She's even used some of my own dragon energy to do it. It's a draining process, to put it lightly, and one I do not recommend you go through unless you are a masochist."

That explained why he wasn't attacking them.

Of course, it could all just be a ruse to make us lower our guard, Rialo said to Anija mentally. *I wouldn't put anything past Jaspus at this point.*

Anija agreed, but aloud, she said, "I noticed you still haven't said why you're 'helping' us, Jaspus. I doubt it's out of the goodness of your heart, of which I'm pretty sure you have none."

Jaspus shook his head. "How cynical. The truth is, I realize I made a terrible deal with Queen Bariwa. I believed that siding with the demons would grant the

Clawfoot Clan more power than we'd ever had before, but I was fooled."

"If you're expecting us to forgive and forget, you are not only dishonest, but stupid," said Rialo. "Dragons do *not* forgive and we especially do not forget."

Jaspus lowered his head. "I don't expect that. All I ask is that you use this information to save our people from Queen Bariwa's enslavement."

Anija eyed Jaspus. He put on a good show pretending to be regretful and even penitent, but Anija still didn't feel like welcoming him back with open arms. Nor did Rialo, who kept glaring at Jaspus as if she could kill him with bad looks alone.

But Jaspus did not, unfortunately, die horribly on the spot. He kept standing there, a penitent expression on his face aided by the way he kept his wings folded to his back. From Anija's experience with dragons, she understood that folded wings was often a defensive posture, a way for one dragon to display weakness and submission.

Jaspus is clearly trying to make himself look weak, Rialo said mentally. *My guess is that Jaspus is trying to make us lower our guard to strike when we least expect it.*

Anija frowned. *If that was the case, then he's doing a piss-poor job of it. Unless he* really *can't tell how skeptical we are of his claims.*

Almost as if Jaspus himself was somehow in on their mental conversation, Jaspus suddenly threw something at them. The object, small and shaped like a square, landed at Rialo's feet. It was some sort of stone tablet that looked vaguely familiar. The form of Draco, the dragon tongue, was carved into it.

Anija looked up at Jaspus sharply. "Were you trying to throw rocks at your sister or something? How childish."

Jaspus sneered. "Of course not. I just noticed how skeptical you all clearly are about my claims, so I thought I'd back them up by giving you a copy of Queen Bariwa's Demonic Covenant."

Anija's eyes widened in shock. "The same one she signed with the demons? What good will that do us?"

"It has some pertinent information regarding the Day of Shadows," said Jaspus vaguely, "along with some other information you Riders might find interesting. Trust me, I had to risk a lot just to get this, so I'm not giving you some worthless trinket or love letter."

Rialo eyed Jaspus skeptically. "Gifts from a god often come with strings attached."

Jaspus nodded. "True. But it is never wise to turn down generous gifts from the mists."

With that, Jaspus flapped his wings and took off into the air. He flew over the peaks of the nearest mountain and vanished, the sound of his flapping wings slowly fading into the distance until Anija could no longer hear him.

Anija looked at Rialo. "I didn't realize you dragons had some sort of code."

"Not a code," Rialo said grimly. "We were exchanging sayings from our parents. A common way for dragons who shared a nest to speak with each other."

Anija raised an eyebrow. "Mind giving me an explanation of what they mean?"

"'Gifts from a god often come with strings attached'

means that gifts that are too good to be true usually are," said Rialo. She gazed at the mountaintop that Jaspus disappeared over. "Jaspus's phrase is basically the opposite saying, that one should not question fortunate gifts that fall into your lap. He's very annoying that way. I was quoting Father while he was quoting Mother."

Anija nodded. Despite having been bonded to Rialo for over two months now, she felt like she was still learning new things about dragons every day.

Regardless, Anija jumped down from Rialo. Landing on her feet softly, Anija walked over to the demonic covenant and picked it up. "Well, I don't really care about whatever sayings your parents told you. I'm going to read this demonic covenant and see if it says anything important."

Rialo snorted. "I doubt it. Jaspus would never actually give us anything useful. At best, he'd just give us a clue that may or may not be helpful if we can figure it out for ourselves. He always liked puzzles."

Anija read the covenant anyway. Nothing stood out to her in particular, however, as it seemed similar to the covenant they had found in the Depths. "Probably, but I don't think it hurts to read it …"

Anija's words trailed off as she got to the part of the covenant that was different from the rest of it. She abruptly stopped speaking, staring wordlessly at the covenant's words, unable to believe her own eyes.

"Anija?" said Rialo, her voice sounding slightly distant. "What happened? Did you see something?"

Snapping out of her shock, Anija looked up at Rialo in fear. "Looks like we're *both* wrong. Jaspus didn't just give us important information. He gave us a leaking dam that will drown us if it bursts."

Rialo frowned, her red eyes darting toward the covenant in Anija's hands. "Tell me what it says."

Anija took a deep breath. She still wasn't sure she believed it, but somewhere deep down inside her, Anija knew that what was written down on the rough-hewn stone covenant in her hands was the truth.

"Old Snow is the original person who summoned the demons. Not his wife."

Chapter Nine

THE PAINTING ON THE WALL OF THE CRAFTERS' WORKSHOP
so closely resembled them that Hal could have mistaken
it for a mirror. Everything was identical to Hal and Keershan's current attire, save for the odd golden armor that
Hal wore. The relic, too, looked to be in better condition
than the one he wore on his head.

"Amazing," Keershan said, his eyes fixed on the
painting.

Hal whipped his head over toward Old Snow, who
had not moved an inch from his position near the forge.
"But it *can't* be, right?"

Old Snow scratched his short, white beard. "The
Relic Crafters were quite wise and had a deeper connection to the gods, I think, than either us or the dragons."

Hal ran his finger along the contours of his painted
counterpart's face.

"Were the Relic Crafters seers of some sort?" Keershan said.

Old Snow strode over to the forge. Running his hand along its surface, Old Snow said, "They regularly communed with the gods. They saw the Fall of the Dragon Riders, the wars that would tear apart humanity and dragonkind, all the way up to the modern day."

Hal turned to face Old Snow again. "If they knew, why didn't they do anything about it?"

"As I said, they weren't warlike," Old Snow said.

"Yet they made this painting anyway," Hal said. "Why?"

"For us," Old Snow said simply. "Though they may not have been able to stop the Fall, they knew that it *would* be undone one day. But to do so, it would require their relics. Namely, the Final Relic."

Hal scowled. "Isn't that a hoax that the Keeper of the Depths made up to try to deceive us?"

"The Keeper of the Depths may have been a liar in many ways, but she did not lie about the existence of the Final Relic," Old Snow said. "Many Dragon Rider legends speak of it, though most are rather vague."

Keershan nodded. "It seemed like they were all talking about different relics; a helmet, a breastplate, a—"

Keershan stopped speaking abruptly. A look of realization crossed his dragonic features. "Yes. *This* is the Final Relic. The golden armor you're wearing in this painting."

"Precisely," Old Snow said. He walked toward them and stopped behind Hal, folding his arms behind his back. "An entire suit of armor, designed to be worn by a future Dragon Rider, more powerful than any other relic.

Powerful enough to kill the Nameless One a second time."

Hal looked at Old Snow in shock. "Seriously? Where is it?"

Old Snow frowned. "That is the issue. I don't know for sure. Although I do know where part of it is."

Hal frowned himself. "You do? Where is it?"

"You're wearing it."

Hal immediately put his hand on his hard, rusty metal helmet. "How do you know? It doesn't look shiny and gold like in the painting."

"Only because it's spent the last five thousand years rotting away in a temple," Old Snow replied. "Did it never occur to you how strange it was that you were able to simply waltz in, pick up the helmet, and put it on? For that matter, did you not ever wonder why I was so helpful in getting you and Fralia out here, or directing Keershan where to go?"

Hal froze. His eyes darted from the painting to Old Snow and back again. "You knew. About the painting. About it all."

Old Snow nodded, a smile on his face. "Yes. Through my years of living in the Tops, I've seen many adventurers come and go. I looked in vain for the one who looked like the man in the painting, wearing the Final Relic, but never saw anyone who came even close to resembling you until you and Keershan showed up."

"Meaning you *knew* we were destined to be bonded and become the first Dragon Rider pair since the Fall?" Keershan said in amazement. He shook his head. "Wow. Even I didn't see that one coming."

"If you knew about this from the start, then why did you not tell us right away?"

Old Snow gave Hal a rather amused smile. "Do you think that the same Halar Norath who hated dragons and thought the whole Dragon Rider thing was the delusional ramblings of a runt dragon would have *ever* believed that he was destined to save the world?"

Hal opened his mouth to argue, thought about Old Snow's response, and closed his mouth. "Yeah. I *was* a jerk, wasn't I?"

"Not more than anyone else in your situation would have been," Old Snow said gently, putting a hand on Hal's shoulder. "The burden you've been tasked with carrying is larger than what most people are even capable of. Why else do you think I've been subtly pushing you in the direction of a leader? I wanted to prepare you for this moment, for you to come to accept your destiny on your own, and make this *your* decision. Not mine. Not the gods'. Not even destiny's."

"What about me?" asked Keershan. He clawed the floor. "I'd like to think I would have accepted the idea earlier."

Old Snow shot Keershan a similar smile. "You needed lessons in bravery. After all, I seem to recall that, when we first met, you were more interested in studying old myths and legends than in reliving them. I recognized potential in you, but like Hal's, it needed to be cultivated."

Keershan lowered his head. "I suppose I wasn't much of a fighter before all of this, huh?"

"It doesn't matter," Old Snow said. He looked from

Hal to Keershan and back again, a proud look on his face. "When I first met you two, I still wasn't entirely sure of your destiny. But after everything we've been through together, I am more convinced than ever that you are the ones who will use the Final Relic to save us all."

Hal glanced at the painting again doubtfully. "Assuming we even *can* find the Final Relic, which seems like a long shot."

Old Snow patted Hal on the shoulder. "That doesn't sound like something one of the Malarsan Army's best Relic Hunters would say, now does it?"

Hal looked at Old Snow again in surprise. "Are you telling me I need to search for it? But what about the Dragon Rider Corps? And the rebellion against Queen Bariwa?"

Old Snow shook his head. "None of that matters without the Final Relic. Of that, I am convinced."

Hal rubbed his forehead. "I don't even know where to begin looking for it. Back when I was a Relic Hunter, we relied on reports from scouts, informants, and the occasional spotter to let us know about possible relic locations. And even then, most of them were dead-ends or worse."

"Understandable," Old Snow said, "but I believe that the location of the Final Relic may be hidden on the painting." He rubbed more dust off of the wall and stepped aside. "Tell me what you see."

Hal and Keershan looked at the portion of the wall that Old Snow had scrubbed away.

To Hal's eyes, it looked like a map of some sort. It depicted an underground maze that he thought was the

Depths at first, though looking more closely, he saw that it wasn't the Depths at all. Rather, it was some sort of series of underground tunnels that were vaguely in the shape of a curled, sleeping dragon.

"It is what I believe is the location of the rest of the Final Relic," Old Snow said. He tapped the middle of the maze. "As for where it is located, I think it's obvious."

Hal was about to say that no, it wasn't, until he noticed Old Snow was poking some writing underneath it. He stepped closer and leaned in to read the writing, which was in an old language that *looked* like a combination of Draco and Malarsan, although it was clearly neither.

Yet despite that, Hal could read it as clearly as day, and what he read sent a chill down his spine.

"What are the Burial Grounds?" Hal said, looking at Old Snow.

Old Snow lowered his head. "Where do you think? Underneath Castle Lamor, right where the Nameless One's remains are said to have been buried."

"So the Relic Crafters put the Final Relic near the Nameless One's body?" asked Keershan. "I'm not sure if that is a smart idea or a dumb one. Doesn't seem like an easy place to get to."

"It isn't," Old Snow said, "particularly now, but I am convinced that we need to go there. At least, you two do."

"Couldn't we beat the Nameless One *without* the Final Relic?" asked Hal, tearing his eyes away from the painting to look at Old Snow once more. "The Dragon Riders of old did, right?"

"Possibly," Old Snow said, "but I suspect the Relic Crafters painted this for a reason."

Keershan hesitated. "Do you think that they thought the Nameless One would come back *stronger* than he was last time?"

Hal had no answer to that question, though it seemed like a fair conclusion to him.

Old Snow rested his chin on his fist. "Maybe. Either way, we were going to have to return to the capital at some point anyway to stop Marial. If we can get the whole Final Relic while we're at it, all the better."

Hal frowned. "You make it sound like we're going on a quest of some sort."

"We may very well have to," Old Snow said. "It isn't like we can stop Marial or anyone else while hiding here in the Tops."

Hal bit his lower lip and looked at the painting again.

He agreed with Old Snow about the need for them to leave the Tops eventually. The only way they could stop Queen Bariwa from resurrecting the Nameless One was to leave Mysteria and put an end to her schemes before it was too late.

On the other hand, if what Old Snow said was true, then the Burial Grounds were where they needed to go next.

And likely heavily guarded by the Malarsan Army. Can't forget the hundreds of slaves and mages they have now, either.

It all sounded so hard to believe to Hal, but on the other hand, he'd heard plenty of unbelievable things that turned out to be true over the last three or four months. It was in the very chamber above them, after all, where

Hal first learned of the Dragon Riders and the role they'd played in the defeat of the Nameless One long ago.

Old Snow is probably right. Hal rested his hand on the sheath of his sword. *But are we really ready to mount a direct assault on Castle Lamor yet? And what about the Glacians? We still haven't decided if we want their help yet or not.*

Old Snow patted Hal on the shoulder again. "It is fine if you haven't made a decision yet. There is still time, though I fear we have less and less as each day passes."

Hal nodded. A shout echoed above. Hal said, "What was that?"

"It sounded like Anija," Keershan said with a frown. "I thought she and my sister had gone off to check on the hatchlings."

"We should go check," Old Snow said grimly.

Hal walked toward the steps as quickly as he could, with Keershan and Old Snow following closely behind. As Hal entered the staircase and began ascending, however, he could not help but think about the Relic Crafters, the Final Relic, the Burial Grounds, and everything that he'd learned down here.

One way or another, we will *have to confront Queen Bariwa.* Hal's boots scraped against the stone steps as he took them one at a time. *Whether we want to or not.*

Chapter Ten

FRALIA FELT HOT.

That was unusual for many reasons, chief among them being that Fralia was sure that it had just turned early spring in the Tops. Old Snow had explained that the worst blizzards arrived at the tail end of spring, which he described as 'winter's goodbye.'

Which I should be right in the middle of myself right now. Fralia rubbed her forehead with the back of her hand. *But* why *should I be in the middle of it?*

The answer came to her quickly. Memories flooded her mind as she recalled her and Cav's battle with the slave and the demonic bats in the skies over the Tops. Every scene of the battle played through her mind in rapid succession, right up to the moment that the slave knocked them out of the sky and they crashed.

After that, nothing. Fralia felt her bare chest. *Clearly, I didn't die, but where am I? Or was that all a dream?*

Fralia felt a warm, damp rag applied to her forehead

by someone she couldn't see. Fralia sat up swiftly, hearing a startled grunt come from somewhere behind her. She opened her eyes.

Fralia was inside a large, cozy tent. A fireball, encased in some kind of glass sphere, hovered near the top of the tent, clearly the source of the heat and light. A large steel pot, bubbling with delicious-smelling beef stew, stood in the center. She spotted a comfy-looking cot, plus a desk, on the other side of the tent, along with a small wooden table covered with plates, bowls, and silverware. Fralia's mouth was rather dry.

And kneeling beside Fralia was a woman with a damp rag in her hand. Her snow-white hair pegged her as a Glacian, complete with robes that looked similar to Jinka's and surprised-looking ice-blue eyes.

Fralia blinked. "Um, hello?"

She must have said something wrong because the woman just crawled away from her. Fralia didn't know what was intimidating. A quick inspection of her body told Fralia that she'd been stripped of her robes and was more or less naked, prompting her to pull her blankets up to her chin.

"Sorry," Fralia said to the woman. "I was just a little startled to see you. Where am I—?"

The woman did not answer right away. Instead, after a moment of staring at Fralia, she rose to her feet and walked toward a tub off to the side that Fralia had not noticed before. The rising steam from it told Fralia that it probably had warm water.

The woman stopped in front of the tub and dropped her rag into it with a soft *plop*. She then grabbed a water pitcher off the table next to it, poured some water into a metallic cup, walked over to Fralia, and handed it to her. "Drink. Snow water."

Fralia took the cup, which was cold in her hands. She was incredibly thirsty, however, and drank greedily.

"Thanks," Fralia said, lowering the cup and looking up at the woman. "I appreciate it, um—?"

"Aople," the woman said simply. "Are you hungry?"

Fralia felt her stomach growl at the question. "A little, yes."

"Let me find food for you." Aople took a long ladle and scooped out a couple of helpings of stew into a wooden bowl. "Here. Eat."

The bowl was pleasantly warm. It definitely smelled like beef with a hint of some spice she could not name.

Fralia popped a spoonful into her mouth and savored the savory taste of meat and broth. "This is really good. What is it?"

"Arctic beef stew," said Aople. "Good for cold nights like this."

"Cold nights—?" Fralia looked up at Aople in surprise. "How long have I been out?"

Aople held up a finger. "One hour. Your friend and his dragon are safe in other tent. Except dragon, but we move him to nearby cave, and our healers work on him now."

"Thanks. But what about Jinka? Is she—?"

A warm smile crossed Aople's face. "She is safe. Thanks to you."

That was a relief to Fralia, though she found Aople's reaction interesting. She wondered if Aople was related to Jinka in some way. That would explain why Aople seemed so happy that the young girl was safe, after all.

Her thoughts were interrupted by the sound of a tent flap opening, briefly punctuated by howling winds outside, before the outside sounds became muted again.

A Glacian man had entered. He was covered from head to foot in colorful, warm-looking robes, the snow on his shoulders and head already starting to melt thanks to the tent's heat.

"Aople," said the Glacian man with a strange accent, "is the mage—?"

The Glacian man stopped speaking when he saw Fralia sitting up and eating stew. "Never mind. I just answered my own question."

Fralia, feeling a bit exposed, brought her blanket up a little closer to her body, though she didn't want to put down the soup. "Who are you?"

The man did a sweeping bow. "Inquirer Dedeket. And you are Fralia Jeniq, daughter of the late General Kolass?"

Fralia froze. Hal had described this man earlier. "How do you know who I am?"

Dedeket rose to his full height, amusement crinkling his eyes. "It is the job of an inquirer of the God-Emperor to know all. For we are his eyes and ears. Plus, we've met before."

Fralia frowned. "We have?"

"Yes. It was at a meeting between the Malarsan royal family and God-Emperor Kryo Kardia. I was still an apprentice inquirer at the time and I met your father, a young but ambitious captain who had brought his family with him. He seemed especially proud of you, his youngest child at the time, I recall. You've certainly grown into a fine young lady since then."

Fralia blushed slightly. She had zero memory of Dedeket's story, but she knew that Father, due to his position in the Malarsan Army, had attended many negotiations and meetings between Malarsan and the Glaci Empire. She'd even accompanied him to a few of them, though mostly in her teenage years when Father was preparing her for her future working for the kingdom. "Thanks, but I don't remember you. At all."

"Not to worry," said Dedeket with a wave of his hand. He nodded at Aople. "I came to thank you for bringing my wayward daughter back to me. Little Jinka has always had an independent streak about her."

Fralia raised an eyebrow. "You mean you weren't worried about your five -year-old daughter wandering off on her own in a dangerous, foreign environment that she hadn't ever been to before?"

Dedeket laughed. "Why should I? She's a special girl. No harm would ever come to her. That is what I was told at her birth, and thus far, it seems true."

That made Fralia raise another eyebrow, but before she could say anything, Dedeket continued, saying, "But it is impossible for a parent who truly cares about their child to not be at least a little concerned when they disappear. And since you and your Dragon Rider friend brought her back to us safe and sound, I wanted to thank you personally."

Fralia smiled. "You're welcome, Dedeket. Although I don't remember what happened after our crash."

Dedeket folded his arms in front of his chest. "You were near our campsite, as it turned out. We heard something and sent a few scouts to investigate, which is how we found out that you were under attack by another dragon."

"Where is it? Is it—?"

"Gone," Dedeket said, jerking a thumb over his shoulder. "We drove it off using our *own* magic. That, and the fact that the blizzard was coming in. I suspect that the dragon went off to find someplace safe to wait out the storm, but I doubt it will return."

Fralia sighed in relief. She'd been anxious about the slave, knowing from experience that the demons did not like to leave loose ends untied.

Glacian magic must be something else.

"Speaking of the blizzard, it doesn't look like it is going to let up anytime soon," said Dedeket, glancing at the tent flap. "It was a struggle just to get here from my wagon. Our resident weather reader thinks the storm won't let up until tomorrow morning at the earliest."

Fralia felt her gut wrench. "I need to get back to town tonight."

"Why? Did you have some urgent tasks to attend to?"

Fralia was supposed to be in her training class with Akon, but she realized that all of Mysteria's activities had likely been canceled tonight as a result of the storm. Despite having a variety of powerful and experienced mages on their side now, the Tops's blizzards were too powerful for even the strongest mages to stop, so the inhabitants of Mysteria usually chose to spend storms huddled up inside keeping warm.

"Stay as long as you like," said Dedeket, gesturing at the tent. "Our heat tents are specially designed to withstand the harshest of arctic winters. Trust me, your Malarsan blizzards are *nothing* compared to the blizzards of the Northern Circle."

Fralia nodded. "Thank you for your kindness, Dedeket. I don't know how I can repay you."

Dedeket's eyes glimmered slightly. "Well, you've already paid me back several times over by saving my daughter. But if you really want to do more, have your people decided whether to accept His Majesty's offer yet?"

Fralia bit her lower lip. Rather than answer right away, she scooped some more soup in her mouth, eating it slowly. "Jinka interrupted us before we could make a decision."

A hint of irritation flashed across Dedeket's eyes. Aople shifted her weight, a guilty look on her face.

Did Dedeket put her up to this? Or is she also trying to get us to accept Kryo Kardia's offer?

"I see," said Dedeket. "I understand, of course, that you Dragon Riders are run by a council of individuals with equal standing. Even so, the kindness and hospitality we are showing you and your friends here tonight are but a glimpse of the support that His Majesty will gladly bestow upon you if you agree to it."

Fralia sipped her snow water. Not only had the Glacians saved them, but they'd probably healed them too, as Fralia did not feel any pain from their crash.

And I have to admit, it would be nice to have more modern amenities in the village. Much better than our current situation.

Even if Kryo Kardia's motives are self-serving, it might be worth it.

"Anyway, I have a question for you, Miss Jeniq," said Dedeket suddenly, his words snapping Fralia out of her thoughts.

"Hmm?" Fralia said, looking at Dedeket over the top of her cup. "What is it?"

Dedeket stroked his chin. "I was curious as to why a woman of your position in Malarsan society would volunteer to be the bodyguard of a Relic Hunter, rather than pursuing something higher, such as a professorship at the academy or even becoming a war mage like your father."

"You definitely know a lot about me."

Dedeket shrugged. "As I said, it is the job of inquirers to know *everything*. And I happen to be even more thorough than the others. Hence how I found out that your first job out of the academy was being the bodyguard of Halar Norath. Even though you were offered many great positions, such as a professorship in the academy and an opportunity to study under Archmage Zora himself. I understood it caused quite a scandal when you decided to become a Relic Hunter's bodyguard."

Fralia put another spoonful of tasty beef stew in her mouth. She wasn't sure that she wanted to respond. It really wasn't any of Dedeket's business.

On the other hand, the Glacians had been rather kind to her so far.

So Fralia said, "Mostly, I wanted freedom."

Dedeket cocked his head to the side. "Freedom? From what?"

Fralia took a deep breath. "Expectations. My other siblings are also accomplished individuals in their own right. Dhan is a war mage like Dad while Orelu is on her way to becoming a professor. Or was last time I spoke to her. Haven't seen either of them in a while."

"I see," said Dedeket. "I can imagine that growing up the daughter of the hero of Malarsan would put a lot of pressure on anyone. Having grown up from rather humble beginnings myself, I can't relate."

"It's hard. I didn't want to be a professor but I also didn't want to be out on the front lines fighting the dragons. I wanted to adventure and see the world. I saw a lot of interesting places before Hal became a Dragon Rider. Still have, to be honest, even if the reasons for going to said interesting places are different."

Dedeket tapped his chin in thought. "Fascinating, yet understandable. Before I go, however, Miss Jeniq, I do have one more, rather pertinent question, something that's been on my mind recently and that even my sources haven't been able to confirm one way or another."

Fralia was not sure she liked where Dedeket was going with this conversation. "Yes?"

Dedeket stared her straight in the eyes with rather frightening intensity. "Did you murder your father?"

Fralia clutched her dragontooth necklace—which had once belonged to her father—tightly with one hand. "No. A demon did."

Fralia did not quite know what Dedeket expected from her. He stared at her for a moment before nodding once and saying, "I thought so. Well, I will leave you and Aople alone. You will be perfectly safe for the night."

With that, Dedeket slipped out the tent flap, briefly giving Fralia a glimpse of the raging blizzard outside before it closed.

Aople, apparently, wasn't one for conversation. She returned to the stew pot, stirring it occasionally while giving herself a bowlful of the stuff.

Why did he want to know if I murdered Father or not? Father died months ago.

Just the thought of Father's passing made Fralia's heart ache.

Fralia was a little worried about the others back in town.

I'm sure they will be fine on their own. Fralia scooped another spoonful of stew into her mouth. *They're probably holing up just like us to wait out the storm. I'm sure they have nothing going on tonight, anyway.*

Chapter Eleven

ANIJA STOOD IN THE HALL OF THE FORBIDDEN TEMPLE, arms crossed in front of her chest. Rialo stood behind her. Outside, she could hear the roaring of the winds and snow from the blizzard that had started up, but she was hardly concerned about that.

No, she was concerned about the three figures who had just emerged from some concealed door, one of whom was hiding secrets from them.

"Anija?" Hal said. "Are you okay? What happened?"

Anija looked at Hal in annoyance. "What happened? *This* happened."

Anija pulled out the demonic covenant from her bag and held it up for everyone to see.

Hal and Keershan exchanged puzzled looks, but it was Old Snow's reaction that interested her the most.

The fact was that he *didn't* react at all, except to twitch a single eyebrow.

Suspicious. What is he hiding?

Perhaps nothing, Rialo offered mentally. *It isn't like we have proof that this covenant is even real. Jaspus doesn't have a reputation for honesty and truthfulness.*

Anija did her best to ignore Rialo. Shaking the demonic covenant, Anija said, "Do you know what this is?"

"A covenant," Old Snow said. "Similar to the one we found in the Depths back in Dragon Valley."

Anija gave Old Snow an extra suspicious glare. "Exactly. Though I bet you *would* know, wouldn't you? I'm sure you've seen this one in particular yourself before."

"Anija, what are you talking about?" asked Hal, putting his hands on his hips. "Where did you even get that from?"

Anija glanced at Hal. "Turns out Jaspus survived the Battle of Dragon Valley and regrets his betrayal. He gave us this to prove his supposed change of heart. Queen Bariwa isn't the one who originally summoned the demons. It was Old Snow."

As Anija expected, that got a reaction from Hal and Keershan. The Dragon Rider pair looked at Old Snow suddenly, like he was a hungry mountain snake rather than a trusted friend and mentor.

Old Snow scratched his short, white beard. "If you think that's what it says, Anija, then read it aloud. It isn't like we have anywhere else we need to go, especially in this storm."

"All right." Scanning the covenant, Anija found the relevant section.

"And to him who originally called us, King Rikas Bariwa, son

of King Bakar Bariwa, king of Malarsan, and defender of the kingdom, we do grant him his heart's desire in exchange for loyalty to our cause."

Anija looked up at Old Snow. "Explain that, old man."

"That is accurate. Though it's missing important context."

Anija's jaw fell open. She'd expected denial, rationalizations, maybe even rage.

Hal said, "Important context—? What are you talking about? I thought you had a falling out with Queen Bariwa precisely *because* she decided to summon the demons."

Old Snow seemed to be choosing his words carefully. He walked over to one of the dragon statues that was missing its head. Arms folded behind his back, he stared up at the statue as if it was a real creature that he could actually speak to.

"I never told any of you the full story about how Marial and I ended our marriage," Old Snow said, his voice tight with emotion. "And for good reason. It doesn't make me look good. It doesn't make any of us look good."

"Who cares about how it makes you look?" Anija said dismissively. She raised the demonic covenant again. "You are the one who put us in this mess in the first place. That's a bad look no matter how you spin it."

Old Snow sighed. "Spinning it implies I know how to do that. Truthfully, there's nothing I can say that would justify my role in our current situation. But I can tell you things that would help you understand it."

Anija bit her lower lip. She was still skeptical of Old Snow, but… "Go on, then. Tell us what happened."

Old Snow nodded, though without looking at any of them. "Fifteen years ago, Marial and I were blessed with the birth of our first—and only—child. He was a boy, our son, and I named him Hiras in honor of the kingdom's first and best king."

Hal slowly nodded. "I think I remember hearing about the birth, though I don't recall much."

Old Snow looked at his feet. "That's because our son was born relatively late into our marriage, and he came out with some deficiencies. Physically and mentally, Hiras was not quite like the other children he grew up with. For that reason, we kept him largely isolated from others, as we were afraid of what they might do to him. In retrospect, that is probably what caused a lot of our problems down the line, though we didn't know it at the time. We were just trying to do our best."

Then Old Snow slumped his shoulders. "Marial, she felt like a failure, I believe. We'd struggled for so long, so long, to have a child, only for him to have to struggle in this world. Marial asked the archmages to heal him, but whatever had gone wrong with Hiras's birth was beyond the ability of even our best mages to heal."

"So Marial went to the demons?" asked Anija.

Old Snow looked over his shoulder at Anija, a shockingly somber look on his features. "No. *I* did."

"So the demonic covenant is right," Anija said. She reached for the knife at her belt. "Which means we can't trust you."

"Please keep listening. Haven't I at least earned that much from you?"

Anija hesitated. "Fine. Finish your story."

Old Snow gave her a grateful smile, though it didn't last long before he looked back up at the headless dragon statue. "I learned of the legends of the demons and the Dragon Riders from my own research into the myths of our kingdom. I initially dismissed them as nothing more than fables, but one day, a demon reached out to me, and offered to heal our son of his defect if we'd summon him."

"So you summoned this demon knowingly?" asked Hal.

"I didn't know what myths were true. For all I knew, the demons had been unfairly painted. And we were desperate, so I agreed to perform the summoning ritual. That was the worst mistake of my life."

Old Snow turned to face them again, though he kept his head low. "The summoning was successful. We brought a demon into the physical world. By doing so, we signed a deal that bonded us with the demons. It was a significant shift, giving the demons a foothold in the royal family. And our son wasn't even healed."

"What happened to your son, then?" Hal said.

Grief crept across Old Snow's face. "Marial became drunk with power. The demons told her about how we could finish off the dragons once and for all, that if we just listened to them, we could end the Dragon War forever. We could make Malarsan the strongest nation on the planet, a force powerful enough to challenge even the

Glaci Empire. But they wanted one thing in exchange for helping us."

Rialo said, "It was your son, wasn't it?"

Old Snow gave Rialo a sad look. "Marial did it. Sacrificed young Hiras to them, spilling his blood on the ritual. Against my will, that is."

Keershan clawed at the floor. "Why? I thought you had summoned the demons to *heal* him."

"Marial had other plans. I should have seen that coming. She always respected strength in a man. It's partly why we always argued. She lusted after power above all else while I often sought out peaceful solutions to our problems."

"I take it that's when you exiled yourself to the Tops, right?" Hal said.

Old Snow glanced around the Forbidden Temple as if looking at the place for the first time. "Yes. After that, I tried —how I tried—to stop Marial, to stop the demons, but by then it was too late. She had used the dark magic of the demons to turn the entire castle against me and kill or silence my supporters among the nobles, if not outright convert some of them into demonic followers themselves. I had no choice but to abdicate the throne, after faking my death."

"Why?" Hal said.

"Because if I had not, Marial would have killed me. I spent the next ten years hiding out, learning all that I could about the Dragon Riders and the true history."

"And now we are here," Anija finished for him. "That's certainly a story."

"A true one," Old Snow replied. He hung his head

even lower. "I apologize for not being upfront about this earlier. As you can imagine, it's a difficult memory for me to return to, as most of our problems can be traced back to my decision."

Anija scowled. "That's putting it pretty lightly, mate. Maybe a little *too* lightly."

Old Snow spread his arms as widely as possible. "Everything I've done so far—all the help and support I've provided, all the information I've given you, all the arrows I've shot—has been my way of repenting of my sins. By opposing my wife, who has completely lost her mind, I have given up my throne, my heritage, my rights, even the power I once wielded. I wouldn't live like this— a simple hermit in the mountains who doesn't even have a pillow to lay his head on—if I *wasn't* sincere about stopping the demons."

Old Snow shook his head. "No. I know my sins and my mistakes, Anija, know them better than anyone except perhaps the gods themselves. Fault me for not telling you all about them if you wish—I won't argue with that—but I will defend myself from any accusations of being friends with demons. I'd rather die a thousand painful, agonizing deaths than ever help a demon."

Anija nodded. Despite how angry she'd been earlier, she was starting to realize just how hasty she'd been in believing Jaspus's manipulations. It made her feel rather foolish herself and also caused her to question if Jaspus gave her that information for precisely that reason.

Then Old Snow sighed suddenly and his shoulders slumped. "But I'm not angry with you, Anija. I hope you understand. I'm just tired, I suppose. It has been a very long day, a long three months, and I'm afraid it will just get longer."

"It's fine, Old Snow. Honestly, I shouldn't have been so quick to judge. Should have known better than to believe Jaspus."

Old Snow nodded. "That is how the demons operate. They take truths and half-truths and twist them or use them as a way to drive a wedge between friends."

"Isn't *that* the truth," Rialo said with a disgruntled grunt.

"Anyway," Hal said. "Now that we have this out of the way, let's call it a night. The blizzard is getting worse."

Hal had a point. The howling winds outside sounded louder than ever, and the Forgotten Temple was much colder than Rialo's dragon cave.

But then Rialo lowered her head until it was level with the humans and she said, "Wait a second. We learned something else from Jaspus."

"Oh?" Old Snow said, looking at her with interest. "What is it?"

Anija took a deep breath. "A month from now, the Nameless One will come back."

Chapter Twelve

"THE DAY OF SHADOWS," SURRELS REPEATED incredulously. He stared at Anija. "Is that really what they're calling it?"

"It's a translation from the demonic language," Keershan said, sitting beside Hal, resting his head on the meeting table. "There are references to it in the old legends."

Surrels shook his head. "Either way, it doesn't exactly sound like a fun holiday for the whole family, now does it?"

Hal looked at the demonic covenant on the table before them before sipping from his coffee. "That's why we need to stop it."

"The question is, how?" Surrels looked around the table at the assembled council. "Because in case everyone forgot, we are still outnumbered a hundred to one at least."

Fralia leaned forward. "We should accept the Glacians' help."

Though paler than normal and with a bit of a cough, she looked rather good for a woman who had been knocked out of the sky by a dragon in the middle of a snowstorm.

It was the middle of the morning after the revelation of Old Snow's true role in the rise of the demons. The blizzard had stopped sometime during the night, covering the landscape in thick snowdrifts. Fralia, Cav, and Onito had flown from the Glacian camp back to Mysteria once the sun had risen.

Hal had called another council meeting to make sure that everyone was on the same page. Fralia and Surrels had taken the news about Old Snow a lot better than Hal and Anija had.

They had just finished listening to Anija and Rialo's report about the Nameless One's coming resurrection.

Which leaves us with the decision of what, exactly, to do about it.

"You said that awfully quick," Surrels said, tugging on his thick winter cap. "I thought you were skeptical about accepting their help earlier."

"I was, but having spent the night with them at their camp, I have to say that I think we could benefit from their help. Plus, after saving Dedeket's kid, they're even more willing to help us than before."

Old Snow, sitting on the far side of the table across from Hal, nodded. "The Glacians have enough resources to back our rebellion, resources we badly need."

Anija rested her chin on her hand. "I'm still skeptical

of that Kryo Kardia guy. I'm not sure making Malarsan a vassal state of the Glaci Empire would be that much of an improvement."

Old Snow said, "Believe me, I don't care much for the idea, either. But at the same time, we are in desperate need of more resources. Rebellions don't fund themselves."

"Even if we accepted their help," Hal pondered, "Would the Glaci Empire even be strong enough to stop the Nameless One? Or prevent Queen Bariwa from resurrecting him?"

"I understand where Hal is coming from," said Rialo. "The Northern Circle is far away, yes? I imagine it would take Dedeket's group weeks, if not months, to return with the news of our acceptance. And it would take even more time for Kryo Kardia to put together a force to help us."

"And we only have a month before the Nameless One comes back," Keershan added. "Granted, that is assuming that Jaspus wasn't lying to our faces, but—"

"This whole conflict might be over within a month's time anyway," Hal said. "We could get the rest of the Final Relic."

Surrels rolled his eyes. "You mean the legendary relic said to be *underneath* Castle Lamor? That is hundreds of miles away from the Tops, probably guarded by soldiers, mages, dragons, and demons? Yes, that seems like a realistic feat."

"But it might also be our best option," Hal said. He looked around the table. "Think about it. We already know, thanks to the crafters' workshop, that I am supposed to use the Final Relic. We know it was designed for exactly this sort of situation. And ask yourself this: Do you think that Queen Bariwa or any of her subordinates or loyalists would think we're crazy enough to directly assault the capital itself?"

"I'm not sure *we're* crazy enough to do that," Surrels replied. "At least, I'm not."

Hal tapped his helmet. "It doesn't need to be all of us. In fact, it might be just enough if Keershan and I went by ourselves."

Fralia shot Hal a sharp look. "You mean you think the two of you should infiltrate Castle Lamor alone? I really hope you've thought this through, because that sounds incredibly dangerous."

"I've given it a lot of thought," Hal said. He reached out and patted Keershan on the head. "*We've* given it a lot of thought, haven't we?"

Keershan nodded. "Last night, Hal and I spent a lot of time thinking about our options. It's easier for two people to sneak into the capital alone than for a whole group of people."

"That's still risky," Fralia said. "In case you forgot, Hal, you are the leader of the Dragon Riders. We need your leadership."

"I know," Hal said. "That's why Anija will be in charge of the Dragon Riders while I'm away."

Anija put a hand on her chest. "Me? Why me? I'm not a leader."

"You're the most experienced Dragon Rider after me," Hal explained. "You'll make a fine leader. Trust me."

Hal meant that, despite the conflicts he and Anija may have had in the past.

"Another thing to consider is that we don't want to leave Mysteria undefended in case of another attack." Keershan gave Fralia a meaningful look. "Especially now that we know that slaves and demons are in the area."

There had been no reports from the scouts since the blizzard had forced the slave into seeking shelter, so it was probably still out there somewhere.

Hal pointed at Keershan. "That's another good reason to get the Final Relic. Queen Bariwa is obviously getting bolder. It would not surprise me if she's planning to send the army to invade the Tops and finish us off."

"It would be even better if we could get the Glacians on our side," Fralia looked around the table urgently. "We should at least put the offer to a vote. Especially in light of this recent information."

"I'm against it," Surrels said immediately. He glanced out one of the nearby windows as if worried that the Glacians might be eavesdropping on them. "Foreign entanglements are a great way to cause us big headaches later down the line."

"I'm with Surrels," Anija said, folding her arms in front of her chest. "I don't trust Glacians as a general rule. Tricky folks, and that's saying something, given how I used to work for the Dark Tigers."

"Obviously, I am in favor," Fralia said.

Old Snow nodded in agreement. "Kryo Kardia may not be a good person, but I think it unwise to turn down potential help."

Rialo snorted. "I am skeptical as well. We dragons do not need help from others."

Everyone looked at Hal and Keershan. Their decisions would decide the council's course of action, as they were the only two who had yet to weigh in on the issue.

Truthfully, Hal was torn. His own encounter with the Glacians, though far from hostile, had not left him feeling confident in the trustworthiness of the Glacians, much less Kryo Kardia himself.

On the other hand, Hal also realized that they very much needed all the help and resources they could get. It was only a matter of time before Queen Bariwa decided to eliminate them once and for all, and Hal was not at all sure that Mysteria would be able to repel a full-on invasion from the Malarsan Army all by itself.

Especially since we know they'll use a lot of their slaves. If they have enough slaves, they might not even need to send their soldiers.

Through their bond, Hal could tell that Keershan felt very conflicted, too, though he was starting to come to his own conclusion on the subject.

Indeed, it took just one eye exchange for the two to know their decision.

Looking back at the rest of the council, Hal said, "All right. We will accept Emperor Kryo Kardia's offer and work with the Glacians to overthrow Queen Bariwa."

Chapter Thirteen

FRALIA DIDN'T KNOW WHAT TO EXPECT WHEN OLD SNOW asked her to stay behind in the Forgotten Temple after the meeting. Of course, she knew that they were going to contact Kryo Kardia, but even with her magical talents and studies, she didn't know how that would work. The only form of long-distance magical communication that she knew of that worked with any real consistency was the communication necklace system, but even that was usually limited to two people speaking through the same necklace.

Once the council made its final decision, the meeting ended. Hal, Keershan, Anija, and Rialo went to inform the Dragon Riders of where Hal and Keershan would be going.

Surrels, meanwhile, left to, as he put it, 'tend to his garden,' which Fralia inferred was the town garden where food was grown.

But Old Snow had asked Fralia to stay here with him,

which Fralia agreed to. She had already told Akon earlier that he could go forward with their magical training exercises without her for the day, as she'd suspected she might be a bit tied up, so she didn't feel guilty for spending more time with Old Snow.

"So what are we doing, exactly?" Fralia said as she picked up a large, thick rough log and handed it to Old Snow.

Old Snow deposited it into the altar. "Contacting Kryo Kardia."

"How?"

Old Snow pulled out a blank sheet of paper from his robes and held it in front of Fralia's face. "Inquirer Dedeket gave Hal this sheet of paper to contact Kryo Kardia with."

Fralia frowned. "But it's just paper."

Old Snow nodded. "So it seems, but Glacian magic, in my experience, is a bit different from Malarsan magic."

Fralia couldn't disagree with that. During her brief stay in the Glacians' camp, she'd marveled at how their heat tents kept the inhabitants as warm and comfortable as if they were sitting in front of a roaring fireplace even in the middle of the coldest blizzards. She'd even asked Aople about it, but the Glacian woman had seemed oddly tight-lipped about their magic.

Maybe she's not allowed to share potentially-sensitive information with people who aren't allies of the empire yet? Or maybe she just didn't know. She didn't look like a mage to me.

Old Snow glanced at the small pile of wood they had placed in the altar. "That should be enough. I know you specialize in air magic, but how much fire magic do you know?"

Fralia raised her finger, and a small light burst into existence. "Just the basic fireball. Watch."

Focusing deeply, Fralia increased the size of the flame until it was about three or four fists put together. She threw the ball into the altar, and the dry wood instantly roared to life. The smell of burning was comforting to Fralia, reminding her of the times when she would curl up with her parents in front of their fireplace back home when she was cold during winter.

"Okay," Fralia said, looking at Old Snow again, "what do we do—Hey!"

Old Snow had thrown the paper in. It landed amid the burning logs briefly before turning to ash.

"What was that about, Snow?" asked Fralia in horror. "That was our only way to—"

The ashes of the paper were glowing a soft ice-blue color, sapping the heat away. Fralia shivered and drew her robes more tightly around her. Old Snow stepped back.

A soft *clap* came from the sparks, and the flickering image of a figure whom Fralia had never seen before rose up from within the cold flames.

Ten feet tall, the figure towered over them both, clad in thick, smooth armor that appeared to be made out of ice. A crown, also made of ice, sat on his head. His white hair spilled down to his shoulders, giving him the appearance of having snow falling from his head.

His skin was a sickly gray tone, but it was his eyes that really caught Fralia's attention. They looked like they were made of ice, as cold and unfeeling as the blizzard that had been raging outside last night. Combined with his sharp features, the figure before them was the very definition of regal power.

"Who summons the God-Emperor of the Glaci Empire, Protector of the Northern Circle, and Ruler of the Ice?" the figure demanded, his voice as deep and booming as a roaring blizzard.

Fralia felt her mouth become dry.

Fortunately, Old Snow stepped forward and, bowing respectfully while gesturing for Fralia to do the same, said, "Hello, Emperor Kryo Kardia. It has been an age since we last spoke."

Kryo Kardia shifted his gaze to Old Snow, which Fralia was grateful for, as his gaze was too intense for her. "King Rikas. You look quite well for a man who has been dead for ten years."

"Reports of my death were greatly exaggerated," Old Snow replied. "You haven't gotten rid of me yet."

Kryo Kardia laughed. "Of course. Although I think you will look much better once you are sitting back on the Malarsan throne after executing your rebellious wife."

Fralia was surprised at how Old Snow and Kryo Kardia spoke so casually to each other.

"And who is the beautiful young woman I have the pleasure of speaking to today?"

"Fr-Fralia Jeniq."

"Jeniq," Kryo Kardia's eyes lit up. "Ah. I spoke to General Kolass a few times and always had respect for his experience and strength. A good man who died before he should have."

Fralia's shoulders slumped. "Yeah. I still miss him."

"My condolences," said Kryo Kardia. He shifted his gaze to Old Snow again. "I take it that Inquirer Dedeket and his caravan successfully reached your town."

Old Snow nodded. "Yes. After much debate, we've decided to accept your support."

A smile crossed Kryo Kardia's lips just then, but only for a moment before it abruptly changed to a flat expression. "Most excellent. It will be a pleasure to provide you and your allies with whatever support you need to defeat Queen Bariwa and take back your throne."

"I am afraid the situation is worse than that."

Kryo Kardia raised an eyebrow. "Worse? How so?"

"Queen Bariwa is attempting to resurrect a long-dead demonic deity known as the Nameless One," Old Snow said.

"I assumed he was only legend. Although, I assumed that the Dragon Riders were myths as well, yet my inquirers inform me that you have quite the collection of Riders under your command now."

"There is more truth in myth than in history these days." Old Snow shrugged. "In any case, you know why it is urgent why we must stop her. The resurrection is merely a month away. Can you provide us with enough manpower and resources to prevent it?"

Kryo Kardia tapped the tips of his fingers together, making soft clinking noises like a couple of ice cubes being knocked together. "If the situation is as grim as you make it, Rikas, I can provide you with anything you need."

Fralia smiled in relief.

Then Kryo Kardia held up a finger. "I have only one condition: That you promise to open trade relations between Malarsan and the Glaci Empire after your wife has been overthrown and to allow Glacians to visit the kingdom as much as they like."

Old Snow frowned slightly. "I am not sure I can agree to those terms without discussing them with the council first."

"Didn't you just say that we have little time? The terms I am asking for now are not terribly onerous."

Fralia didn't see Kryo Kardia's requests as being that bad. It wasn't as if he was demanding that Old Snow make the kingdom part of the empire, after all.

Finally, Old Snow nodded again. "All right. I accept, but with the caveat that we will review the deal in a year."

Kryo Kardia raised an eyebrow. "A year from today?"

"Yes," Old Snow said. "I believe Malarsan will be in more stable shape by then. We may even be able to meet in person next time."

"It is not a bad idea, I suppose. I accept."

Fralia sensed that he wasn't exactly happy with Old Snow's counter offer.

"All right, then," Old Snow said. "When can we expect the first shipment of men?"

"Two weeks," said Kryo Kardia. "I can send men from the nearby provinces of Hosar and Knil, as they are the closest countries to the Malarsan border."

"Sounds good. I will inform the rest of the council."

Kryo Kardia bowed his head. "I thank you, Rikas, for your willingness to work alongside me to free your people from Marial's oppressive rule. May our partnership be long and fruitful."

"Let us hope," Old Snow said with less enthusiasm.

"Do not worry about reaching out to Inquirer Dedeket. I have my own ways of contacting him."

With that, Kryo Kardia swung his right arm forward and his image disappeared. The fire turned back to a more natural orange-red and the cold air was replaced with comforting warmth.

Fralia looked at Old Snow. "You're a good negotiator."

Old Snow rubbed the top of his head. "Thank you, Fralia, but I am afraid that Kryo Kardia may have gotten the best of me. At least I was able to buy us some time."

"You mean the one-year deadline?"

Old Snow nodded. "I believe I made the best decision, but I am aware that other nations have fallen for the exact same reason. Often, all Kryo Kardia needs is one foothold."

"If the Glaci Empire is so strong, why has he never successfully conquered Malarsan before? I know we have our own magic and army, but they're so much stronger than us."

Old Snow chuckled. "No one wants to admit this, but it's mostly because of the dragons. Their fire."

Fralia had a hard time imagining a being as imposing as Kryo Kardia being afraid of anything. "Fair enough, but I don't see why I had to be here. I felt a bit useless."

Old Snow tapped his chin thoughtfully. "Because you didn't talk? No, Fralia, you played a very important role, even if you didn't say very much."

Fralia stared at Old Snow in confusion. "I don't follow."

Old Snow gestured at the flames. "You have met Emperor Kryo Kardia, which will be important for future negotiations with the Glacians. And since you are the only member of the council other than myself to have met him, you will have a better idea of how to deal with him in future negotiations."

Fralia nodded slowly as she took in Old Snow's words. "I see, but you know Kryo Kardia better than me. Seems like you would be a more effective negotiator with him in the future than I would."

Old Snow gave her a mysterious smile. "I won't be around forever, Fralia. This is just my way of preparing you and the other youngsters for taking over. Now let us go and inform the others and see Hal and Keershan off."

"What if Emperor Kardia learns about the Final Relic and tries to steal it from us?"

Old Snow laughed. "He wouldn't be able to use it. A Rider's relic always returns to them. Worry instead about how Emperor Kryo Kardia may decide to take advantage of our alliance in the future."

With that, Old Snow walked toward the exit. Fralia followed, unsure if Old Snow was correct about the relics or if he was perhaps a bit too optimistic.

Worry about one thing at a time, Fralia told herself. *One thing at a time.*

Chapter Fourteen

ANIJA USUALLY DIDN'T THINK OF HERSELF AS AN authority figure. That probably came from years of working for Shadow Mask in the Dark Tiger Guild, plus her general rebellious, individualistic nature.

It wasn't that Anija did not like bossing people around—she definitely did—but rather it was that she didn't want the *responsibility* of bossing others around. She'd gotten enough of a glimpse of the pressures of leadership to know that it could be a very heavy burden to bear.

Don't worry, Rialo said in Anija's mind. *If you want, you can sit back and relax while I tell other people what to do. As a big sister and current chief of the Clawfoots, I am used to giving orders.*

Anija looked up at Rialo's head. She sat on the dragon's back, clad in her winter furs. The sun was starting to peek out from behind the clouds, providing some faint but much-appreciated warmth that had been missing these past couple of days.

I'd like to take you up on that offer, sister, but unfortunately that isn't how Dragon Rider pairs work, Anija said. *We're a team.*

She and Rialo stood on the southern end of Mysteria, near what used to be the gates for the town. Thanks to help from Fralia's mages, they had managed to repair them after years of neglect, but Anija was not exactly confident that the walls would withstand a serious assault from an invading force.

The other ten Dragon Riders were gathered around them. It was an impressive sight. She noticed Ragnol standing about a dozen feet away, regaling a female Dragon Rider with some sort of story he was undoubtedly exaggerating. Another couple of Dragon Riders—twin brothers Erine and Wrine, who had been bonded to a pair of dragon twins—were currently mock-fighting each other for the amusement of the non-Dragon Riders watching.

The Dragon Riders, of course, were not the only people here. In fact, most of Mysteria was present, the sounds of their voices filling the cold mountain air, along with their footsteps crunching the leftover snow from last night's blizzard.

Everyone had gathered for one reason: To see Hal and Keershan off on their quest to retrieve the Final Relic. The two were supposed to be leaving soon and no one wanted to miss their departure. Even many of the non-bonded dragons hovered overhead or sat on the ground nearby.

Seeing how universally popular Hal and Keershan were reminded Anija of how she wasn't.

Once everyone knows that we are being left in charge, they'll have to listen to us, no matter our personal charisma.

Easy for you *to say,* Anija told Rialo. *Maybe dragons don't need charisma to lead, but we humans certainly do. Although I suppose I could always go full Shadow Mask and threaten to execute anyone who refuses to obey my orders.*

Keershan encircled the area before landing on the ground several feet away. Hal stood on his back, covered in his old Relic Hunter armor, a new sword at his side and a shield hanging off his back. His rusted helmet completed the look, giving him a very warrior-like appearance.

"Residents and Dragon Riders of Mysteria," Hal raised his voice so that everyone could hear him. "Although I'm sure most of you know, Keershan and I want to clarify where we are going and why."

"I heard you were going to attack Castle Lamor and kill the queen," shouted an earth mage leaning against the walls of the town. "By yourself."

Hal laughed. "We are going to find the legendary Final Relic."

Hurried whispers spread among the assembled Mysterians, and even the dragons talked among themselves.

Hal looked around at the crowd before him. "This mission is too important to put off, because we have received information that in a month's time, the Nameless One will rise again during the Day of Shadows."

As Anija expected, this news caused a bit of a stir among the Mysterians.

"Next month?" said a grayish-white dragon whose name escaped Anija. "But that's too soon to do anything!"

"If we leave now, we should reach Castle Lamor in time." Keershan said.

"Are you certain you should be traveling by yourselves?" asked Ragnol doubtfully. "I've read the reports from our spies in the field. The world beyond the Tops has grown noticeably more dangerous for us. Perhaps—"

"We will be fine," Hal said. "Two people can travel much more quickly than a small group."

"You mean three people."

Anija whipped her head toward the gates. Old Snow walked with Fralia on his left and Surrels – the knees of his pants rather muddy for some reason – on his right. Old Snow had his bow and arrow slung over his shoulder, along with a traveling bag.

"You will need my help," Old Snow said. "I know the city better than anyone here."

"We agreed to the offer," Fralia added. "Emperor Kryo Kardia can get us a small army in about two weeks. The caravan he sent will be dropping off supplies for us later today before making their way back north."

"Fralia will be our liaison with the Glacians while I am away," Old Snow said.

Anija hadn't thought of Fralia as being a diplomat, but it made sense. Her status as the daughter of one of the four generals meant she was probably better suited for the task of negotiating with foreign powers like the Glaci Empire than most.

"Old Snow, are you absolutely certain you want to come with us?"

Old Snow laughed. "Hal, my friend, if safety was my top concern, I would still be in Castle Lamor with my wife. I believe that you need my help to pull this off. The rest of the council will be able to manage in our absence."

More whispers exchanged among the crowd, more looks of uncertainty or even worry. Despite that, Anija sensed that Old Snow's words had actually calmed a considerable portion of the crowd, who had been worried by Hal's statement about him and Keershan leaving the town to stop Queen Bariwa.

How is he so damn persuasive? Seriously, I'm almost convinced at this point that the old man could persuade the Nameless One to become a saint if he wanted to.

He was the king of Malarsan for a while, Rialo noted. *I imagine he has a lot of experience in public speaking and persuading people to do things.*

"All right," Hal said with a nod. "I suppose we can use all the help we can get."

"How long will you be gone?" asked Akon, a water mage who Anija recognized as Fralia's second-in-command.

Keershan said, "We hope to be within a couple of weeks at most."

"And Anija and Rialo are in charge of the Dragon Riders while I am away," Hal added. "So make sure to treat them with the same respect you'd treat me and Keershan."

Rialo rose up, while Anija tried not to squirm in her seat.

It was hard to tell, but Anija thought that most of the Dragon Riders seemed fine with Hal's decision to make her leader. It probably helped that Anija and Rialo were already his second-in-command, so it wasn't that big of a change.

So why does it feel *like more responsibility than I've ever had in my life?* Anija wondered.

Because that is what true leadership often feels like, Rialo replied. *Perhaps you now understand exactly how I felt when Father made me the chief of the Clawfoot Clan before his death. Only you at least had an inkling of yours coming.*

Anija couldn't argue with that.

Not that she said anything, however, because Hal was still speaking. "Now that we have cleared up all of that, it's time for us to go. Old Snow, are you ready?"

Old Snow nodded. He said goodbye to Fralia and Surrels, along with Anija and Rialo, before walking over to Hal and Keershan. Old Snow climbed onto Keershan's back.

With Old Snow grasping his waist safely, Hal looked at the Mysterians and waved goodbye. The people of Mysteria shouted well-wishes. Hal shot Anija a brief smile.

My job seems like child's play compared to what he's *going to do. He needs the luck more than me.*

As if on cue, Keershan started flapping his wings rapidly, sending snow flying everywhere, before launching into the sky. Keershan did another circle in the air above everyone's heads before taking a sharp turn south, heading in the direction of the capital, Castle Lamor, and, perhaps, the Final Relic.

And Anija found herself praying to the gods to keep them safe.

Chapter Fifteen

Hal remembered the days it had taken to climb down the Tops after killing the Defacer. Now they had no reason to walk. Keershan soared above the peaks.

Of course, with all the snow that still covered the ground below, Hal could barely make out the trail they had once used to travel to the town of Giant's Foot below. Even so, he could remember the feelings of anxiety and even despair that had played through his heart during that initial journey.

Amazing how many things have changed since then, Hal thought. *I didn't even want to be a Dragon Rider back in those days. Now I can't imagine* not *being a Dragon Rider.*

Same, Keershan replied. *Well, not about the 'not wanting to be a Steed' part, but about our life and how different it is. I'd like to say it's better, but I'm not sure I can.*

Losing your home is hard, Hal agreed. *But it will be worth it in the end. If we can stop the Nameless One, stop Queen Bariwa, then maybe we can build a home for both of us.*

Hal could tell that Keershan was thinking not just about Dragon Valley, but his late father, Chief Bronda.

Hal, too, had lost his father, although not nearly as recently as Keershan. It was another one of those things that had deepened their bond, even beyond merely being Dragon Rider and Steed.

It made Hal think about Lamb's Hand. In all of the craziness of the last few months, Hal had not had a chance to visit his hometown or even hear news from it. Queen Bariwa had threatened to wipe it off the map if he continued to oppose her.

Now that Hal thought about it, he and Keershan did have parallel lives in many ways. Both had lost their homes, their parents, their careers, and had risked their own lives several times.

And now, we're both going to face Queen Bariwa directly, for both of our peoples.

He heard a grunt behind him and glanced over his shoulder at Old Snow. The former king of Malarsan was holding tightly to Hal's waist. His white beard, hair, and brown robes fluttered in the wind. Though Keershan's natural body heat protected them from the worst of the cold, he still wondered how Old Snow put up with it as well as he did.

He's a tough old man for sure, Keershan said mentally. *One of the toughest people I know, human or dragon.*

Hal could not argue with that.

They flew for a couple of hours, reaching the back of the Desolate Tops—the part that was hardest to get to and was more isolated than the front—by early evening. This brought the small town of Giant's Foot into view.

Most of its buildings were covered in snow, but Hal could see lights coming on already.

That was when we first met Anija. She was trying to steal my relic, never even suspecting that she would get her own at some point.

The town had become an invaluable ally to the Dragon Riders. As the only settlement for many miles, it was their closest tie to civilization in the area.

'Civilized,' however, it was not. Due to its position, it had few law enforcers of any sort, and those few who were there were more interested in booze and prostitutes than their work.

It helped that Old Snow was on good terms with the town's residents, especially with Agate, the woman who ran the local inn and had been a consistently useful source of rumors and information on what was going on in the wider kingdom, which she would relay to the Riders' scouts whenever they passed through the town.

Can we spend the night in Giant's Foot? Keershan asked. *I'm a little tired, plus it's getting dark.*

Hal grinned. *You just want some of Agate's fried lamb, don't you?*

Can you blame me? Even Salard would descend from the heavens to enjoy that.

Hal chuckled, but said, *You've got a point. We may have to rough it from here, but that doesn't mean we can't have a nice bed to sleep in tonight, at least. Let me ask Old Snow first.*

Hal looked over his shoulder at the old man and yelled, "Old Snow! Keershan and I are thinking of spending the night in Giant's Foot. What do you think?"

Old Snow, who seemed to have been lost in thought, snapped his head toward Hal. "Of course. I haven't seen

Agate in a while, and we need to be well rested for what's to come."

Assuming Bloka doesn't decide to kick us out, Keershan added dryly.

Bloka was a giant of a man himself, who was the town's self-proclaimed protector. Though he'd given Hal's party some trouble during their first journey, Bloka had since turned out to be a reliable supporter of the Dragon Riders.

Keershan flew toward the town square, the largest open space in the cramped village. As they drew closer, Hal noticed movement in some of the windows, although that wasn't a surprise. Any time they passed through, it caused a big stir. The children, in particular, seemed to like the dragons.

That was why Hal found it odd when they landed and no one appeared.

Hal's danger instincts kicked into overdrive. He looked around the dark town square briefly, noting the well, the executioner's platform with a rusted guillotine that had seen better days, and about a dozen lamps— essentially glorified, very tall torches—rising from the cobblestone street. He smelled the usual stench of dirt and animal droppings that filled the air and felt the cold bite at the exposed parts of his skin.

But it was entirely silent.

It was as if they had walked into a graveyard.

"Keershan, Old Snow, do you notice anything out of the ordinary?"

"Maybe everyone is asleep?" Keershan said.

Old Snow shook his head. "Giant's Foot may not

have the nightlife of a major city, but the Giant's Toenail, at least, should be busy."

The inn, despite having all the lights on and the doors open, looked strangely empty. Usually there was a steady stream of fur hunters, criminals, and town inhabitants streaming in and out. It may have been a little early, but Hal would have expected to see at least a few of the regulars show up.

That was when someone burst out, screaming his head off. The man rushed toward them.

It was Bloka, running toward them faster than Hal had ever seen him move. He looked as if he was possessed, his eyes wide and fearful.

Bloka tripped over something and landed flat on his face not far from them. Hal and Old Snow leaped off of Keershan's back and rushed over. Hal reached him first and knelt beside the large man, who had stopped screaming and looked for all the world like a corpse.

"Bloka?" Hal shook his shoulder. "Can you hear me?"

Bloka raised his head. Blood was splattered all over his face, deep wounds had been cut into his flesh, and he appeared to be missing quite a few teeth. The blood looked and smelled quite fresh, making Hal wrinkle his nose.

Yet it was not the obvious injuries that made Hal feel afraid. No, it was the sheer look of absolute terror that was written all over Bloka's face. It was as if he had seen into the depths of hell itself.

"Run," Bloka gasped, his voice shockingly weak. "Leave, save yourselves …"

"Why?" Old Snow said. "What happened here? Who attacked you?"

Bloka trembled and tried to rise before falling back down onto the ground, hyperventilating.

"Um, guys?" Keershan said. "We're not alone."

The inhabitants of Giant's Foot emerged from the surrounding buildings. Hal knew them all, either on a first-name basis or at least from seeing them around town.

But the people all wore strange, spider-like masks over their faces. They walked as if in a stupor, feet shuffling unnaturally across the ground. There was absolute silence, aside from boots clicking against cobblestones and clothing swaying in the wind. Despite not being dressed for the weather, they did not appear to feel the coldness of the night.

The villagers formed a loose circle around the town square, cutting off all potential avenues of escape except for the sky.

Old Snow had already drawn his bow. Keershan clawed at the ground.

Pure terror crossed Bloka's bloody features, and he jumped to his feet. Hal tried to catch him, but Bloka moved too fast.

Bloka did not get far before something long and dark lanced out of the open doors of the inn and slammed into his head. He collapsed on the spot, blood rapidly leaking out of his cracked skull, his body utterly lifeless.

Hal drew his drill sword and raised his shield. "What the hell was that?"

An odd clicking sound came from the inn's open

doors, and a second later, a gray-haired, heavyset woman stepped out.

It was Agate.

But she was hard to recognize with the huge, black-and-red spider covering the upper half of her face, its spindly legs digging into her skull.

"Welcome to Giant's Foot, Dragon Rider," said Agate in a voice that was a mixture between hers and some other creature's voice. "Check in to my inn and never check out."

Chapter Sixteen

FRALIA NORMALLY DID NOT DREAM WHEN SHE SLEPT.

Her father had suggested this was because dreaming was the mind's way of thinking about the events of the day, and she already did a lot of thinking on her own. Her mother had said it was because the gods did not speak to Fralia very often, as she apparently did not need divine guidance like many people.

Fralia didn't really care much for dreams, anyway. In her experience, dream magic was probably the least reliable form. One could never tell if it had any basis in reality, or if it was all the ramblings of people who had done more drugs than magic.

That was why Fralia was surprised when she, not only had a dream that night after Hal, Old Snow, and Keershan left, but even *knew* it was a dream.

She found herself watching a scene from her childhood. A young girl—around the age of seven or eight—

was sitting at a desk that was comically large compared to her small form. With long, black hair and a determined expression on her face, she was a spitting image of Fralia at that age.

She even has ink stains on her face from all of the ink I used when I was writing essays, Fralia thought with a smile.

Young Fralia did not seem to notice her. She carefully dipped her quill into a near-empty inkpot sitting next to her paper and then, just as carefully, finished writing a sentence that Fralia could not read from her current position.

She was in the primary study of her parents' mansion back in the capital. It was a large room with built-in shelves covering the walls, full of hundreds upon hundreds of books on magic, history and politics. Even in a dream, Fralia could smell the scent of ink and paper that pervaded the study, feel the warmth from the candle which lit her younger self's many papers.

But why am I dreaming about this? Fralia glanced around the study with a frown. *And why am I lucid?*

"Perhaps it is because you feel much like you did during this study session," said a familiar male voice behind her, deep but kind and caring. "You have been dealing with a heavy weight on your shoulders recently, after all."

Fralia froze.

"It's okay, Frali," said the voice again. "You can turn to look. I won't bite."

Fralia whirled around on her heels.

Standing a few feet away was a mountain of a man.

Clad in dark brown-and-black armor, the man had short hair of the same hue as hers, with kind green eyes that looked out from a face that had put the fear of the gods into even the mightiest dragons.

Fralia was at a loss for words. The only thing she could say was, "Is that … is that you …?"

Her father smiled. "Long time, no see, Frali."

Tears streaming, she practically tackled him. He barely budged. Fralia hugged him tightly. He wrapped his arms around her in a gentle, comforting way that Fralia had not felt in a very long time.

"Father … Father …" Fralia said. "I'm sorry … I'm sorry …"

"It's fine, Frali," said Father as he patted her on the back. "It's not your fault. You didn't kill me. The demons did."

Fralia could barely see his face through her blurry eyes. "But how—?"

Father smiled. "The world of dreams is a place in itself. Think of it as a bridge between the worlds of the living and the dead. Under the right circumstances, the dead can speak to the living. Your mother has explained much to me recently."

"Is she here too?"

Father caught her chin and made her look him in the eyes. "Unfortunately, your mother couldn't join me. It's difficult for the dead to speak to the living even in the world of dreams, and besides, she thought you would want to hear from me more than her, due to your guilt."

Fralia sniffled. "Because if I didn't distract you, you wouldn't have died."

"Don't say that," Father chided. "You didn't know what the Dark Priest was going to do. I wanted to thank you."

Fralia blinked. "Why?"

"Because I value truth. Seeing you stand up to me back then confirmed that I raised you right. I just wish I could have lived long enough to properly meet your friends and let them know how much I appreciate them taking care of you. Especially Halar."

Fralia blushed slightly. "But you can't come back."

Father nodded. "I can't even stay here long. But death isn't always a bad thing. If you could see the things I've seen, well, I'm not allowed to say."

"Not allowed?" Fralia said. "Who isn't allowing you?"

"It doesn't matter. I came to warn you and your friends."

Fralia, wiping away her tears with the sleeve of her robes, said, "About the resurrection?"

Father wore a slightly exasperated but amused expression. "Frali, you're only talking about the problems you can *see*. I'm warning you about the problems you *can't*." He sighed. "I forgot how blind the living are. There is a traitor among your friends, someone working within to take you down."

A shock like a lightning bolt went down Fralia's spine. "A traitor? Who is it?"

"I don't know. My vision of the physical world is limited. All living beings look much alike to me, except for people who were important to me in life, such as you and your siblings. Even your face is starting to get blurrier the longer I am dead. However, I *can* see a person's soul. And the soul of the traitor is blacker than a pit full of bloodsuckers."

Fralia shuddered. "What do souls normally look like?"

Father furrowed his brow. "Bright, I suppose is the best word for it. Good—or at least decent—people tend to have souls which shine like stars."

Fralia touched her chest. "What does *my* soul look like?"

Father smiled. "Always the curious one, aren't you? Haven't you wondered at why your town has not been attacked by the Malarsan Army yet, despite how outnumbered you and your friends are?"

Fralia bit her lower lip. "I just thought the Tops were too treacherous."

Father chuckled bitterly. "Trust me, Queen Bariwa would sacrifice every soldier in the army if she thought it would get rid of you and the others. No, she knows that she doesn't need to do much until the traitor finishes their job."

"What job?"

"The complete and utter destruction of the Dragon Riders," said Father. "The traitor is trying to take them down from within."

Fralia's mind raced. The implications were horrifying. Someone on their side—maybe even one of her own friends—was actively working against them. For all she knew, the traitor had been among the group who saw Hal, Keershan, and Old Snow off, and she hadn't even known it.

"How will I discover them?" Fralia said. "Unlike you, I can't see peoples' souls."

"You don't need to," said Father. "Stay aware. Although darkness can't always be seen, it can always be felt. They can't hide their darkness forever. Trust the instincts I helped you train over the years."

Fralia rubbed the back of her neck. "What if I don't have proof?"

Father looked around suddenly as if he had lost something. "Uh-oh. It looks like my time is up."

"What will happen now?" asked Fralia urgently. "Will we ever see each other again?"

Father averted his gaze. "I wasn't told that, either. Jamas might know. He's been dead longer than me."

"Jamas—?"

Father gave her a soft smile through the mist starting to fill the room. "Either way, just seeing your face again makes it worth all the trouble I had to go through to get here."

Fralia brushed her tears away. "What about Orelu and Dhan?"

"Funny thing about being a spirit," said Father. "Although I can't be *everywhere* at once, sense of place is a bit more flexible when you don't have a body."

Fralia felt shock jolt her. "You mean you're talking to them now?"

He waved a hand. "See?"

Through the mist, Fralia caught glimpses of two other people. One was a man clad in black war mage armor while the other was a young woman in red mage robes. They stood talking to mirror images of Father, seemingly unaware that all three of them were standing in the same room together.

That was, until they looked toward each other, shocked.

And they can probably recognize me, too.

Then Father squeezed her shoulder again, returning Fralia's attention to him. His expression hadn't changed much, though now he looked a little sadder.

"I'm proud of you, Frali," said Father. "You and your siblings. I know you will play an important role in the future, more important than you can even imagine."

Fralia blinked. "Is that another thing that someone else told you that you aren't allowed to tell me?"

Father shook his head again. "No. Just fatherly pride speaking. I don't see the future any clearer than I did in life. I do hope, however, that you will restore your relationships with each other. For your sakes, if not for mine. Now, it's time for me to go."

With that, Father walked toward the exit to Young Fralia's study. Through the open doorway, Fralia caught a glimpse of shining light that seemed warm and safe.

Then Father looked over his shoulder and said, "Oh, and Frali?"

"Yes, Father?" Fralia said. "What is it?"

Father smiled grimly. "Next time you see Old Snow, tell him he can't keep sacrificing his soul."

Without further explanation, Father stepped through the doorway and closed it behind him.

As soon as he left, the mist, which had been gathering

at the corners of the room, soon expanded, completely obscuring Fralia's view and plunging her back into dreamless sleep.

Though not before this question dominated her mind: *What was Old Snow doing to his soul?*

Chapter Seventeen

THE NEXT MORNING AFTER HAL'S DEPARTURE, ANIJA AND Rialo were the first to greet the Glacians as their caravan entered the village. They unloaded all the treasure they had brought with them. Anija had to admit their gifts *were* very nice.

It wasn't just gold and silver, either. There were long, sharp swords made out of some sort of blue metal, armor made of the finest steel that money could buy, and even some armor designed specifically for dragons.

Akon and his mages used their magical skills to sort through it. Even at a glance, Anija could tell that the Dragon Riders had taken a big boost in terms of strength and wealth.

"Of course you did," Dedeket had remarked when Anija said something to that effect to him. He spread his spindly hands. "This is but a glimpse of the absolute power and wealth that His Majesty wields, a single sip of the most delicious wine in the world. With our alliance now cemented, you will have access to treasure and resources most can only dream of."

Even Rialo seemed impressed, especially when they brought out a large, golden bust of Chief Bronda's head.

That was another thing that Anija noticed. The gifts which had no immediate practical use were obviously designed by people who knew a lot more about the Dragon Riders than they let on. Dedeket himself even gave Fralia a carved image of General Jeniq as Kryo Kardia's way of showing respect for her father's memory. They also had a gift for Hal specifically, which Anija had placed in his home to await his return.

Clearly, someone had done their research.

In any case, once the Glacians finished unloading their treasure, they wasted no time in departing. Dedeket claimed that the first retinue of Glacian soldiers would be arriving soon to support the rebellion and that the rebels could contact Kryo Kardia anytime through the magical flammable papers that they gave them.

Soon the Glacians' caravan—now looking much emptier—made its way back north. Anija tried to offer them something in exchange, but Dedeket cut her off, saying that this was simply their gift to the Dragon Riders.

The Glacians' departure did, however, allow Anija to focus on another, more immediate problem that the Dragon Riders faced: The lack of bonding between humans and dragons.

Anija stood in the middle of a large stone building

that may have once been a warehouse for weapons, though that was just a guess on her part. It was cold and dark aside from the handful of lamps. It also smelled of metal and dust.

A stack of relics sat on the table before her. They had once belonged to General Stayling Omaros's Dancing Army with the intent to use them during the Battle of Dragon Valley to subdue and conquer the dragons living there. Thanks to Hal's persuasion, the Dancing Army had been converted to their side.

Ten of the relics had been successfully used so far to create new Dragon Rider pairs, but there were still about two dozen or so relics that had yet to be used.

And Anija was going to find out why.

"So no one has volunteered to bond recently?" Anija said to the elderly woman standing next to her.

Dark-silver hair hung from Wilme's head. She stood with a surprising amount of alertness.

"Aye," said Wilme. "The last new Dragon Rider pair was two weeks ago."

Wilme had been one of General Omaros's strategists. In her youth, she had apparently been a top archer in the Malarsan Army, although her strategic mind had allowed her to rise through the ranks until she had all but become a general. Wilme, however, apparently wasn't very ambitious, and so had always rejected offers for promotion mostly because she apparently liked shooting arrows better than commanding armies.

As a result, when the council decided who to put in charge of protecting and distributing relics, Wilme had been the obvious choice. She was careful and methodical, almost fanatically so, and was already trusted by the rest of the rebels. Even Anija had grown to trust her. Not a mean feat, as Anija didn't trust many people, and the few she did had earned it several times over.

"That's not good," Anija said, rubbing her forehead. "We have a dozen Dragon Riders, but Queen Bariwa has hundreds of slaves. We need more."

"Easier said than done," said Wilme. "Although many of us are willing to work *with* the dragons, most of us are still very wary of them."

Anija sighed. She knew that all too well. Centuries of hostility and conflict.

From what Rialo had told Anija, dragons felt similarly. Right now, Rialo was back at her nest, partly to look after her young, partly to brainstorm with Kikow and a handful of other Steeds about how to bridge the gap.

"It's only a matter of time before Queen Bariwa decides to attack us. The fact that Fralia and Cav got attacked by a slave less than a mile from the town's borders should be a wake-up call for everyone."

"True," said Wilme, "but you are still asking a lot from the others. Although I've never bonded myself, I do know that it's a very intimate process."

Anija nodded. That was putting it mildly. She'd felt like she'd bared her whole soul to Rialo when they bonded.

"But I do have an idea," said Wilme. "We could do a big bonding ceremony within the next week or so. A mass gathering between humans and dragons in which new Dragon Rider pairs are created," Wilme explained. "In essence, humans and dragons get together to have fun, get to know each other, and then bond together as Rider and Steed."

"So it's basically like a big party, then."

"Similar," said Wilme. "It's an ancient tradition that goes all the way back to before the Fall."

Anija eyed Wilme in surprise. "When did you suddenly become an expert on Dragon Rider history?"

Wilme shrugged. "I've learnt quite a bit from Keershan and Old Snow. Bonding ceremonies were apparently common."

Anija didn't see any harm in throwing a party. Truth be told, the village could probably use it. Ever since the Battle of Dragon Valley, it had felt like they'd been working hard nonstop. While that was understandable given their current circumstances, Anija knew that even dragons couldn't work forever without some kind of rest or fun.

Heck, even Anija thought the idea of a big human-dragon party sounded like fun, and she normally avoided parties like the plague. Unless she had been hired to steal from a dumb rich person during a party, that was.

After checking with Rialo, Anija said, "All right. Go ahead and start organizing it."

Wilme rubbed her hands together eagerly. "I was thinking sometime within the next week or so. Now that we have the Glacians' gifts, we could distribute those at the ceremony, too."

"Excellent idea," Anija said.

As they planned out the ceremony, Anija could not

help but feel a sense of happiness and excitement rising within her.

I only wish that Hal and Keershan could be here to see it, but what they are doing is probably even more important than this. Hopefully they're making good progress, wherever they are.

Chapter Eighteen

HAL'S STOMACH CHURNED AT THE SIGHT OF THE SPIDER-like creature clasped over Agate's face like a mask. The rest of her body looked normal, aside from ugly black lines running through her veins, making them bigger and more prominent.

"What have you done to Agate?" Old Snow said, his voice tight, bow pointed at her.

Agate made a sickening chirping sound that cause the hairs on the back of Hal's neck to stand on end. "The human woman is no more. She struggled longer than the others, but in the end, she could not resist the swarm."

"The swarm?" Hal said.

Keershan shook as he said, "The scariest demon in all of the legends. The spiders operate in a hive mind. Ruled by a swarm queen, the demon can overrun entire cities, turning humans into extensions of itself."

"Glad that you know about me," said the woman in front of them. Hal guessed she was likely the queen.

Hal glanced at the other possessed people. "Is it possible to free them?"

"The legends said it was impossible. The swarm feeds on minds and souls. Even if you managed to remove a spider, they would likely not survive the process."

Hal felt his heart sink into his stomach. "That means that everyone here is dead."

"You don't have to put it in such *stark* terms," said the swarm queen. "I prefer to think of it as freedom. Humans are such fickle creatures, having to make all sorts of individual choices each and every day. Truth be told, most of the villagers surrendered peacefully to our control. They know we will do more with their bodies than they could on their own."

"Agate would never say that," Old Snow said. "She was one of the toughest and most independent women I've ever known."

The swarm queen rubbed her chest again. "This is why we gave her body to the swarm queen. As an example to others."

"Did Queen Bariwa send you?" Hal said.

"Yes. The human queen has become increasingly impatient as of late. She no longer cares about killing you herself. And it has been ages since we were given the freedom to control humans. Even longer since I feasted on the soul of a Dragon Rider. Those are the most delicious."

"Freedom?" Hal questioned. "Sounds like you are on a tight leash."

Keershan clawed the ground. "The swarm is considered extreme even by demonic standards. The Nameless

One would keep them locked up and only use them when other demons failed to destroy his enemies. And even then, he'd make sure to lock them back up as soon as they completed their task."

Hal gaped. "Even the Nameless One feared these things?"

"Not so much 'feared' as respected," said the swarm queen. She spread her arms. "The swarm's sole desire is to spread across the world and bring all beings into our hive. Human, dragon, it doesn't matter to us. Queen Bariwa certainly didn't understand what she brought by summoning us, though she will soon enough if she survives the Day."

"Foolish woman," Old Snow said, shaking his head.

Hal raised his sword, feeling Keershan's dragonfire building up in his soul. "If it's a fight you want, then let's fight."

The swarm queen tilted her head to the side. "Are you so certain that you want to fight us? *All* of us?"

More shuffling footsteps around Hal made him look around at the rest of the swarm.

It appeared that the entire town of Giant's Foot was assembled in the town square now. About three hundred or so people wore identical swarm Spiders on their faces.

"She has a point, Hal," Old Snow said. "Unless you are willing to kill everyone here, I am not sure we can defeat them in a fight."

Hal gritted his teeth. He didn't want to admit it, but Old Snow had a point. If they were just simple demons, Hal wouldn't have hesitated to slaughter the whole lot of them. Demons were not human, after all, and certainly didn't deserve to live.

But this was different. These were humans, humans who had been forcibly possessed by demons against their will. Killing humans was a different ballgame to Hal, especially since he'd known some of these humans in the past.

But what were they *supposed* to do? It wasn't like they could simply throw down their weapons and surrender. For that matter, the swarm queen certainly wasn't interested in negotiating a peaceful way out of the village.

And I'm getting tired. Hal rubbed the sleep out of his eyes. *It's been a long day.*

The swarm-possessed villagers shuffled in closer. They were starting to move in now, partly to cut off potential escape routes, partly in preparation for when they decided to swarm Hal and the others.

If they do that, then we'll have to fight back. Even if we win, we'll still be responsible for the deaths of many innocent people.

Not really, if you think about it, Keershan told Hal mentally all of a sudden. *They're already dead. The swarm spiders ate their souls. What we're looking at right now is basically dead meat.*

"Dead meat?" Hal whispered to Keershan, deciding to speak aloud so Old Snow could follow their conversation. "That's kind of harsh, wouldn't you say?"

Keershan shrugged. "Maybe, but it's also accurate. While I'm not thrilled about killing these people, I'm afraid that may be our only choice."

Old Snow frowned softly, keeping his bow trained on the swarm queen. "Perhaps. A much bigger problem is what will happen if we let them spread across the kingdom, as I doubt Marial will bother reining them in until the Nameless One returns."

"And by then, it will be too late to stop us, humans," said the swarm queen, making another chittering sound likely meant to replicate human chuckling. "Make your choice. For it will be the last you ever make."

Hal scowled. More than anything, he wanted to stab the swarm queen in the face and shut her up permanently, but he wasn't sure that would work. What they needed was a way to stop the swarm queen, to get rid of her and her swarm without needlessly harming or killing the innocent people she possessed.

That was when a crazy idea occurred to Hal. He had no idea if it would work. He didn't think any legends may have spoken of it. And he wasn't sure he wanted to mention it to the others, either, for fear of the swarm queen noticing.

So Hal sheathed his sword.

"Hal, what are you doing?" Keershan said in a panicked voice.

"Perhaps he has given up already," the swarm queen said, her words laced with smug triumph. "It would be wise, for no one can survive the swarm."

"Except for the strongest-willed old woman in the world," Hal said. "Right, Agate?"

The swarm queen stepped backward. "You do realize that the elderly woman is gone, yes? Her soul has been subsumed by the hive."

"Liar," Hal said. "I know she's still in there, fighting against your will. She just needs help."

The swarm spiders started to chitter, which gradually turned into laughter. It was the most spine-tingling sound that Hal had ever heard, a noise that would live on in his nightmares for the rest of his life.

The swarm queen laughed the loudest of all. She laughed so hard that she seemed unable to speak for a moment, before finally saying, "Amazing. We cannot remember the last time that anyone made us laugh. Truly, Dragon Rider, if we did not have explicit orders to kill you, we would spare you to act as our jester, for you are quite humorous."

"I'm not joking," Hal said. "And I'm not that funny in general, so I don't even try. I'm just speaking the truth."

The swarm queen stopped laughing, as did the rest of the swarm. "Truth? What truth?"

Hal pointed at her chest. "That Agate is still alive in there and that you haven't fully eaten her soul yet."

The swarm queen chittered angrily. "Jesters should not make statements about things that they know nothing about. It has been a day since we arrived and conquered this town's population. We leave no survivors, especially among the strong."

"But that's why I believe Agate is still in there," Hal said. "She was a strong-willed woman. She wouldn't let herself get conquered by anything, much less a bunch of ugly spiders that need to be squashed."

The anger radiating off of the swarm was almost palpable at this point. Hal could sense that the swarm queen's anger was flooding through the hive. It was probably messing with their ability to think or notice anything else other than Hal, which was fine. If his theory had any grounding at all, then making the swarm upset was a necessary first step to saving everyone.

"We are not mere 'bugs' to be squashed by arrogant humans," said the swarm queen. "We are the swarm. Cities and nations have fallen under our power. Even the demons in the darkest shadows whisper our name in fear. You have no idea what you are talking about."

"It's true that I don't know everything there is to know about you," Hal said, "but I don't need to know every little detail about you and your fellow insects to know that your days are numbered. Once Agate fights back, even you won't be able to stop her."

The swarm queen shook her head. "Our ages in darkness have caused us to forget just how foolish you humans can be."

Hal smirked. "Foolish? Or smart enough not to be scared by a bunch of spiders?"

That seemed to do it. The swarm queen extended her hand toward Hal, and what looked like a long spider leg lashed out toward him. The leg wrapped itself around his neck, choking him. Old Snow turned his bow toward it.

Come on, Agate. Hal stared at the swarm queen, trying not to tear his gaze away from her. *I know you're still in there … come on …*

That was when he saw it. An involuntary twitch of the fingers on the swarm queen's left hand. He might not have made the connection if not for the swarm queen herself glancing at her hand.

But the twitching didn't stop. Soon, the entire left arm was moving on its own.

"What is this?" said the swarm queen. She glared at her rogue left arm. "Stop moving."

"No," the voice that came from the swarm queen's mouth sounded very tired but also very determined. "You might control the rest of my body, but you can't control *me*."

"Agate?" Old Snow said, lowering his bow in disbelief. "Are you still in there?"

"No!" the swarm queen snapped. "The woman is dead. I—"

"Yes, Old Snow, I'm still here," said Agate, interrupting the swarm queen. "It's difficult to speak and it feels like I'm having to fight through a whole bunch of spider web, but I'm here, all right."

Hal smiled. He immediately grabbed the spider leg around his neck and, channeling dragonfire through his hands, burned right through it.

The swarm queen howled in pain, but so did the rest of the swarm, eerily enough.

Rubbing his neck, Hal said, "I knew you were still in there, Agate. Fight!"

"No," said the swarm queen. "I will devour you whole …"

Hal wished there was a way he could help Agate, but he was practically powerless.

Or am I?

Focusing on the relic on his head, Hal mentally reached out to Agate. He didn't really know what he was doing. He didn't even know if what he was trying to do was even possible.

But damn if he wasn't going to try.

Then Hal felt it. A click, in the way one might feel the joining of two puzzle pieces together. He felt his mind connect to Agate's in a way he'd never done with any other human before, and the next time he blinked, his surroundings had changed.

The dark night sky overhead had been replaced with a domed cavern, strewn with thick spider web everywhere. It was humid and smelled too much like death and blood.

Hal was drawn to the scene in the middle of the chamber. Agate—half-covered in torn webbing and lying on the floor—was struggling against a giant spider that looked just like the swarm queen, except bigger and deadlier. The queen was trying to get its pincers into Agate's body.

Raising his sword, Hal ran forward. Dragonfire exploded along the blade of his sword, and with a final yell, he beheaded the spider queen before she even noticed he was there.

Then his world blinked again and he found himself back in Giant's Foot. The air was full of the screams of dying swarm spiders.

Wherever Hal looked, he saw the disgusting creatures curling their legs and then falling off of the faces of their victims onto the ground, turning to dust upon impact. Their victims also collapsed, although it was impossible to tell if they were dead or simply unconscious.

The swarm queen was still holding on. But then

Agate reached up with both hands and ripped the spider off her face. She tossed the body onto the ground at her feet, where it, too, turned into dust that blew away in the wind.

Then Agate looked up at Hal, Keershan, and Old Snow with a soft smile on her face, said, "Thank you …" and then fell over onto the ground face-first, leaving them to stare at her in shock.

Chapter Nineteen

As it turned out, the situation with the swarm spiders and the villagers of Giant's Foot was more complicated than it first appeared. Those who survived went around collecting the bodies of those who had passed, planning to give them a mass burial in the morning.

Hal offered to help but was urged to get Agate home. Her house was apparently attached to the back of the Giant's Toenail. Hal and Old Snow placed her onto her bed and opened the window so Keershan could participate in their conversation.

Agate, despite being exhausted by her harrowing experiences, agreed to speak with them. She required food and water, however, as she apparently hadn't eaten.

Sitting down on a stool, Hal said, "How did the swarm take over the town?"

Agate, propped up against her pillows, chewed on her bread for a long time before answering. Hal noticed that she had little pinpricks in the sides of her face from where the swarm queen's talons had dug into her skin. They looked a bit painful.

"It happened so suddenly," said Agate. "Around nightfall, everyone heard screaming from the Makar family's house on the edge of town. Some of the defenders, led by Bloka, went to check on them, but when they returned, they were all wearing those damn spiders on their faces."

"Except for Bloka," Hal said.

"I don't know how he avoided it." Agate sighed. "In any case, it wasn't long after that until the Swarm spread through the village like wildfire. I tried to gather as many survivors in my inn as I could, blocking the doors and windows, but it wasn't enough."

"What were their plans for you guys after capturing you?" Keershan said.

"I don't remember much, and they never talked. But I was under the impression they were waiting for someone to show up."

Hal grimaced. "Us. They must have been expecting us. But how?"

"Remember the traitor?" Old Snow said, glancing at Hal and Keershan. "The one that Jaspus warned us about?"

"Are you saying that one of our friends warned the demons we were heading out and helped them coordinate this attack?" Keershan demanded. "That's insane! We're all in this together. And Jaspus is a known liar besides."

Hal rested his chin on his fist. "Jaspus may lie about

most things, but that doesn't mean he's always wrong. It would explain why the swarm knew they could wait for us here, even though no one outside of Mysteria should have known."

Keershan clicked his teeth together anxiously. "But if there *is* a traitor, then who is it?"

Hal didn't have an answer to that question. Even Old Snow seemed at a loss for words. The ex-king simply sat on a wooden stool identical to Hal's, hands folded over his lap, a troubled expression on his face.

"Regardless of who it is, we may need to rethink our travel plans to the castle," Old Snow said. "It's clear Marial knows more than we thought."

"Should we return to Mysteria and warn everyone about the traitor?" Keershan said.

"Don't you worry about that," Agate rubbed her puncture wounds. "I will send one of my boys up there to warn them."

"That's very generous of you, Agate," Hal said, "but the villagers have been through enough as is. There's no need—"

"No need for what?" Agate questioned. "To put our lives on the line for a cause we believe in? To help friends who saved us? I may not be a Dragon Rider or a mage, but I live in Malarsan, too. If there is any way I can help save this country, then I absolutely will."

"Thank you, Agate," Old Snow said. "We need all the help we can get."

Agate nodded, then looked at Hal and asked, "How did you do that? Enter my mind and kill the swarm queen from within?"

Old Snow tapped his bearded chin. "If I had to guess, I'd say that Hal did something called a mind-jump."

Keershan poked his head through the open window even more, accidentally slamming his shoulders against the side of the inn, making it shake. "I know what that is! It's so rare that only a handful of Riders could pull it off."

"It reminded me of our first encounter with the splotchlings," Hal said. "When I used my bond with Keershan to help him fight off their control. I suppose I wanted to see if I could do something similar with Agate. Surprised it worked, honestly."

Old Snow nodded. "Mind-jumping essentially allows a Dragon Rider pair to temporarily 'expand' their bond to include other living beings, allowing for things like telepathy and similar mental abilities."

"But only temporarily," Keershan added. "And it doesn't always work, either. Frankly, I'm just amazed it worked at all, but also really excited. I know I've said this, like, a-million-and-a-half times already, but it's just so cool getting to see legend come to life, isn't it?"

Hal stretched his shoulders. "I guess, but I wish I could do it again. It could be useful."

"Practice may help," Old Snow said, "although as I said, even the best Dragon Riders struggle with it. It wouldn't surprise me if you could do it only once, and that's it."

"I hope not," Keershan said. "I can see lots of situations where mind-jumping might be useful."

Hal shook his head. "Regardless, we still have a long

ways to go before we reach the capital. Perhaps by then, I'll have gotten better at it."

"Hopefully," Keershan said. He yawned again. "While this is all fascinating, I think we probably should call it a night."

"Wait," Agate raised a hand. "I have something else I learned from the swarm queen when she possessed me. Something I think you, in particular, would want to hear, Hal."

Hal perked up when Agate said that. "What is it?"

Agate took a deep breath. "Your hometown of Lamb's Hand has been destroyed, and nearly everyone within it is dead."

Hal felt his world fall out from underneath him. "What if the swarm queen lied?"

"I sensed that there was at least some truth to it. I've gotten pretty good at spotting liars over the years."

Hal's hands balled into fists.

That would mean that everyone is dead. Mother, our neighbors, my childhood friends, the local farmers and shopkeepers. Everyone *is dead.*

Old Snow leaned forward. "You said *nearly* everyone was killed."

Agate pursed her lips and looked out the window of her room. "I think the queen may have spared some people. Kidnapped them to use as hostages against you guys."

Hal felt a jolt of hope shoot up his spine. "Did she say who?"

Agate shook her head sadly.

"It would probably be people who are close to you, Hal," Keershan said.

Agate brushed a few stray strands of gray hair from her face. "It was framed as a rogue dragon attack. Their story was that a lone dragon sought vengeance for the defeat of his people by burning Lamb's Hand to the ground."

Hal felt something firm rub against his shoulder and looked to his left. Keershan was rubbing his snout against Hal's shoulder in an obvious gesture of comfort, his big green eyes showing concern.

"I wish I could be of more help."

Old Snow rested a hand on top of Agate's hand. "Trust me, you've been of enough help to us. Just relax and sleep. We'll stay here tonight and keep you safe."

Agate nodded. With that, Hal and Old Snow left her room while Keershan pulled his head out of the window. Hal listened closely until he heard Agate snoring through the wooden door.

He glanced down the dark hallway, his hands balling into fists. "You know what we need to do."

Old Snow nodded. "Of course. As soon as Agate mentioned your mother's peril, I knew what you would say. I'm just surprised you haven't said it yet."

"Didn't want to scare Agate," Hal said.

Agate didn't seem very easily scared to me, Keershan said mentally all of a sudden. *But yes, probably best not to say what we were thinking aloud.*

Hal nodded. He and Old Snow made their way down the hall, side by side, young man and old, the two looking so radically different from each other, yet connected in a way that neither of them could quite explain.

And Hal said, "We're going to the capital, and we're going to kill Queen Bariwa."

Chapter Twenty

To Anija, it was finally starting to feel like early spring in the Desolate Tops.

A week had passed since Hal had departed. The air was significantly warmer, thanks in no small part to the hot sun overhead. Although there was a soft, cool breeze in the air, it was much more comfortable than the biting wind from the last couple of months.

Granted, it wasn't like the weather was going to *stay* this nice. According to Fralia and the other air mages, it would cool down again in the coming week.

You humans should grow more fur or something.

Anija rolled her eyes at Rialo. *Easy for a dragon to say.*

You do know that you can borrow some from me, right? Anija focused on their bond and felt heat suddenly rise within her. It was almost *too* hot, forcing Anija to cut off the connection before it gave her heatstroke. *Maybe I'll keep that in mind for the next blizzard.*

They stood in Mysteria's 'square'. It was basically an open spot where meetings were regularly held, the ideal spot for the bonding ceremony.

It was currently crowded with humans and dragons, echoing with jokes and gossip. It frustrated Anija to see, however, that the humans and dragons largely segregated themselves. She did notice a couple of water mages playing with some baby dragons, including Rialo's daughter Yiko.

A wooden platform held most of the unused relics. They sat atop a large stone table, gleaming dully under the light of the sun. A few people glanced at them fearfully, as if they would come to life and attack them.

What a silly fear. I'm a lot more likely to attack them for refusing to bond than the relics are.

I suspect that the others wouldn't be very happy if you did that, Rialo said. *Just a guess.*

It was just a joke, Anija replied. *I'm not that* violent. *Just a little peeved is all.*

Despite Anija's joking, she had to admit she was pleased by the turnout. When she announced the bonding ceremony to the Mysterians a week ago, Anija had been worried that few people, human or dragon, might show up. She had not made it mandatory to attend, largely because she didn't see how she could do that. Combine that with the general reluctance among the Mysterians to bond at all, and she'd expected it to fail.

But Wilme had been smart. She'd announced that the bonding ceremony would include a large feast and festival for the town, essentially turning it into a large party.

That was deliberate on Anija and Wilme's part. By framing it as a fun party instead of a solemn ritual, they hoped to make it more appealing to the other Mysterians.

Thus far, the framing had worked. Using what little resources they had, Anija and the other council members had been able to organize a fun, lighthearted event that involved nearly the whole town. Even Anija, not usually one to enjoy parties or socializing, had had a fun time. She hadn't realized just how much stress that she—and by extension, the entire town—had been under for the past couple of months until she felt it leave her shoulders.

Wilme is a smart woman. Anija spotted the elderly woman making her way through the crowd toward the wooden platform. *She could easily lead the town if she wanted. Glad she's on* our *side now.*

Agreed, Rialo replied. *But it looks like the main event is about to start.*

Anija nodded. Wilme was not the only council member approaching the platform. Surrels and Fralia were also approaching from different angles. Anija sensed everyone would reach the platform at the same time, which would be the start of the bonding ceremony.

Better get ready, Anija said as she scrambled off of Rialo's back. *No need for you to do anything except stand there and look pretty.*

Rialo snorted. *I don't want to look pretty. I want to look fearsome.*

Anija rolled her eyes as she set foot on the wooden

platform at the same time that Wilme, Fralia, and Surrels reached it. The four of them met in the middle near the stone table piled high with the unused relics, their rusty, metallic scent wafting off the objects in the cool breeze.

"Is everything in place?" Anija asked Wilme.

Wilme nodded, her gray hair done up in a bandanna behind her head. "Yes. Thus far, everyone seems to be in a good mood, and we haven't had any problems."

"Aside from Jols and Bimi getting drunk and trying to fight each other for some reason," Surrels added. "Reminds me why I don't like breaking up fights between soldiers."

"The mages are also in place for the ceremony," Fralia said. "Ragnol has not reported any suspicious activity outside the town walls recently."

Surrels leaned in closer toward the group. "Be that as it may, the *real* suspicious activity might not be happening outside at all, but rather *inside* the town."

Anija scowled. She knew what Surrels meant.

A day after Hal and his party left town, a messenger from Giant's Foot had arrived. Not only did he tell them about the swarm, but he also warned them of a potential traitor in Mysteria, working to destroy the town from within.

Such news had disturbed the council, so much so that they agreed not to tell the rest of the town about it. That may have been a controversial decision at the time, but Anija didn't want to needlessly worry or scare the people, especially since they didn't have hard evidence of the traitor's existence yet.

Fralia, in particular, had argued against keeping the

traitor's existence a secret but had been outvoted by Anija, Surrels, and Wilme. Even now, Anija noticed a disapproving frown tug at the corner of Fralia's lips.

"Aye," Anija said grimly. "How's the investigation been going?"

Surrels shrugged in frustration. "Like trying to find a blackberry in a pitch-black room the size of a castle."

Anija bit her lower lip. "Not well, then."

"Understatement of the century," Surrels said. "We have no real clues to the traitor's identity, other than some admittedly rather questionable statements from people who are probably not very trustworthy. And trying to do it *without* letting anyone know you're doing it? Might as well ask me to cut down an entire forest by myself."

Anija frowned in annoyance. "If you think this is pointless, then I can find someone else to investigate the traitor."

Surrels held up his hands, palms facing her. "I didn't say this was *pointless*. It's just going to take a lot more time than I thought."

"We are a rather small town," Wilme noted. "Everyone knows everyone at this point. I can't imagine it's easy to hide an investigation here."

"Another understatement," Surrels grumbled.

Anija shook her head. "As long as you keep looking, I'm sure we'll find some clues if nothing else. And anyway, that's an issue for another time. We need to focus on the bonding ceremony right now."

Fralia raised a hand suddenly. "What about Hal and the others? Have we heard any updates on them?"

"Unfortunately, no," said Wilme. "The Giant's Foot messenger was our last contact with Hal and the others. We have no idea where they might be right now or what their current status is."

Wilme was correct, even if Anija wished she wasn't. They had heard nothing whatsoever from Hal, Keershan, and Old Snow since the arrival of the Giant's Foot messenger with his story about the swarm and the traitor. The messenger had left them with a message from Hal, promising that they still planned to reach the capital well before the Day of Shadows.

That was all fine and dandy, but given how the entire kingdom beyond the Desolate Tops and its foothills was crawling with enemy soldiers, mages, and even dragons, Anija did not feel very good about their odds of survival.

Yet there's nothing we can do about it, either, at least until the Glacians show up with backup and we can actually start to turn the tide.

That was another minor frustration. The Glacians had yet to return with the promised backup. Granted, they had said it would take two weeks minimum, but Anija still felt uneasy.

I feel it, too, Rialo said telepathically. *The tension. I felt this way right before you and your friends entered Dragon Valley for the first time.*

On that cheery note, Anija clapped her hands and said, "All right! Let's talk about this later. For now, we have a bonding ceremony to do."

The council members broke their huddle. Fralia raised her hands, which glowed green. Anija felt a funnel of air form in front of her mouth, so she said, "Can everyone hear me?"

Her voice sounded ten times louder. Every head, human or dragon, turned to look in her direction, some looking slightly annoyed at being interrupted, though most looked curious about what Anija had to say.

Magic really is *useful. I should learn a few spells myself.* She'd never had the time—nor the inclination—to do it before.

Placing her hands together, Anija said, "Thank you all for coming to this event! I feel like it has been a great success so far and a wonderful way for us all to take it easy for a change. Am I right?"

Lots of nodding heads.

"But we didn't do this event *just* to have fun. We are holding this bonding ceremony to try to make more Dragon Rider pairs. Those who are interested in becoming Dragon Riders, please step forward and line up. Humans to the left, dragons to the right."

Human and dragon alike wore uneasy expressions.

Then a young woman walked up to the wooden platform. She was a fire mage, based on her red robes. She had long, blonde hair and a small set of glasses on her nose.

The mage did not come alone, either. A brown-scaled dragon with gold eyes also approached the platform. He respectfully bowed to Rialo for a moment before turning his attention to Anija and the council, the scent of smoke wafting off his large form.

Fralia stepped toward the mage. "Shalla! I didn't know you were here."

Shalla seemed a bit awkward. "Apologies. Everything has just been so crazy these past few months that I didn't have time to tell you."

"You know her?" Anija said.

Fralia nodded eagerly. "Shalla is—was—my father's right-hand. She served him faithfully up until his death."

Shalla stood up, a shy look on her face. "Yes. After your father's death, I was assigned to General Omaros's Dancing Army as a support mage."

"So you don't think I killed my father?" Fralia asked.

Shalla shook her head. "Not anymore. I used to, like everyone else, but after everything I've seen, I've realized just how wrong I was."

"Welcome aboard, Shalla," Anija said. She looked up at the brown dragon. "And your name is—?"

"Mizromi. Chief Rialo knows me."

Rialo scratched at the earth. "He's one of the Clawfoot Clan's lesser chiefs. In fact, he and my father are actually brothers, which technically makes him my uncle by your human standards."

"Your uncle, eh?" Anija said. "Mind if I call you Uncle Miz?"

Mizromi grunted. "I would prefer it if you did not."

"Fair enough," Anija said. She looked from Shalla to Mizromi and back again. "Do you know each other or—?"

Mizromi nodded. "Shalla and I have become acquainted over the past few months. I've also been speaking with Rialo about what being a Steed is like and have decided I would like to be of more direct help, especially if it lets me avenge my brother and fulfill his last words."

"Same," said Shalla. She was twisting the folds of her robes together in an obvious nervous habit. "I-I used to be really scared of dragons—still kind of am, to be honest—but I've also felt called to bond with Mizromi, and now I'm ready."

Wilme picked out a relic from the pile and handed it to Anija, who noticed that it was a necklace similar to hers, albeit with fewer jewels and a little rougher. Even so, she could feel power surging through it.

Anija raised the necklace and said, "Shalla, Mizromi, are you two certain that you are ready to bond with each other and become a new Dragon Rider pair? Because once bonded, only death can undo it."

Shalla and Mizromi exchanged quick glances with each other, but then Shalla said, "We are sure."

"Absolutely *certain*," said Mizromi. "We wish to do whatever is necessary to save our peoples and protect our land from the demons."

They sound a lot more committed than I was.

Probably because they are less selfish than you are, Rialo said with false innocence.

Resisting the urge to roll her eyes, Anija lifted the necklace over Shalla's head and rested it around her neck, before stepping back.

She and Hal had both witnessed the other ten Dragon Riders pair with their Steeds two-and-a-half months ago. Even so, she still found it an interesting sight to behold.

Shalla would have looked like a statue if not for the

rising and falling of her chest indicating that she was still alive. Mizromi also went very still.

Then their eyes glowed a brilliant golden color, brighter and brighter until they suddenly stopped, returning to their normal coloration.

But Shalla and Mizromi looked a little different now. There seemed to be a glowing effect covering their bodies. It looked like they had stars shining within them.

Anija had seen this effect before. It was a temporary effect that lasted for a couple of hours at most, although it would just as often disappear within minutes of the bonding succeeding. Keershan had told her that legends spoke of a star being 'birthed' every time a new Dragon Rider pair was formed, but Anija didn't know if that was true or not.

It's pretty. Anija watched as Shalla's and Mizromi's bodies continued to glow. *Not particularly practical, but pretty nonetheless.*

Then Shalla and Mizromi blinked and shook their heads, dazed.

"So?" Anija said. "How do you two feel?"

Shalla ran a hand along the back of her neck. "Like this is what I am meant to be."

Mizromi agreed. "I feel whole, for want of a better term."

Anija nodded eagerly. She'd felt the same way. It was a sign that the bonding process had worked and that the Rider and Steed were indeed meant to be one.

The crowd was now looking at Shalla and Mizromi with renewed interest. In fact, as Anija watched, humans and dragons alike began to line up. Not everyone lined up to participate in the bonding process, but enough did that Anija suspected they would be here for a while.

But then Anija heard a cry of surprise from Wilme, and spun to see something that stunned her to her core.

All of the relics that had been sitting on the stone table were gone.

Chapter Twenty-One

FRALIA HADN'T NOTICED A THING UNTIL WILME CRIED out. The stone table was now very empty, completely devoid of all of the relics that had once been piled high upon it.

"What the hell?" Surrels said.

Anija looked at Wilme. "Did you see what happened?"

"They were right here. Counted them myself."

Fralia felt dread rise inside her soul.

A banging sounded behind the wooden platform. Fralia saw a large, cloth bag full of clanking metal objects disappear into an alleyway.

Anija rushed toward the edge of the platform and jumped down, with Fralia and Surrels not far behind her. As they jumped, Fralia twisted her hands in midair, creating an air cushion to soften their landing before they darted after the thief.

The bag was so big and bulky that it was damn near

impossible to see the thief himself, but Fralia thought it was a person.

As soon as they entered the alley, Fralia shouted, "Drop those relics!"

The thief turned a corner.

Cursing, Fralia and the others followed. The thief stopped in front of a stone wall that looked too tall for him to climb.

"Hey!" Fralia called.

The thief turned slowly, which was when Fralia realized that it wasn't human at all, but a humanoid snake-like creature. Most of its body was hidden under the dark robes, save for its serpentine face, which peered out from its hood. Its exposed feet—looking like a mixture of human feet and snake tails—bit into the stone street.

"So the daughter of the Dragonslayer has come after me," said the thief. "I would have expected you to remain with the other mages. Coming after me isn't very smart."

The thief's voice was surprisingly smooth and even elegant, very unlike his monstrous appearance. He almost sounded human despite not looking it, although Fralia didn't let her guard down.

"Are you another demon?" Fralia demanded. "Because you sure look like one."

"You are correct," said the thief. "I have no name, but if you must refer to me by something, call me Hanok."

"I don't care," Anija said. She drew her sword. "Drop the relics and we might only cut off *one* of your legs."

Hanok tilted his head to the side. "Now your threats are a bit more credible, seeing as you are a Dragon Rider.

Even so, I find that you modern Dragon Riders simply lack the sheer ferocity of the original Dragon Riders who defeated the Nameless One all those years ago."

"We can probably kill you just fine," Surrels said, also pointing his sword at the demon. "Assuming you aren't smart enough to simply give us the relics."

Hanok snorted. "And risk the queen's wrath? Please. I'm not *that* foolish."

"How did you even get into the village, anyway?" Anija demanded. "Ragnol is supposed to be protecting the gates."

Hanok actually stepped backward at the appearance of Anija's dragonfire, though he didn't run. "You think *I* am your most pressing problem, humans? You truly are blind, or do you not know that the very existence of your little village is in danger?"

"Regardless of that, we need those relics," Surrels said. "Without them we're basically screwed."

"You certainly picked an interesting moment," Anija said. "The balls of you to try stealing from us when nearly all of our dragons and mages are assembled in one place. I forgot how audacious you demons are."

Hanok shook his head. "I actually picked the perfect time to steal from you, although I understand why you may not know that."

"You're good at bluffing, you know that?" Anija said. "Because for a second there, I almost believed you."

"We demons are masters of deceit and lies," Hanok admitted, "but even liars can speak truth at times. And what I just said was the absolute truth, however much you may deny it."

Fralia didn't shudder, but she did feel dread rise within her. She didn't know if Hanok was indeed telling the truth or if he was simply messing with them, but either way, he needed to be stopped before he escaped with the relics.

Maybe I can hit him while he's talking. It wouldn't be hard to knock the bag out of his hands with a powerful gust of wind. I might even knock him down, too.

That was when a portal appeared behind Hanok. Its shadows writhed and twisted, looking almost like a living creature itself. Cold air blasted at them.

"Here's where I make my exit," Hanok smirked. "Farewell, humans. Next time we see each other, you will know that I speak nothing but the—"

A column of dragonfire suddenly rained down on Hanok, completely encasing the demon. He screamed as the fire consumed him, dropping the bag of relics onto the ground. Anija simply looked up and said, "Thanks, Rialo!"

Looking up, Fralia saw Rialo standing on top of a nearby building. Seconds later, Rialo cut off her flames, revealing that Hanok was no more. In his place was a smoking heap of black ash that smelled like burnt flesh and organs. There was no hint of Hanok's original body at all, although Fralia was hardly going to mourn his passing.

The relic bag was only blackened slightly by Rialo's firebreath. The portal had closed too.

Anija said, "Good job, girl! Fried him to a crisp like he deserved."

Rialo snorted. "I'm not very impressed with demons who behave as if they are Salard's gift to the world."

"Yes, well, next time warn us," Surrels waved his hand at his face. "Nearly cooked my eyebrows off."

"At least he didn't get away with the relics," Fralia said, wiping sweat off her forehead. "That has to count for something, right?"

"Let's take them back so we can resume the—"

Anija was interrupted by a terrible ripping sound as the bag—already weakened by the flames—tore outright ...

Revealing nothing more than a bunch of steel metal helmets.

"What the—?" Anija said in shock. She emptied the entire bag, finding more and more mundane objects with each shake. "These aren't the relics."

"Does that mean we had fake relics from the start?" Surrels said in shock. "That our bonding ceremony was doomed to failure?"

Fralia shook her head. "Remember what Hanok said about the traitor in our midst?"

A loud horn blared, followed by the magically magnified voice of Ragnol saying, "Citizens of Mysteria! The Malarsan Army has been spotted marching on us. All men to arms!"

Chapter Twenty-Two

Anija, Surrels, and Fralia climbed onto Rialo's back and took off into the air.

Rising into the sky, her hair billowing out behind her, Anija noticed the other Dragon Riders already flying with them. That included Mizromi and Shalla, the two soaring beside them. The Dragon Riders appeared to be converging toward the south end of the village.

The Malarsan Army was marching on that gate.

Hundreds upon hundreds of soldiers marched across the rocky, barren hills between Mysteria and the rest of the Tops. Dozens of mages, clad in colorful robes, walked among them, hands and staffs glowing with suppressed moulash.

But now they had dragons. Probably fifty or so slaves walked among the soldiers, moving stiffly, their eyes glowing a sickening green color. Each dragon was clad in thick armor that bore the insignia of the Malarsan Army, and the biggest among them carried a Malarsan flag on its back, which flapped violently in the wind.

At a glance, Anija knew there was no way they could defeat them. She'd always known that they were outnumbered, of course, but it was another thing to see it.

"Holy crap," Surrels said, raising his voice to be heard over the howling winds and flapping of dragon wings. "Did they send the entire army just to destroy us?"

"Looks like it," Anija said. A white flag rose from the center of the army. "Don't tell me they want a truce."

"They probably want to talk with us, as we're the leaders," Surrels said. "Look who's leading them."

Peering down again, Anija saw that a large, silver-scaled dragon led the army. It was Jaspus, and riding on his back, clad in fiery red armor, was General Dugden Tikos himself.

General Tikos was even bigger than Fralia's father. He rode Jaspus like he was a horse he had broken, reins in a tight grip as he led the army toward the village's walls.

"He has a reputation for his honesty," Surrels reminded them. "So we probably should see what he wants."

Anija didn't like the idea of getting close to the enemy but saw no choice. Perhaps they could buy themselves some time.

Barking out orders to the other Dragon Riders to keep their distance, Anija urged Rialo down. They passed over the walls, which were starting to fill with warriors and mages of their own, and landed about fifty yards from General Tikos and Jaspus.

"Hello, sister. Wonderful seeing you again, despite the circumstances."

"If I could go a thousand lifetimes without seeing your smug face again, I would, brother," Rialo replied. "Unfortunately, fate had a different road in mind for us. Surprised to see you letting a human ride you."

Jaspus winced. "Technically, it's against my will, so—"

"Silence," said General Tikos in a harsh voice. "Dragons are to be seen, not to talk."

The general dropped down, armor clinking. A small, head sized bag hung at his waist, swaying as he stepped toward them.

Anija had to admit she was a bit nervous to be standing before the Malarsan Army like this, even though they did not appear ready to attack yet. That General Tikos felt he apparently didn't even need a dragon to approach them made her wonder if he was insane or had bigger balls than a well-endowed male dragon.

"Greetings, council of Mysteria," said General Tikos. He gestured at the army. "I have led the Malarsan Army all the way out here to wipe you from the land once and for all."

Anija scowled. "We're not blind. We can see that."

General Tikos nodded. "I know. I simply want to make sure you do not get any crazy ideas."

"Such as fighting back with all of our might against your forces?" Anija said. "Because if you think we are just going to roll over and let you steamroll our village into oblivion, you have another think coming."

General Tikos folded his arms in front of his chest.

"On the contrary, I fully expect you and your fellow Dragon Riders to put up a massive resistance against our forces. Although I am certain that we will overwhelm you, I'm not expecting an easy win without significant losses on our part."

Anija smirked. "We'll make those *significant* losses into *crippling* losses. Unless you want to turn around and leave now with your dignity intact, that is."

General Tikos chuckled. He glanced at the walls of Mysteria behind Rialo. "Rich of you to throw around words like 'dignity' when you live in such hovels. Perhaps you should be more careful to live up to your own standards."

"Not our fault we're the kingdom's number-one enemy and can't afford anything better," Anija replied.

General Tikos tilted his head to the side. "Wrong. You could have chosen, at any point, to surrender. To give up your delusions of fighting Queen Bariwa and her plans for the kingdom. If you had given up sooner, you might have simply earned yourself a life sentence in the castle's dungeons, rather than the death sentence that has been handed down from on high."

"Your idea of a life sentence sounds like a death sentence to me," Anija said. "Besides, it's too late for that now. For better or for worse, we're the plucky rebels going up against your oppressive regime."

General Tikos nodded. "Agreed. I was simply remarking how regretful it is that everything has come to this point. But what's done is done and cannot be undone, as the gods say. We can only live with what has happened before us, though every moment allows us to shape what comes *after* us."

"Surprisingly insightful words from a crazy guy like you," Anija said.

"I am many things, Anija Ti, but 'crazy,' I am not," said General Tikos. His eyes darted to Fralia. "I especially do not look forward to having to put to death the beloved daughter of one of my former colleagues. Back when he was still alive, I had nothing but respect for Kolass, so I was greatly disappointed when I heard that you had sided with the rebels."

It was Fralia's turn to scowl now. "If you really believed that, you wouldn't be leading the Malarsan Army to kill us all. You wouldn't be obeying Queen Bariwa. You'd be helping us."

General Tikos laughed. "Ah, to be young again and still have such an idealistic view of the world and how it works. It makes me miss my youth."

"What do you want?" Anija demanded. She gestured with her sword at the army standing behind General Tikos. "Clearly, you didn't come here *just* to destroy us, otherwise you would have destroyed the village already. What made you want to have a chat with us?"

General Tikos smiled. "First off, my main mission here *is* to kill you. Queen Bariwa made it abundantly clear to me that I am not to leave a single man, woman, child, or dragon alive here. Everyone—and I do mean *everyone*—must perish for the crime of revolting against Her Majesty's rule."

Anija said nothing to that. She just waited for

General Tikos to get to the point, which she noticed he wasn't very good at doing.

General Tikos snatched the bag off his belt and held it up for them to see. "But before I do that, I wanted to show you exactly how doomed you are."

General Tikos pulled something out of the bag and hurled it toward them. Rialo stepped backward instinctively, perhaps thinking the object was some kind of weapon, but Anija felt a hollow feeling expand inside her stomach.

It was Hal's relic, gleaming slightly under the warm sun above.

And it was covered in blood.

A heavy silence fell. Fralia sucked in a breath, and Surrels swore softly. Anija was too shocked to speak.

General Tikos nodded. "That belonged to the Dragon Rider known as Halar Norath and his Steed, Keershan. Until I killed them both myself."

Chapter Twenty-Three

ANIJA'S WHOLE WORLD SEEMED TO SPIN. SHOUTS ERUPTED behind her. She was vaguely aware that the villagers of Mysteria had somehow heard what General Tikos said and were in an uproar.

I'd be in an uproar, too, if I could feel anything right now.

"You're a liar," Fralia's voice cracked with emotion. "We would know if they were dead."

General Tikos tilted his head to the side again. "Would you, really? Do you happen to have a communication necklace that we are unaware of?"

Tikos has a point. We really don't *have any way of verifying if he is lying or not.*

General Tikos spread his arms. "We caught Halar Norath and his dragon attempting to sneak into the capital's walls a few days ago. After a fierce but short battle, he and his dragon were both killed by me and General Mokoa. As for Old Snow, he didn't last much longer after that."

Anija felt a deep rumble run through Rialo's whole form and realized Rialo was growling at General Tikos in a way she had never heard before.

"You evil, wicked little human," said Rialo, her words slightly distorted by her anger. "First you take my father, and now you take my little brother? How many more members of my family must you take before you are satisfied?"

"All of them, eventually," said General Tikos. "But do not worry. We would rather enslave you than kill you. The more dragons we have, the stronger the kingdom is."

"And the easier it will be to resurrect the Nameless One, right?"

General Tikos shifted his gaze to Surrels. "I don't know what you're talking about."

He probably doesn't want to spoil the surprise in front of his men so soon, Rialo said mentally. *Regardless, I say we fry him to a crisp and send his remains back to Queen Bariwa with a note saying that she is next.*

That would *be fun, but* …

Anija shook her head. Hal's alleged death had shaken her to her core. Or maybe it wasn't just his death, but the sight of his bloody relic, evidence that he had indeed met a terrible end, that, perhaps, General Tikos had not been lying after all.

It also had to do with Anija's insecurities about her leadership. She'd assumed that Hal, once he returned, would take back the reins of leadership over the Dragon Riders from her, that this weight would no longer be on Anija's and Rialo's shoulders alone.

Now, however, the weight felt heavier than ever, and her legs and back, weaker.

Anija, Rialo said urgently. *Don't let Tikos get into your head. Remember who we're dealing with here. The demons are masters of deception and falsehoods. That includes humans who work with them, such as General Tikos.*

I know, Rialo, Anija replied. *I know. But goddamn, when will we actually* win *for once?*

Rialo seemed to have no answer to that question, or perhaps she was simply interrupted, for General Tikos spread his arms and said, "Now that you have seen evidence of the deaths of your greatest heroes, will you surrender? Or fight?"

"What happens if we surrender?" asked Surrels.

General Tikos smiled in a rather demonic way. "We raze your village, put all of you to death, and take your dragons—the ones we don't kill—as our slaves. The same result as if you choose to fight, albeit with slightly less death and carnage on your part."

Anija gulped. She felt her old habits starting to return, the coward who pragmatically analyzed any situation and always made sure to retreat whenever things got too dicey. Such an attitude made sense when she was a lone thief whose boss didn't care if she lived or died.

But as the current leader of the Dragon Riders and primary protector of an entire village of people, retreat simply was not an option. It wasn't like there was anywhere *to* retreat to at this point, anyway.

There is a saying that my father always quoted, Rialo said. *Do you want to hear it?*

Go ahead, Anija replied, feeling numb.

When we are few, we must become *strong,* Rialo said. *Numbers are not everything. We dragons have been outnumbered by you humans for most of our history, yet we've continued to survive. It is quality, not quantity, that matters in war. And we have the superior quality force by far in my estimation.*

That's rather optimistic of you, sister.

I see it as realistic, Rialo said.

Rialo had a point. Whatever their odds, they couldn't just give up.

Especially if Hal and Keershan are still alive somewhere. Yet even if they aren't, they'd want us to keep fighting. To be not just leaders, but heroes.

Anija felt a rumble of agreement run through Rialo's mind. *You know what to do.*

Without hesitation, Anija jumped off of Rialo's back. She heard Fralia and Surrels calling her back, but she ignored them.

She marched straight up to General Tikos. She picked up Hal's relic along the way, putting it under her arm.

The general was even bigger up close. As she stopped less than six feet away she was almost certain that he could crush her with his fists alone.

But she knew that General Tikos was also not as big as a dragon.

"You are an audacious one," General Tikos said, and Anija caught a hint of respect in his voice. His hands twitched. "What is to stop me from killing you right here and now?"

Anija leaned toward General Tikos. "Absolutely nothing. Although if you think killing *me* would make your life easier, you really are a dumb motherfucker."

A vein popped in General Tikos's forehead. "Watch your language, thief."

Anija snorted. "Thief? I'm not a thief. I'm a Dragon Rider."

General Tikos chuckled. "Halar said much the same thing. 'I'm a Dragon Rider, not just a Relic Hunter.' My ax beheaded him just as easily."

White-hot anger rose up inside Anija, and it wasn't just hers. Rialo's anger made Anija feel stronger and more alert.

Even General Tikos seemed to notice. His hand went to the handle of his ax at his side, although he didn't draw it yet.

"I don't know if Hal is alive or not," Anija said, "but one thing I *do* know is that Dragon Riders don't run. We don't give up, even in the face of impossible odds. And we certainly don't let demon-worshiping bastards like you scare us, whether with lies or the truth. We're stronger than you, smarter than you, and all-around *better* than you. And we're going to beat you."

General Tikos frowned. "I was mistaken. You aren't just audacious, young lady. You are downright delusional."

"Says the guy who doesn't realize he's going to be thrown away by the demons once they don't need you anymore," Anija replied.

General Tikos's frown disappeared, replaced with a soft, triumphant smile. "You know what I am famous for, don't you, young one? Out of the four generals, I am the only one who is not some sort of mage. And do you know why that is?"

Anija blinked. "No. Is it because you're lazy?"

General Tikos barked out a laugh that made Anija's bones shake. He leaned in closer to her, his eyes briefly glowing red. "Because, whereas the others relied on human magic to kill dragons, I drew upon the power of darker magic. Demonic magic."

That was when Anija noticed General Tikos's veins were becoming black. It was something that she remembered seeing in Jaspus, only it was even uglier up close.

"Demonic magic is beyond what any human mage can do. I have delved into the forgotten places, immersed myself in pure shadow and still have yet to reach its bottom. I do not think there is one."

Anija felt a chill run up her spine. "So you're a true believer, then."

General Tikos nodded. "And if that means sacrificing my whole soul to the Nameless One, then so be it. It will be worth it to achieve immortality and power the likes of which even the gods envy."

General Tikos leaned even closer. "So forgive me, Dragon Rider, if I do not find your powers terribly intimidating."

Anija gripped Hal's relic tightly in her hands. "You know what, General? Some people say I talk too much, that I'm not respectful enough. And maybe there's some truth to that. But you know what else is true?"

The general stared blankly at her. "No. Wha—"

Clang.

Anija slammed Hal's relic into General Tikos's face as hard as possible.

The blow was driven by her dragon strength as well, and the general was sent sprawling in the dirt, landing at the feet of a shocked-looking Jaspus.

It wasn't just Jaspus, however. The surrounding soldiers stared in surprise.

Raising Hal's relic above her head, Anija called out, "Did you see what I just did, you bastards? We're the Dragon Riders of Mysteria. You kill one of us, we kill *ten* of yours. If you want to run, now's the time. Otherwise, pray to the gods that your deaths will be quick *and* painless."

Anija didn't know where those words came from, but she meant every one of them, and then some. The dragonfire running through her veins made her willing to take on anyone who tried to attack her and her clan.

The Malarsan Army was apparently intimidated. Even the slaves looked less than eager to attack her.

General Tikos rose to his feet, rubbing his face. "Men of Malarsan, destroy the Dragon Riders. Raze their village to the ground. Do not let even one survive."

With that, a war cry rose up among the Malarsan Army. Weapons and armor clanged together, mages began conjuring elemental balls in their hands, and the slaves snapped their teeth.

But an even louder war cry broke out among the Dragon Riders and people of Mysteria. Roars broke out across the Tops as dragons emerged from within the caves and peaks above. Looking over her shoulder, Anija saw the other Dragon Riders soaring over the village walls toward the Malarsan Army, letting loose a combined war cry that even she found a bit intimidating.

General Tikos slashed his ax, and Anija jumped back to avoid getting her head taken off her shoulders. His eyes and veins were nearly pitch-black now, making him look even more demonic than before.

"Don't go anywhere, Dragon Rider," said General Tikos, his voice sounding slightly less human now. "For your insults, I will crush you with my own bare hands. Just like I did to Halar."

Then General Tikos—along with the entirety of the Malarsan Army—rushed toward her, screaming bloody murder, their collective movement sounding like rolling thunder clouds across the sky.

Chapter Twenty-Four

"We shouldn't be here," Old Snow said as they walked. "This is unnecessary. We could get ourselves killed."

Hal, who walked ahead of Old Snow, looked over his shoulder, giving Old Snow a hard glare. Over the last three days, they'd discussed this very thing. "I *have* to know, Old Snow. If I don't, I'll never be able to live with myself."

"But it's a distraction," Old Snow said. He gestured in a southerly direction. "We should be heading south, toward the capital. The Day of Shadows is coming very soon."

Hal hated it when Old Snow was right. "You could have gone on ahead of us, you know. Sneaked into the capital, scouted it out, and then given us a report when we got there. We would have been fine on our own."

Old Snow chuckled. "Given how we've seen multiple

wanted posters all over the kingdom with surprisingly accurate depictions of you and Keershan, I doubt it."

"Old Snow's got a point, Hal," Keershan said, who walked beside Hal. "I know why you wanted to come out here, but without Old Snow, I don't think we would have gotten this far on our own."

Hal scowled. He kept walking up the hill, his leather boots crunching the dry, dead grass underfoot. "This is my home. My mother is here. If you think I am just going to ignore my home and my mother—"

A strong hand suddenly landed on Hal's shoulder, making Hal stop and look again. Old Snow had grabbed his shoulder, once again displaying his unusual strength, a hard but gentle look in his eyes.

"I understand your concern quite well, Hal," Old Snow said, "but you need to remember that the demons are liars. They can and will say anything they think will get them what they want or make you act in the way they want. And they won't feel guilty about it, either."

Hal shrugged off Old Snow's hand and whirled to face him. "You think I don't know that? I know exactly who and what these things are. I also know that they are good at following through with their threats. Especially Queen Bariwa."

"You're still not thinking this through," Old Snow said. "This is exactly what they want us to do."

Hal's hands balled into fists. "If you're so against us coming out this way, then why did you come with us at all?"

"Because I care about you and want to stop Marial before she ruins everything," Old Snow argued. "You are the one who will wield the Final Relic, but the future is not set in stone. Putting your life in danger for no good reason is a good way to rewrite the future, and not in a good way, either."

Hal opened his mouth to continue arguing, but then Keershan put his head between them and said, "Guys, can we stop fighting with each other, please? I know you two disagree on a lot of things, but we're still friends, remember?"

Hal pursed his lips and looked away. "I'm sorry, Old Snow. I just have to know."

Old Snow nodded once. "Yes. And perhaps I shouldn't be so quick to complain. Even so, I still think this is unwise."

Keershan shrugged. "However wise or unwise it may be, we're not that far from your hometown, right, Hal?"

Hal nodded. He pointed up the hill. "Should be just over that hill. Come on."

With that, Hal resumed walking up the hill with Keershan marching beside him and Old Snow following behind them. Although Old Snow was silent at the moment, Hal could still sense the old man's disagreement with their current direction.

Admittedly, Hal had known it for the past four days, since Agate had told Hal that Lamb's Hand had been destroyed and everyone killed.

Learning that had changed everything for Hal. He had argued with Old Snow that they needed to verify that information, and the only way to do that was to detour through Lamb's Hand on their way to the capital, rather than take the direct route they had originally planned.

Old Snow, naturally, had been against the idea, arguing that they had no time to do that, and besides, demons are liars.

How many times has he said that exact phrase over the last four days? Has to be at least a million times. Or feels like it, anyway.

Not that Hal entirely failed to understand Old Snow's point of view, however. The demons *were* liars and couldn't be trusted to tell the truth about anything.

But it was a risk that Hal was willing to take. He'd missed his hometown ever since he started this Dragon Rider journey. Every day, he'd find himself wondering how his mother was doing or if he would ever smell the hay and see the sunset over the tiny village of Lamb's Hand like he'd done every day growing up there.

Old Snow just doesn't understand. He doesn't have a hometown like me—relatives, friends, neighbors, traditions. He's still very much the high and mighty king of Malarsan, even if he's not sitting on a throne or wearing a crown.

Are you sure about that, Hal? asked Keershan in his mind suddenly. *Old Snow might understand more than you give him credit for.*

Hal glanced to his left. Keershan walked beside him, not actually looking at him, but he could sense the dragon awaiting his answer.

Keershan, unlike Old Snow, had not voraciously argued with him about the detour through Lamb's Hand. Keershan had been supportive ever since Hal made that decision, although Hal knew Keershan well enough to tell that the dragon had something on his mind at this point.

I've already given him the benefit of the doubt enough, Hal said. *If Old Snow still disagrees, no one's stopping him from going on to the capital and waiting for us there.*

Perhaps, Keershan said, *but splitting up is not very wise, especially these days, when there seem to be enemies around every corner.*

You don't think this is a trap, too, do you?

Keershan was silent for a moment. *In my Dragon Rider research, I once read a story about a Dragon Rider very much like you. He came from a small village but left after finding a dragon egg and bonding with the dragon inside. He eventually returned to his hometown after hearing about a great danger threatening its existence, but ...*

Hal, feeling a bit impatient, said, *But what?*

The threat was an illusion cast by a mage who was an enemy of his, Keershan continued. *The mage made all of his old friends and relatives and neighbors look like grotesque monsters. He slaughtered them all without even thinking about it, only discovering the truth* after *the last of them died and the mage ended the illusion.*

Hal grimaced. *What a sad story. I didn't think Dragon Riders could be fooled so easily.*

I don't know if the story is true or not, Keershan said with a shrug. *But it has always stuck with me for a reason, I think, and I'm worried we might be walking into that reason very soon.*

Hal snorted. He didn't want to dismiss Keershan's story, but neither did he want to let it scare them away. Especially if it was not true. Anyone could spin a scary story. Very few could prove it happened. He just wouldn't be happy until he knew for sure.

Then they reached the crest of the hill that overlooked Lamb's Hand. Hal turned his attention to the plains below, a mixture of eagerness and anxiety rising within him.

Hal's soul burned at the sight that greeted him below.

The village of Lamb's Hand had been so named, according to Hal's mother, because of the golden-colored grain which grew there in abundance. In addition to sheep and cattle, Lamb's Hand was where a lot of grain for the kingdom was grown and produced. Hal himself had many memories of working the fields with his friends, neighbors, and family, picking heads of grain that would eventually be refined and sold to people throughout the kingdom.

Looking at the blackened mess below, one would never know that.

It looked like a massive fire had ripped through Lamb's Hand. Fields of blackened ash stretched on for miles before him, looking like a blanket of ash spread over the face of the land. The scent of aged smoke wafted up below, along with ashes that were caught in the wind and sent swirling in some grotesque parody of a tornado.

The village itself, located in the center of the grain fields, appeared to be nothing more than a collection of burned and ruined buildings. He saw no humans working or playing in the fields, no sign of the horses which pulled the grain wagons behind them, nothing to indicate that any sort of life existed down there anymore.

"By the gods," Old Snow said as he stepped up beside Hal. He rested a hand on Hal's shoulder. "I am so, so sorry."

Hal did not immediately respond to Old Snow. The sight of his hometown below, ruined and destroyed with everyone he had known and cared for dead, it numbed his heart.

Hal felt Keershan's sadness for him through their bond and felt Keershan press his snout against his arm. Hal rubbed Keershan's nose, feeling the rough, scaly skin of the dragon's face, a sensation he was very familiar with by this point. The warmth from Keershan was comforting as well, though it didn't quite do away with the feeling of falling he was experiencing at the moment.

It appeared as if Agate's report was true: The village of Lamb's Hand had been razed to the ground, and everyone within was likely dead.

That thought broke through Hal's numbed heart and mind. He felt heat rising within him, not dissimilar to the heat from Keershan's dragonfire, only even hotter.

"My house," Hal said. He looked at Keershan and Old Snow. "We need to go to my house."

Old Snow frowned. "Hal."

"We need to see," Hal said. "I need to know. If my mother is ... if she's still ..."

Hal couldn't even finish the sentence. He just climbed onto Keershan's back, joined by Old Snow, and then the three flew into the air.

From above, it was hard to distinguish between individual buildings, but eventually Hal spotted it. The blackened remains of a one-story wooden farmhouse, its fencing torn, the building itself little more than a burned-out husk.

Even before Keershan landed, Hal jumped off his back, sending smoky ash flying into the air as he rushed over.

The front door had apparently been ripped off its hinges already, so Hal scanned the kitchen and the living room.

"Mother!" Hal called, raising his voice as high as he could to make sure she could hear him. "Mother, are you still here? Moth—"

Hal started coughing, having accidentally inhaled some of the ash. He heard footsteps creaking on the old floorboards behind him and turned to the doorway.

"She's not here, Hal," Old Snow said. He glanced at the burned-out interior. "I'm not sure anyone has been for a while."

Hal felt his heart tighten. He'd never have imagined Lamb's Hand becoming an ash town, yet here he was, standing among the ashes of friends, family, and memories.

His shoulders slumping, Hal walked out of the house. Keershan stood a few feet away looking sad too.

"You were right," Hal said as he and Old Snow's boots crunched through the soft ash. "This was a waste of time. No one is around. The village has been gone for a while."

"No one is around?" said an ice-cold voice that Hal had not heard in a while. "Don't speak so soon."

Old Snow nocked an arrow into his bow and aimed it at the building.

"Who's there?" Hal said. "Show yourself."

What sounded like ashes stirred up in the wind—although Hal realized it was supposed to be some kind of laughter—seemed to come from the house. "Trust me, human, you do not wish to see my true form. But I can show you *a* form."

The soot on the front steps of the house began to vibrate. A massive cloud floated in the doorway, only to start taking form.

In seconds, a spindly, gray-robed demon, eyes glowing red as fresh blood, stood in the doorway. It gripped a long, thick staff, which was topped with a jewel as black as its heart.

Anger rose up within Hal. "The Dark Priest."

The Dark Priest, the demon which had killed Fralia's father, grinned. "You sound very excited to see me again."

"I'd be more excited to see your grave," Hal said. His eyes narrowed. "Last I saw, you and the necrodragon had crashed into the streets of the capital from ten thousand feet in the sky. I'd like to think that even demons couldn't survive that."

The Dark Priest sighed. "Do you know what happens to a demon when it dies, Dragon Rider?"

"I've never given it a great deal of thought."

The Dark Priest spread his arms. "We demons are not individuals as you perceive them. We all are born of the dark well from which the Nameless One himself has come. When we 'die' in the physical world, the seed which we were born from returns to the well, to be reincarnated eventually."

Hal scowled. "Meaning demons never truly die."

"Not necessarily. The Nameless One rarely offers a second chance. Some of my brothers and sisters who failed before the Fall will never be free."

"Why did the Nameless One give you a second chance?" asked Hal. "You failed to kill us before."

The Dark Priest flashed a frightening grin. "I can be very persuasive. Who else do you think came up with the plan to raze your hometown to the ground, knowing it would drive you to forget your *real* mission?"

Hal gripped his sword tightly. "So it was a trap after all, then. Fine. I'll kill you again and again and again, however many times it will take until you stay dead for good."

The Dark Priest gripped his staff with both hands. "Are you so sure? What would your mother think of that?"

The Dark Priest waved his staff. Some sort of portal opened in the air to the Dark Priest's side, showing nothing but endless shadow until the vision of a figure—like a reflection in a mirror—appeared.

It was Hal's mother. She was sitting in a stone cell. Her brown dress was torn and ragged, her hair straggly and thin, and her skin looked very pale.

"Mother?" Hal said, taking a step forward.

"Waste not your breath, Dragon Rider," said the Dark Priest.

Hal glared. "Where is she?"

"Back in the dungeons of Castle Lamor."

Hal's hands shook with suppressed rage. "You spared her. Why?"

"Simple," said the Dark Priest. He gestured at the image. "Surrender yourself to the queen of Malarsan, and your mother will be freed, even given her own mansion and estate in the capital. Fight me, however, and both you and your mother will perish."

Chapter Twenty-Five

THE NUMBNESS IN HAL'S HEART GAVE WAY TO ANGER. He had gotten angry seeing the Dark Priest standing in the doorway of the remains of his childhood home, but positively explosive rage filled his soul when the Dark Priest made his offer.

Dragonfire exploded along his sword's blade, and Hal snapped, "If you lay even one finger on my mother, I will burn you to ashes, and then burn your ashes to nothing."

"You may do so if you wish," said the Dark Priest without a hint of fear in his voice, "but however much throwing a tantrum will make you feel better, I guarantee that it won't save your poor old mother. Indeed, quite the opposite."

All Hal wanted to do was run his sword through the Dark Priest's chest and end his miserable life. The rage running through his veins right now was almost more than he could handle.

But then a calming hand rested on his shoulder.

Looking to see who it was, Hal saw Old Snow's bearded face frowning at him gently.

"Lower your sword, Hal," Old Snow said. "We may not be able to fight our way out of this."

Hal wanted to ignore Old Snow, but for some reason he found the old king's words too persuasive to ignore. He sensed that Keershan was also trying to calm him down, although he'd been mostly unaware of Keershan's presence in his mind until he started thinking about it.

Taking a deep breath, Hal dismissed the dragonfire on his sword and lowered his weapon, though he didn't sheath it. He wasn't going to go that far.

"So you do listen to your elders, after all," said the Dark Priest. "An admirable trait, if a bit useless."

Old Snow stepped forward, taking his hand off of Hal's shoulder. "Sometimes it isn't so admirable, Dark Priest. Particularly when one's elders are corrupt and evil."

The Dark Priest cocked his head to the side. "To whom are you referring, if I may ask?"

"Marial," Old Snow said. "The Marial I know would never have ordered the destruction of one of her own towns simply to lure an enemy."

"The Marial you know is no more," the Dark Priest replied. "Queen Bariwa did indeed order the destruction of the entire village of Lamb's Hand, along with all of its inhabitants, save for the Dragon Rider's mother, although I imagine she wishes she had perished with her neighbors right now."

More anger rose up inside Hal, but before he could respond to that, Old Snow said, "Then I would like to make you a counteroffer, demon. I have something I know that both Marial and the Nameless One want more than anything: Myself."

Even the Dark Priest raised its eyebrows in surprise. "You are willing to give up yourself?"

"For Hal's mother."

"What?" Hal said. He grabbed Old Snow's shoulders and turned him around to face him. "What are you even saying?"

"Yeah," Keershan said. "You can't just give up yourself. We need you and your guidance. Without you—"

"You will be fine," Old Snow said, looking from Hal to Keershan and back again. "Both of you. So long as you continue to look for the Final Relic, I have faith that you will win."

Hal gritted his teeth. "But surrendering yourself is exactly what the demons want. We can't lose you."

"I understand your distress, but you need to look at it from my point of view."

"What do you mean?" asked Keershan.

Old Snow sighed, his shoulders slumping, making him look a lot older than he was. "Although I may have been ousted from power ten years ago, I am still King Rikas Bariwa, king of Malarsan. While in exile, I've had to endure seeing and hearing about the suffering of my people under my ex-wife's leadership. You don't know how hard that is for a king who truly cares about his people, to sit back and watch as they suffer while you are powerless to help."

Old Snow looked toward the image of Mother in the portal. "But perhaps I can begin making up for that failure of mine by giving myself up as the ransom for your mother. It's a start, anyhow."

"And an end," Hal added, "because the demons *will* kill you."

Old Snow had an odd smile on his face. "We all die someday, Hal. It's just that not everyone gets to choose how they go out."

With that strange saying, Old Snow turned once again to face the Dark Priest and spread his arms. "Take me, demon. Take my body, my soul, whatever you want, it's yours."

The Dark Priest stared at Old Snow for a moment. Demonic faces could be difficult to interpret at even the best of times, and right now his face was downright opaque.

Finally, the Dark Priest said, "Thank you for the offer, human. Unfortunately, Queen Bariwa doesn't want you."

"She doesn't?" Old Snow said, sounding almost hurt. "Then what *does* she want?"

The Dark Priest pointed at Hal. "Him. Specifically, his relic."

Hal touched his dragon helmet. "Doesn't she have enough already?"

"That is for us to know," the Dark Priest replied. "Do not worry your mortal head about it."

Hal scowled. He raised his sword again, channeling his dragonfire along the blade's edge. "We won't give you or Queen Bariwa anything. We might be willing to spare your sorry life if you decide to leave us alone."

The Dark Priest smirked. "You know I could never do that, Dragon Rider. This is my second chance. I sincerely doubt that the Nameless One will be gracious enough to give me another. Unlike other gods, His Darkness is not known for his mercy."

"Like that's our problem," Hal said. He pointed his sword at the Dark Priest. "Go to hell."

The Dark Priest tapped his chin. "Your kind words are noted, Dragon Rider. But in case you have forgotten already, we still have your dear mother."

His mother was moving now. She raised her head and looked around at her surroundings in confusion. She did not seem to see or notice them, however.

But then Hal noticed a dark tendril snaking through the bars of her cell. Mother did not seem to notice it. She was too busy tugging at the chains on her wrists and ankles, apparently trying to loosen them.

Hal wanted to scream at Mother to notice the tendril, but he knew his voice wouldn't reach her. He could only watch helplessly as the tendril curled along her body until it got to her neck, which Mother finally seemed to notice. She screamed and thrashed, but the tendril did not let go.

Hal glared at the Dark Priest. "Whatever you're doing, stop it. Or else I'll send your ashes back in a casket to the Nameless One personally."

"That is not my doing," said the Dark Priest, holding up a hand to feign innocence. "It is likely one of my hungry brothers or sisters. Most demons cannot control themselves around helpless humans. Their souls tend to be the tastiest."

Anger hotter and redder than anything Hal had felt washed through him. He could feel Keershan getting angry with him. His first instinct was to hop onto Keer-shan's back and go all Dragon Rider on the Dark Priest. He had turned demons to ash before.

He could easily—and happily—do it again.

But his reason pointed out that, however justified his anger might have been, his mother was still in danger. She had given up fighting the tendril now, lying limp in its grasp, although Hal could see the fear and disgust in her eyes as the shadow extension wrapped around her.

So Hal, hating himself, threw his sword down onto the ground. "Fine!"

That single word echoed through the air, causing the Dark Priest to turn his attention back to Hal. The Dark Priest leaned closer to them, a curious expression on his face. "Fine? What do you mean?"

Hal glared at the Dark Priest. "You know exactly what I mean, Dark Priest. I mean you win. You can have me. Just let my mother go and stop torturing her."

A wicked, triumphant grin appeared on the Dark Priest's face while Keershan said, "Hal! What are you saying? I know you care about your mother, but—"

"If I don't give myself up, they'll kill her, Keershan," Hal said, looking at Keershan. "I couldn't live with myself if I left my mother to die in their care. This is our only choice. Wouldn't you do the same for your mother?"

Keershan looked heartbroken for a moment, but then a look of determination appeared on his face and he nodded. "Yes, I absolutely would. And as your loyal Steed, I am coming with you."

"So the Rider *and* his Steed have agreed to give them-selves up," the Dark Priest observed. "This has gone even better than I could have hoped. His Darkness will be quite pleased. Are you certain that this is what you want?"

"Yes," Hal said as he and Keershan nodded as one. "It is."

The Dark Priest made a strange hissing sound. "Most excellent indeed. Although as a demon I will never understand the bond between mother and child, that does not mean I can't exploit it to my advantage."

Hal scowled, but then looked at Old Snow. "Old Snow, go back and tell the others. They'll need to know."

Old Snow's face was also difficult to read, although Hal got the impression that Old Snow was not happy about this decision. "Are you certain? If we lose you, then we won't get the Final Relic."

Hal shook his head. "I know this will mess up our plans, but there are other Dragon Riders. Anija or one of the others can do it in my place."

Old Snow raised an eyebrow. "Despite what the Crafters' prophecy showed?"

"The future is not written in stone," Hal said. He exchanged a quick look with Keershan. "Besides, someone has to survive. And you are definitely a survivor, old man, regardless of how you feel about yourself."

Old Snow smiled, although it was a sad smile. "Then I'll just have to keep on surviving, I suppose."

Hal nodded. He turned toward the Dark Priest once more. "All right, Dark Priest. We're ready to go when you are."

"I have always been ready to go," said the Dark

Priest. "Fortunately, we demons have a way of fast travel that mortals are not privy to."

The Dark Priest snapped his fingers. The portal vanished, and a second later, a pool of shadow emerged under Hal and Keershan's feet. The pool grew wider and wider, until it surrounded them on all sides for a good ten or fifteen feet. Old Snow had retreated out of its range, watching them with regret and sadness in his eyes.

Then shadowy tendrils rose up from within the pool and wrapped around Hal and Keershan's wrists and ankles. The tendrils were shockingly cold to the touch, making Hal grunt in pain, while Keershan growled. Hal immediately started channeling dragonfire heat through his veins, though it still felt like having a frozen towel wrapped around his wrists.

Glancing over his shoulder at Old Snow, Hal said, "See you later, old man. Safe travels."

A chuckle came from the Dark Priest. "You expect me to let him go, despite what he now knows about our plans?"

Without warning, the ashes scattered around the farmhouse began to shift and rise. Demonic warriors formed out of dust, clad in gray and armed with swords and axes, red eyes gleaming from their inhuman faces. Old Snow raised his bow but was outnumbered already.

"These are our ash demons," said the Dark Priest, gesturing at the small army. "They are the tortured spirits of those who perished in ash towns, driven by their anger and grief, unable to tell between friend and foe, guided solely by jealousy of the living."

Horrified, Hal and Keershan immediately began

trying to free themselves from their tendrils. But like quicksand, the tendrils strengthened the more they struggled, and then they started to sink into the shadowy pool rapidly.

"No!" Hal shouted, yanking as hard as he could. "You bastards! Leave Old Snow alone! You got what you want already."

The Dark Priest's eyes gleamed with evil amusement. "The Nameless One does not forgive or forget. Like all who oppose the Nameless One, your former king shall perish."

The last thing he saw, before he and Keershan vanished under the shadows, was Old Snow firing arrow after arrow at the ash demons.

And the last thing he heard was the Dark Priest's wicked laughter.

Chapter Twenty-Six

HOW LONG HAL WAS IN SHADOWS, HE DIDN'T KNOW. IT could have been five minutes or five years.

He was in the very essence of darkness itself. It was what Hal imagined the world must have been like before the gods created it, that nothingness where life and death were equally irrelevant.

Utter silence rang in his ears like a gong. His blood felt like ice. There was a scent of rot, and the bitterest taste lingered in his mouth for what seemed like an eternity.

And then it was over, and Hal found himself lying on the hard stone floor of a jail cell. It was grimy, and the air was dank. A particularly large dried blood patch lay mere inches from his face, dimly illuminated by a single torch on the hallway outside, burning not merrily, but resolutely, as if it was the only thing standing against the shadows.

Yet it was infinitely preferable to the endless darkness that Hal had found himself in not too long ago.

Or was *it a long time ago? I can't tell.*

Drawing in a deep breath, Hal forced himself to sit up. He drew upon the dragonfire in his bones, attempting to warm himself up quickly and become strong.

But Hal could not feel the warmth of the dragonfire anymore.

At first, Hal thought maybe he was doing something wrong, so he tried again, but nothing happened. All he could do was sit there and feel as cold and miserable as ever.

Keershan, are you there? Keershan?

But Hal did not hear Keershan, either. It was as if his bond with Keershan had been completely severed.

As far as he could tell, he was indeed alone in whatever dungeons or jail he'd ended up in, in more ways than one.

I failed. Hal looked at his hands in despair. *I gave the Nameless One exactly what he wanted, and I didn't even fight against it.*

The door's squeaky hinges echoed as it opened. Footsteps approached, and light spilled into the dungeon.

Three figures appeared on the other side of the bars of Hal's cage.

Hal had no trouble recognizing them. One was General Mokoa. A ball of shining magical light in her hands contained a little water within it. Her skin looked noticeably paler than the last time he'd seen her.

The second was the Dark Priest. He walked with his arms folded in front of his chest, looking quite pleased with himself. The shadows seemed to cling to him in a way that they did not to the others, as if the shadows were a part of him.

And the third and final was, perhaps, the most dreaded of them all: Queen Bariwa herself.

Queen Bariwa looked decrepit. Her skin was as pale as a corpse's, her pitch-black veins standing out. A tar-like color appeared to partially fill her eyes, the whites of which now had a red hue to them. The stench of death rose above her perfume.

"Long time, no see, Halar Norath," said Queen Bariwa, her voice hoarser and more ragged than before. "You look even more like an abused, abandoned puppy than the last time we met."

Hal scowled. He rose to his feet, despite his exhaustion. "And you look more and more like a corpse every day, Your Highness."

Queen Bariwa chuckled. "Bark at me all you like. But I know you can't bite me, no matter how much you may want to."

Hal's hands balled into fists. "Well, you have me now, Queen Bariwa. The Dark Priest promised to free my mother if I surrendered. Have you done that yet?"

The Dark Priest inclined his head. "It is done. Your mother has been released. Not that it will do you much good, as she doesn't even know you are here."

Hal sighed in relief. He was honestly surprised that the Dark Priest had upheld his end of the deal and freed Mother. Granted, the Dark Priest could have been lying, but Hal doubted it somehow. He sensed that the Dark

Priest was telling the truth this time, which would be a first.

Hopefully Mother will find a way to support herself, now that she doesn't have me or Father to rely on.

"What about Keershan?" Hal said. "Where is he? And why can't I feel him anymore?"

"That may have to do with the fact that we took your relic," said the Dark Priest.

Instinctively, Hal reached up to touch his head, only to feel his own short, scratchy hair.

As soon as Hal registered the sensation of his own hair against his palm, Hal launched himself at the bars. Grabbing the bars—as his arms were too thick to fit through the small openings—Hal snarled, "Give me back my relic!"

"Why?" asked the Dark Priest in obvious amusement. "I told you that is what we wanted, did I not? And when you said we could have you, I took that to mean we could have *all* of you, including your relic."

"What did you do with it?" Hal said. "I swear to the gods that if you are using it to enslave a dragon, I—"

"Nothing so puerile, Rider," said Queen Bariwa. "I have plenty of other relics to use. Including relics that you personally retrieved for me."

Hal glared at Queen Bariwa. "Then what *are* you doing with it?"

"I gave it to General Tikos for use in the upcoming invasion of your little Dragon Rider village," said Queen Bariwa. "He is a master of psychological warfare and intimidation tactics. I imagine he'll find a *very* good use for it."

Hal gripped the cold, dirty bars even tighter. "When will the invasion happen?"

"In about four days from today," General Mokoa replied. She smirked. "And it will be glorious."

Hal glared at General Mokoa. "I take it that you are going to be part of it?"

"With both General Jeniq and General Omaros dead, the Malarsan Army can't afford to put all of our eggs in one basket anymore. Although I'd love to get revenge on General Jeniq's daughter and the former Dark Tiger for how they humiliated me in Dragon Valley."

"You have your role to play here, General," Queen Bariwa reprimanded. "Be grateful I did not have you put to death for that blunder."

General Mokoa shut up very quickly.

"Why are you invading Mysteria so soon?" asked Hal. "Our information indicated that the Day of Shadows is still a week and a half away."

Queen Bariwa smiled. "Your information is wrong. The Day of Shadows is actually starting in four days, on the same day as the invasion. Did you honestly believe that we would leak such important information to a fool as traitorous as Jaspus? We deliberately fed him incorrect information."

"So, around the same time General Tikos is grinding your tiny little village into the dirt, the Nameless One should be rising," General Mokoa brushed her dark hair out of her eyes, which gleamed in the glowing sphere of water in her hands.

Hal felt his heart tighten. "You're monsters. All of you."

"Monsters?" Queen Bariwa repeated. "Is that all that the first Dragon Rider has to say to me? I was expecting more."

Hal scowled. "Where is Keershan? I swear by the name of every god in the heavens, if you killed him—"

"He's still alive," General Mokoa said. She winked at the Dark Priest. "Though not for much longer, right?"

"Correct," the Dark Priest said. "Your dragon will be the final sacrifice in the ritual and thus begin the resurrection of the Nameless One. Currently, he is imprisoned and unconscious in another part of the castle that you couldn't reach even if you tried."

"Is that the real reason you have enslaved the dragons, then? To have ready sacrifices for your dark ritual?"

"Indeed," said the Dark Priest. "Dragons are unique creatures. They are living engines of destruction in some cultures and bringers of wisdom and light in others. Their energy, if sacrificed with the correct incantations, can even bring back the dead."

"It's an ancient rite," said Queen Bariwa, "said to be even older than the Nameless One. Although it does require a large population of dragons to perform correctly."

Hal's grip on the bars tightened so much he would have broken them if he still had his dragon strength. "Enslaving dragons, just to sacrifice them for your evil god, if there's any justice in the world at all, you will suffer the consequences of your actions."

Queen Bariwa smirked at Hal. "I find it rich that one

of my best former Relic Hunters is now lecturing *me* on the evils of enslaving and abusing dragons. Or did you forget that you and the hundreds of other Relic Hunters in my employ are what made this possible?"

"It's true," General Mokoa piped up. "If you and your peers hadn't retrieved hundreds of missing relics scattered around the kingdom, this wouldn't even be possible."

Hal ground his teeth together in frustration, but he also realized that he couldn't deny what either of them said. Hal had indeed recovered dozens of relics on his own over his years of service to the queen. And he wasn't the only one. The Relic Hunter Corps was perhaps the second largest wing in the Malarsan Army, which had always seemed odd to Hal until recently when he found out exactly *why* the Relic Hunters existed at all.

"Even so," Hal said, "Only because I was tricked. I was taught that the relics would end the Dragon War and stop all the senseless killing and dying on both sides. If I'd known what you were actually trying to do, I would have killed you myself."

Queen Bariwa regarded Hal with amusement. "But the Dragon War *is* over, Halar. And it *was* thanks to the relics. I do not recall, however, ever promising what would *happen* to the dragons or the relics after the war. You may accuse me of many things, but a liar, I am not."

"That's not what your husband said," Hal muttered.

Queen Bariwa's eyes widened with anger. Her hand shot out and grabbed his collar, pulling him against the bars.

"Do not mention *him* around me unless you wish to

die a painful death," said Queen Bariwa, her voice lower and deadlier than it had been even a couple of seconds ago. "And because I am not trained in the art of execution, it would be *very* painful indeed."

Hal gulped. Although he was bigger, taller, and stronger than Queen Bariwa, something about her intimidated him greatly.

Hal, however, did not want to show fear, so he said, "That begs the question: Why haven't you killed me yet?"

Releasing his collar and stepping away from his cell, Queen Bariwa said, "Because *he* wishes to see you once he returns."

Hal immediately understood who Queen Bariwa was referring to. "The Nameless One. He knows who I am."

"Of course," said Queen Bariwa. "I have kept him informed about the opposition we have faced. He has not been very pleased, but he is nonetheless interested in seeing you."

"Why?" Hal said. "Because I've been such a thorn in his side?"

Queen Bariwa smiled coldly. "You shall see soon enough. In any case, I believe we are done here."

Hal's captors departed, leaving him in the dark once more.

Hal walked over to a wooden seat built into the wall of his cell. He sat down on it, the wood creaking ominously under his weight, although it fortunately held.

Hal was currently experiencing a whirlwind of emotions that he found difficult to parse. He was happy that Mother had been set free, that she had not been killed like everyone else in Lamb's Hand.

The rest, however, was something straight out of Hal's worst nightmare. Keershan would be the final sacrifice for the Nameless One's resurrection. The Day of Shadows would come too soon. Old Snow was likely dead. Mysteria was going to be invaded in four days, and no one even suspected it.

And Hal was completely and totally powerless to do a damned thing about it.

Hal sank his head into his hands, rubbing his forehead with his fingers. *I should have listened to Old Snow. If we'd just kept going to the capital, we might have avoided this situation entirely. But I didn't, and now I—we—are suffering the consequences of my actions.*

Not for the first time, Hal missed Father. He wished he could ask his father for advice, but barring that one unusual dream he'd had a few months back, Hal had no way to reach out to or contact him. He was well and truly on his own, and he knew it would just get worse from here.

Much, much worse.

Chapter Twenty-Seven

FOUR DAYS LATER, ON THE DAY OF SHADOWS ...

Hal was awakened by a metal bowl sliding across the stone floor.

"There's your gruel, dog," said a harsh voice on the other side of the cell. "Eat up, because it'll be your last."

Rubbing the sleep out of his eyes, Hal looked down at the bowl at his feet. It was the same gray gruel he'd been fed twice a day every day for the past four days now. He wasn't even sure it counted as 'food,' looking more like wet clay and tasting about as appetizing.

Hal's jailer was a big, fat man who wore a black hood. Even so, Hal could see the wicked smile he'd worn every day of Hal's captivity.

"What are you waiting for, prisoner?" said the jailer. "Eat."

Hal scowled but took the bowl of gruel anyway and

started slurping it up. The gruel tasted and felt like quick-sand, but Hal gulped it down anyway.

Normally, the jailer would shove Hal's food bowl into his cell and leave him alone for the next twelve hours. This time, however, the jailer lingered, his pig-like eyes staring at Hal with unnerving intensity.

Hal raised his bowl. "Can I have seconds?"

"No," the jailer said curtly. "Her Majesty wants you to get ready for the big event."

Hal felt his heart sink into his stomach. "Today is the day."

He knew it was. He'd just… tried avoiding thinking about it.

"Yep," said the jailer. He knocked on the bars with his knuckles. "General Mokoa will escort you in an hour. So you still have time to pray to the gods."

"Thanks for the advice. It is comforting."

"Make all the quips you like. Won't save you." With that, the jailer walked away, chuckling to himself.

The past four days had been as close to hell as Hal would experience in this life. Though he had not been beaten, he had been kept isolated. He received no news from the outside, saw no one except the jailer, and was fed one bowl of gruel and one cup of water every day. They did give him a bucket to relieve himself in, but they didn't change it out, meaning the stench of his own waste was constantly in his nostrils. He caught little sleep on the cold stone floor.

As a result, even though it had only been four days, it had felt more like four years. Hal had quickly lost track of time, thanks to having no access to the sun or any sort of timekeeping device. For all he knew, the jailer might have just been lying when he said that today was the Day of Shadows. It wouldn't be the first time the jailer— whose name he still did not know—had pulled a cruel prank on him.

Somehow, though, I suspect that he's telling the truth this time. I can sense the darkness.

That was an unusual thing to say and probably didn't make sense, but to Hal, it did. Over the past four days, he'd sensed a growing darkness gathering underneath his feet. It felt ready to burst out and flood the whole kingdom like a raging river.

That was likely the Nameless One's presence growing stronger and stronger every day. Though Hal had not seen any demons since getting here, he saw them frequently in his dreams. Dark nightmares featuring ghoulishly laughing creatures ripping his skin from his flesh, dropping him in a pool of blood where he would slowly and painfully drown to death.

Whether those dreams were from the Nameless One —perhaps as a way to torture Hal—or simply came from his own subconscious, Hal still didn't know.

Hal tried to reach out to Keershan. Like every other time he'd tried it over the past half week, he felt and heard nothing.

If the Day of Shadows has indeed come, how do I know that Keershan hasn't been sacrificed already? He might not even be alive anymore.

That thought—and others like it—had greatly troubled Hal. He tried not to think them, but between the isolation, the bad food, lack of sleep, and general tiredness he experienced, it was difficult to think anything even close to resembling a positive thought.

Hal also worried about the other Dragon Riders in Mysteria. Today was also supposed to be the same day as the invasion of Mysteria. If that was the case, then for all Hal knew, his friends were likely being slaughtered even as he sat there in his cell thinking about them.

And that was what had gotten to Hal more than anything else: The idea that, not only was he helpless to save himself, but he was also helpless to save his friends.

Keershan, Old Snow, Fralia, Anija, Surrels, Rialo, and everyone else. I'm sorry. I failed you.

Not that he hadn't *tried* to escape, but his attempts had been quickly thwarted. Everything that he had considered had failed, including one foolish attempt to overpower one of his captors.

Hal heard the familiar sound of the dungeon doors opening, along with footsteps rapidly making their way toward his cell. He rose to his feet, hiding his empty food bowl behind his back. It may have seemed like a lame weapon, but if Hal was going to die, he might as well go down fighting.

Has it really been an hour yet, though? Feels like it has only been a few minutes since breakfast. Maybe Mokoa is early.

Regardless, Hal waited with bated breath, listening closely to the footsteps. They were definitely coming his way. They were so close now that it sounded like they were walking right next to his ears.

So when the hooded figures appeared in the hallway on the other side of the bars of Hal's cage, he wasn't surprised to see them. He was surprised, however, to see that they weren't General Mokoa and her soldiers. Nor were they the demons or even Queen Bariwa herself, coming perhaps to taunt him one last time before his execution.

No, they were two hooded figures whose hidden faces made it impossible to identify them initially. Somewhere in the back of his head, Hal compared them to the Defacer—the very first demon he fought and killed what seemed like a lifetime ago—only to realize that these figures weren't demons at all when they spoke. One of them smelled like a tree for some reason.

"Hal?" said a voice that Hal thought he'd never hear again. "Are you in there?"

Hal rushed over to the bars and gripped them harder than ever.

The hooded man standing before him lowered his hood, revealing the familiar, kindly smiling face of Old Snow.

But his face was a lot more scarred than the last time Hal had seen him. A particularly nasty gash ran down one cheek.

"Yes, Hal, it's me," Old Snow said. "I'm here. And I'm going to break you out."

"I thought you were dead. Queen Bariwa said—"

"Marial is a liar, first and foremost," Old Snow said calmly. "Though the best deceptions often have a hint of truth mixed in with them. For now, we need to get you out of your cell."

Hal turned his attention to Old Snow's hooded companion. "Who is 'we,' exactly?"

"You don't recognize me?" said a familiar feminine

voice within the hood. "I suppose it has been a long time since the Dark Forest, human."

The woman lowered her hood as well, revealing the face of a woman whose skin resembled tree bark and whose hair looked like branches and leaves mixed together in odd patterns.

Hal's jaw dropped open. "Tremas?"

Tremas had been a tree spirit from the Dark Forest. An ally of Old Snow, Tremas had been the one to save Hal from a demonic infection that would have killed him if left untreated. It had been several months since then and Hal nearly had forgotten about her, but he couldn't say he was unhappy to see her.

"The one and the same," said Tremas. She raised her hand, which terminated in root-like fingers. "Stand back. This will get loud."

Hal stepped backward hastily as Tremas grabbed the door of his cell. With a few grunts, she tore it straight off its hinges.

Old Snow stepped into Hal's cell and began checking Hal over. "Can you walk? Are you injured or sick?"

"I'm fine," Hal said. "We need to go."

"And you need more than I can offer." Old Snow reached into his robes. "I don't have a gourmet meal for you, but I do have something else you may find useful."

Old Snow drew out Hal's drill sword and held it out to him hilt-first. With trembling fingers, Hal took his sword and, flipping it upright, slashed it a couple times for practice, a smile on his face.

"Where did you get this?" asked Hal, appreciating

the heft of the sword in his hands. "I thought the demons had confiscated everything."

"They did," Old Snow said, "but I suspected you'd want your things back. Tremas."

Without another word, Tremas tossed her bag into the cell, which clanged loudly against the floor. Hal immediately spotted his old armor stashed inside.

"They were kept in the armory. Either Marial has not learned from her mistakes, or her minions don't know how to properly hide confiscated weapons."

Tears of happiness threatened to pour out of Hal's eyes, but he sniffled them back and, looking up at Old Snow and Tremas, said, "How—?"

Old Snow frowned. "It wasn't easy, especially after you and Keershan disappeared. I was very nearly overwhelmed by the Dark Priest's forces, only escaping through faking my death. That's where this new scar came from."

Hal smiled. "Again?"

Old Snow shrugged. "What is the saying among the tradesmen of the kingdom that the royal foreman once told me? 'If it isn't broken, don't fix it'? Regardless, surviving was the easy part. The harder part was finding and rescuing you before the Day of Shadows."

"That's where I come in," said Tremas with a bow. "Old Snow came to my forest asking for my help."

Hal stared at Tremas in shock. "And you agreed?"

Hal was shocked because he remembered quite well how Tremas had explained that the tree spirits were largely neutral in the conflict between the demons and the Dragon Riders and didn't care who won one way or another. Indeed, the only reason Tremas even helped them last time was to repay a mysterious favor for Old Snow, although to this day he still didn't know what he'd done for her.

"Of course," said Tremas. She smiled wickedly. "For a price, naturally."

Hal glanced at Old Snow. The former king *did* look a bit older and more tired than usual, which was how he'd looked the last time he'd paid Tremas. Hal still wondered how he 'paid' her, although he supposed that was something he'd worry about later.

But then Old Snow flashed Tremas an unexpected smile. "You make yourself sound worse than you are. You seemed eager to help when I explained how dangerous the Nameless One's resurrection would be for everyone, including the tree spirits."

Tremas averted her gaze. "Only because the demons recently tried to burn down my forest unsuccessfully. If the demons did not want me as an enemy, they shouldn't have intruded on my forest."

Hal shook his head. "I am so grateful for your help, regardless of your motives. I promise you once this whole mess is over with, I'll pay you back a hundredfold."

Tremas gazed at Hal. "I only ask one thing of you Dragon Riders if you win: That you leave me—and my forest—alone."

Hal nodded. "I promise."

"Anyway, to continue our story, we then made our way to the capital," Old Snow said. "Once we entered the city, we retrieved your weapons and armor, sneaked into the Castle dungeons, and now we're here."

Hal looked at Old Snow in surprise. "How did you find me? I thought that no one outside of the Castle even knew I was here."

"It was an educated guess," Old Snow replied. "Truthfully, I didn't even know if you were still alive or not. But I was betting on Marial deciding to take the lazy option and imprison you like a normal prisoner, rather than take the smart precautions one would take if they were imprisoning a Dragon Rider."

Hal looked down at his hands, not meeting Old Snow's gaze. "Former Dragon Rider, you mean. They took my relic, and I can't feel Keershan anymore, although I know he's still alive."

Hal felt Old Snow's hand rest on his shoulder, causing him to look up at Old Snow's kindly face.

"Former Dragon Rider?" Old Snow repeated. "Son, your relic isn't what makes you a Dragon Rider. It's just a tool to help you bond with Keershan. It's your bond with Keershan that will lead us to him."

Hal bit his lower lip. "But I can't feel him. That's the problem. I don't know where he is."

"And?" Old Snow said. "Have you already forgotten that this isn't the first time you lost your relic and had to rely on your bond with Keershan alone to communicate with him?"

Hal was a bit confused at first until a memory of a throne room flashed in his mind. "That's right. The first time we came here, I was able to communicate with him in the throne room without a relic. Yet that was when we were in the same room, which we clearly aren't now."

"So?" Old Snow said. "The legends of the Dragon

Riders are not always accurate, but they talk of Riders and Steeds telepathically sensing and talking with each other over vast distances thanks to their strong bonds. Your bond with Keershan is strong, is it not? So you should be able to do it. Remember how you felt the first time you did it. And then do it again."

Hal realized that Old Snow had a point. His previous attempt to talk with Keershan had proved that, with or without a relic, their bond existed, and that was back when their bond had been much weaker than it was now.

Drawing upon his memories of that night in Queen Bariwa's throne room, Hal closed his eyes. He focused as intently as he could on his bond with Keershan, seeking to draw upon that connection between them, to find and use it as he always did.

Again, Hal felt nothing at first, but after a few more intense seconds of thought, Hal suddenly felt something. It was a weak sensation at first, like the faint beating of a heart through layers of clothing.

But the more he focused, the stronger the sensation became, until Hal soon felt a familiar presence in his mind, one he had thought he might never feel again.

Keershan? Hal said mentally, his tone hesitant and unsure. *Are you there? Can you hear me?*

Keershan's weakened but still recognizable voice said, *Hal? Is that you? Or is this another trick of the demons?*

It's me, Keershan. The real *me. Not a demon. Where are you?*

Hal was filled with relief and happiness as Keershan's emotions flooded him through their bond. *I'm not sure. It's dark and scary. Can you sense my physical body's location?*

Yes. Old Snow and I are on our way now. Just hang tight, okay?

Okay, Keershan said, *but please get here quickly. The ritual is about to start.*

Opening his eyes, Hal looked up at Old Snow and Tremas. "I talked to Keershan. He's still alive. And I know where he is."

Old Snow smiled broadly. Slapping Hal on the shoulder, he said, "Then get your armor on, Hal. We have a dragon—and a kingdom—to save."

Chapter Twenty-Eight

ANIJA DODGED ANOTHER SWING OF GENERAL TIKOS'S broadsword. Landing on her feet, Anija fired another fireball at the massive General, striking him in the chest. His eyes glowed red, and he thrust his hand forward.

Shadowy tendrils launched out from General Tikos's hand toward Anija, who swung her dragonfire-coated knives through the air. The daggers cut through the tendrils without effort.

Gripping his ax with both hands, General Tikos said, "You're quick. But how much longer can even a Dragon Rider avoid my ax?"

Anija smirked. "Pretty long. Turns out that being a Dragon Rider comes with some perks. Like using my Steed's power to make myself strong."

General Tikos smirked back. "Does it make you more perceptive of dangers around you as well?"

Anija felt something cold and burning wrap around

her ankles. The unnatural shadows rose up her legs like slimy snakes, squeezing the warmth out of them.

A massive shadow alerted Anija just in time to see General Tikos's ax coming down.

Instinctively, dragonfire erupted around Anija's legs, instantly incinerating the tendrils. She leaped backward, the ax slamming into the ground where she'd been standing.

Breathing hard, Anija thrust her hands forward. A ring of dragonfire erupted around the general.

"The real question is, does selling your soul to the devil make *you* less perceptive?" asked Anija. "Or have you always been this crazy?"

General Tikos grunted and swung at the flames, but it was clear he was stuck for the time being. Sweat had broken out on his forehead, and he already looked uncomfortable in his thick, heavy armor.

Taking a moment to breathe, Anija scanned the battlefield around her, trying to spot Rialo.

It didn't take Anija long to find her. Rialo stood on the other side, trading blows with Jaspus and another slave. The three dragons were roaring and snapping and slashing at each other, blood and scales flying everywhere. Anija felt Rialo's feral rage burning through her bond, a driving force that kept her going despite being outnumbered.

As for everyone else, the battle was far too chaotic for Anija to make sense of what was happening. Mysterians and Malarsans clashed with screams of metal and flesh, mages on both sides cast spells to help or hinder their friends and enemies, and the Dragon Riders and the

unbonded dragons were either ripping through the
enemy ranks or taking care of the slaves. She certainly
didn't see Fralia or Surrels, nor did she know if they were
even alive.

At least the bastards haven't reached the village yet. Anija
glanced over the gates that remained standing. *Until they
do, I think we're doing okay.*

That was the problem, though. Anija knew that they
were horribly outnumbered and that the only reason they
hadn't been completely destroyed yet was because
everyone was motivated by her speech. The Dragon
Riders had higher morale than the enemy, but how much
longer that would last was anyone's guess. She certainly
spotted a lot of corpses from people on their side
covering the battlefield already, though the enemy had
lost a fair number of troops, too.

*Hope the other council members are okay. Because I can barely
take care of myself.*

A strange whirling sound filled Anija's ears. General
Tikos raised his ax and swung it in a circle.

Ice-cold wind exploded outward, instantly putting out
Anija's dragonfire. The freezing gale also struck Anija
and, though her flames had taken the brunt of it, she felt
it bite at the exposed parts of her skin.

It wasn't the natural cold of the Tops. It felt as if
General Tikos had somehow channeled his own ice-cold
cruelty through his ax.

Twin tendrils rose out of the earth and wrapped
around her wrists. Ice-cold pain ripped through her. She
dropped her knives to the ground, where the dragonfire
harmlessly dissipated.

The general swung again.

A young black-and-brown dragon swooped down from the air and tackled General Tikos. Crying out in surprise, he fell to the dirt with the young dragon, which immediately began biting and scratching.

"Yiko!"

Yiko was too busy tearing General Tikos a new one to respond to Anija. The young dragon was almost as ferocious as her mother. For a moment, Anija thought that Yiko might just maul General Tikos to death all on her own.

But then there was a cry of pain and the general got to his feet. He held Yiko by the throat with one hand, his other holding his ax. General Tikos appeared unaffected by Yiko's claws that tore at his wrist and forearm, glaring at the hatchling as if she was an ant.

Anija ripped her hands out of the tendrils' grasp and hurled one of her knives at General Tikos. The knife flew end over end through the air until it slammed into the gap between General Tikos's armor plating along his flank.

General Tikos roared and threw Yiko at Anija, sending them both rolling.

Dazed, Anija looked at Yiko, who lay near her. The hatchling seemed to be struggling to maintain conscious-ness, her eyes dimmer than normal.

That was when Anija noticed Yiko's throat. A fresh scar lay there, like a hot iron had been pressed against her scales in the shape of General Tikos's hand. There was a smell of fried flesh.

Rialo's parental anger suddenly shot up inside Anija, giving her the strength to rise.

General Tikos removed Anija's knife with some effort. Blood flowed freely down the side of his body.

"Is this the best that you can do? It will take more than that to kill me."

"I dunno," Anija said. "Seems to have distracted you well enough."

General Tikos smirked. He crushed the knife in his hand and dropped it at his feet, the weapon little more than a crumpled heap of metal. "Just a distraction. That's all you are good for. You certainly aren't as strong as Halar, I can tell you that much."

Anija scowled. "How the hell would *you* know, anyway? It's not like you've fought Hal."

"I can just tell," said General Tikos. "I've been a general for years, and served in the Malarsan Army even longer. My combat instincts have been honed to near perfection. And in my experience, thieves like yourself are usually too weak to bother with."

Anger shot through Anija's body. "Then perhaps you and your pals should pack up and head home. We didn't pick this fight."

General Tikos smirked even more. "Oh, but you did. You picked this fight the moment you let Halar and the others wrap you up in it. You could have quit anytime, betrayed them at any moment. Instead, you chose to help them destroy the castle, oppose us at Dragon Valley, and now lead them against us here. Don't act like you don't belong here. All of us do."

Anija scowled, though truthfully, she found it difficult

to refute General Tikos's points. Hell, she remembered how much she'd hated having to tag along with Hal and the others on their quest and how it had only been relatively recently that she had changed her mind about it.

"So what?" Anija said. She felt Hal's relic hanging at her side, having tied it to her belt earlier to avoid losing it during the battle. "Maybe you have a point. But that doesn't mean we're going to lose."

General Tikos shook his head. "Such optimism is admirable, if incredibly naive and unfounded. Soon, my forces will utterly demolish yours. Yet even if, by some miracle of the gods, you were to win, it wouldn't last long. The Day of Shadows is upon us."

General Tikos gestured toward the sky overhead.

Although it was the middle of the day, Anija *did* think the sky looked a bit darker than it should have been. Or rather, darkness was leaking into the sky from somewhere far to the south, from—

The castle. Where the Nameless One's body is.

As if reading her mind, General Tikos said, "Exactly. In truth, this battle really doesn't matter. Who wins and who loses, who lives and who dies all will be irrelevant when the Nameless One returns to this physical plane. His power is vaster than that of any human mage or dragon. You'd do well to beg him for forgiveness, even though he does not give it even to his loyal servants."

Anija bit her lower lip. "You know what? All you do is talk. I thought you were supposed to be the quiet one."

General Tikos chuckled. "How can I be silent in the face of absolute victory waiting just around the corner for me and mine to seize with our hands?"

Anija drew another knife from her belt. "Let's see how you like getting a knife to the eyes."

Anija took another step, only to feel a sudden spike of pain in her head.

Anija … help …

Anija looked to her right. Although a handful of dragons and quite a few dead soldiers lay scattered around Rialo, her Steed was currently surrounded by about four slaves that slashed and bit at her. A handful of earth mages stood on the outskirts of the battle, using their magic to destabilize the ground under her.

Even worse, Rialo was bleeding and missing scales everywhere. Her movements, though still quite fast and vicious, had clearly slowed down at this point.

Rialo, Anija thought, taking a step toward her. *Hang in there. I'll—*

General Tikos's ax swooped through the air. Anija, acting purely on instinct, ducked and rolled, barely avoiding it. Even as she rolled to her feet, however, General Tikos thrust his hand toward her, and shadowy tendrils erupted from his wrist.

The tendrils wrapped around Anija's wrists and ankles and lifted her off the ground. Anija cried out as the cold tendrils bit into her exposed skin, making her drop her knife and lose focus.

She looked up into the gleaming eyes of General Tikos, who stared down at her with gleeful malice in his dark eyes.

"Bonding with a dragon gives you its powers, but also its pain," said General Tikos. "A convenient weakness for us to take advantage of, wouldn't you say?"

Another tendril suddenly erupted from General Tikos's palm and stabbed into Anija's stomach. White-hot pain flowed through Anija's body like a wave, and she could only scream in pain.

"Feel the pain, Dragon Rider," said General Tikos, his voice much lower. "Let it wash over you, for it is the last thing you will ever feel."

Chapter Twenty-Nine

FROM HER POSITION ON THE WALLS OF THE VILLAGE, Fralia saw what happened to both Anija and Rialo. She wished she could help them, but unfortunately, Fralia had her own problems to deal with.

Namely, defending the walls of Mysteria against the invading soldiers below.

When the battle started, Rialo had immediately told Fralia and Surrels to retreat to the village walls. Someone needed to command the troops from the back. But even there, the number of Malarsan soldiers was over-whelming.

Granted, the Dragon Riders did a good job forming a loose 'wall' of dragon teeth and dragonfire that drew the attention of a good chunk of the Malarsan Army. However, the Malarsan Army was massive, so another large chunk of soldiers simply bypassed the Dragon Riders entirely in favor of directly attacking the compar-atively weaker and less defended village.

Thus far, Fralia and her mages had done a good job keeping the enemy at bay. Fralia used her air magic to send approaching soldiers flying. The earth mages were led by Hokart, an experienced member of the former Dancing Army. They had formed a deep moat around the village walls. The water mages, led by Akon, had filled the moat and turned the surrounding ground to mud. The fire mages provided cover for the Mysterian soldiers and fried any Malarsans that somehow managed to cross the moat using the narrow land bridges that spanned it.

Unfortunately, the other side had mages, too. Mud dried to solid ground, courtesy of the enemy earth mages, while the opposing water mages used the moat as a weapon as well. The air mages were the trickiest, emptying the lungs of their enemies, which wasn't always obvious until multiple soldiers all dropped dead at the same time. Only their fire mages did not participate in the attack, distracted by the Dragon Riders or the ally dragons that had come down from the surrounding peaks to aid them.

Not like they even need *the fire mages at this point.* Fralia watched with dismay as an enemy earth mage crushed three of their soldiers with a fist made of stone, only to get immediately beheaded by one of their warriors. *They could demolish this entire village with just the earth mages.*

Perhaps it could have been worse, but Fralia failed to see how. After all, the battle *started* with them finding out that Hal, Keershan, and Old Snow were dead.

When Fralia saw General Tikos throw Hal's bloody

relic onto the battlefield and heard him gloat about Hal's death, it had almost shattered her.

After all, Hal was one of her best friends, if not her *best* friend. Though the two may have started out as a simple Relic Hunter and mage bodyguard duo, the two had grown close over their journeys together, since the day that Old Snow told them about the Dragon Riders in the Forgotten Temple what seemed like a lifetime ago.

And if Fralia was going to be truly honest, she sometimes felt a bit more strongly about Hal than if they were *just* friends.

But it wasn't just Hal. She'd grown close to Keershan and Old Snow, too. Keershan, like her, had been a brainy bookworm, or the dragon equivalent, anyway. His genuine interest and curiosity in human magic had led to many interesting discussions with him, including Keershan theorizing about the possibilities of dragons learning human magic. She'd never get to have another discussion about magic with him ever again.

As for Old Snow, he'd become a father figure to her in a way that she hadn't even realized until recently. With her actual father dead and her own grandparents nowhere near close to her, Fralia didn't realize just how much she needed that father figure in her life. Losing Old Snow was nearly as painful as losing her actual father.

"Fralia?" said a voice behind her. "Do you have a minute?"

Wilme looked rather harried with her messy gray hair.

"What's the matter?" asked Fralia. "Do you have an update?"

"Our scouts in the field say the battle is getting worse. We've lost a lot of soldiers and mages already, plus a few dragons. Surrels is doing his best to lead the soldiers, but he thinks it won't be long before the enemy breaks through our defenses."

Fralia grimaced, recalling how Surrels had rushed out to lead the soldiers against their former brothers-in-arms. "Tell me something I don't know."

Wilme leaned in close to Fralia, said, "I believe I may know who the traitor is. I was looking around the town square and found some disturbing evidence. It's Shalla."

Fralia felt her heart twist. "Surely you must be joking."

"How I wish I was," Wilme said.

Fralia's mind raced, still half-focused on the raging battle. "Can you show me your evidence?"

Wilme pulled a bracelet out of her bag and handed it to Fralia.

It was a relic. "Where did you find this?"

"On the stage where the bonding ceremony took place. Shalla was trying to take it, which didn't make sense because she already has a relic. When I confronted her, she fled to the Forgotten Temple."

"Where is Mizromi?"

She used a blast of wind to knock a soldier back.

Wilme sighed. "I don't know. And Shalla may have left the village already."

Fralia bit her lower lip while hurriedly refilling the lungs of a choking mage. That sounded incredibly suspicious to her. And she had to admit, she could not recall seeing either Shalla or Mizromi anywhere on the battlefield among the other Dragon Riders. Granted, the battlefield was chaotic and difficult to follow, but she still felt like she would have seen them if they were around.

Another gust of wind sent two men skittering back from their assault. Fralia could help here—but she wasn't the only one who could help.

Looking at Wilme, Fralia said, "Wilme, will you command the air mages for me while I go and confront Shalla?"

"Are you sure that would be wise, Fralia?" asked Wilme. "I'm not a mage."

Fralia put her hands on the old woman's shoulders. "But you *are* one of the most brilliant tactical minds in our group. If anyone can successfully lead our mages against the Malarsan Army, it would be you."

Wilme pursed her lips. "Thank you, Fralia, but—"

"And I remember my father always praising you," Fralia said, drawing upon her old memories. "Whenever he and General Omaros worked together, he'd always comment on how smart and tactical you were. He even talked about recruiting you into *his* army, though I don't think he ever actually did."

Wilme blinked. "I never knew he said that about me."

Fralia smiled. "Now you do. Can you do it?"

A confident grin crossed Wilme's elderly features. "Of course!"

"Thanks," Fralia said. "I know you'll do a good job."

"I'll do my best," said Wilme. "But Fralia, be careful. I don't know if Shalla is by herself or not, but if she's really the traitor, then she won't come quietly."

Fralia nodded. She knew that already, but appreciated Wilme's concern nonetheless.

Slapping Wilme's shoulders one last time, Fralia rushed past Wilme down the stairs leading from the walls to the village itself. She ran as fast as she could, her eyes on the Forgotten Temple in the center of the village, the tallest building in the settlement. It looked as ominous as ever, perhaps even more so, knowing the confrontation that Fralia would inevitably have there.

I just hope that Wilme is wrong. Each step of her feet took her closer and closer to the Forgotten Temple. *Because if she's not, then losing the battle might be the least of our problems.*

Chapter Thirty

Despite Hal's youthfulness and bond with Keershan making him stronger than normal, Hal still struggled to keep up with an elderly man and a walking tree. The irony was not lost on him, though he focused on using his bond as a mental compass to guide them.

Leaving the dungeons, as it turned out, was not nearly as difficult as Hal had feared it would be. Old Snow and Tremas had already killed the jailer in charge of keeping Hal in his cell. Hal had also worried that General Mokoa and her men would find out he escaped, but Tremas told him not to worry, as she'd left a special 'gift' for General Mokoa in his cell that would ensure that she wouldn't be bothering them anytime soon.

On that ominous note, Hal had led Old Snow and Tremas out of the dungeons and into the castle itself. As it was the middle of the day, Hal had expected the place to be busy—but not like this.

It was practically crawling with servants, soldiers, and

mages. It seemed to Hal that Queen Bariwa was not taking any chances of some sort of outside interference on the Day of Shadows.

As it turned out, that didn't actually matter very much, because they took a series of hidden tunnels that Old Snow called the steps. These were a series of hidden entrances that led to hallways and stairs built into the walls of Castle Lamor. Considered one of the Castle's greatest secrets, the steps were designed with the safety of the Malarsan royal family in mind. They led to a variety of secret exits that would allow the Malarsan royal family to safely flee in the event of an attack.

The steps seemed almost like a parallel castle within Castle Lamor. Old Snow navigated them through the maze-like series of steps and corridors that all looked the same to Hal. It made him grateful that Old Snow had been the king of Malarsan at one point, as he was sure he would have gotten lost in here on his own.

They didn't run into anyone, though Hal could hardly relax. Although the steps were *supposed* to be a secret known only to the royal family, a handful of servants knew of them. That also didn't even account for the demons, which could be anywhere.

But one way he knew they were getting closer to where Keershan was being kept prisoner was the growing sense of *evil*.

It felt like they were walking straight into the beating heart of pure malice and cruelty. It was difficult for Hal to concentrate on his bond. Every human instinct in his body told him to turn, flee the castle, and keep running all the way to the very ends of the world itself.

But Hal's Dragon Rider instincts kept him going. Running now might save himself, but it wouldn't save Keershan, the others, or Malarsan.

Hal didn't say much until it felt as if they were right on top of the sensation. Coming to a stop, Hal said, "We're here."

They were in an unremarkable hidden hallway in the steps. It was as dusty and dim as the rest they'd walked through.

Hal pointed at the door to his right. "Beyond this, we'll find Keershan. And something evil."

Tremas nodded. "I feel it as well."

"You do?"

"Aye," said Tremas. "As a tree spirit, I am more attuned to the movings of spiritual good and bad in the world than you humans. Personally, I find it more surprising that you sense it, although perhaps I shouldn't."

"Why not?" Hal said.

Tremas pointed at Hal's chest. "The Dragon Riders of old also had a strong connection to the spiritual realities that normal humans ignored or could not sense. Indeed, the entire idea of bonding is itself not entirely physical. Or have you never wondered why Dragon Riders are so special?"

As this revelation buzzed through Hal's mind, Old Snow said, "While this is interesting to discuss, I believe we should keep moving. We don't have much more time before Marial destroys everything."

Without waiting for either Hal or Tremas, Old Snow opened the door, and the three of them stepped through.

They emerged into a bigger hallway. There were two statues with their backs to him. It appeared that this steps entrance, like all the others, was elaborately hidden in a way that no one would ever think to search for.

Despite the early spring warmth, the air felt as cold as the dead of winter.

"So where is Keershan?" asked Tremas, looking to her left and to her right. "I see nothing."

Hal peered around the statue.

The hallway opened up to a balcony overlooking the central courtyard of the castle.

Hal heard a pained dragon roar. *Hal ... help ...*

Without hesitation, Hal ran out from behind the statues and onto the balcony. Being careful to remain hidden, Hal knelt behind the railing and peered down at the scene below.

Once, shortly after Hal completed his Relic Hunter training, he'd gone to Castle Lamor along with the other top graduates to attend a party thrown by the queen herself. Apparently, it was a tradition started by the previous queen of Malarsan to invite them to the castle garden.

Hal remembered how he'd been blown away by the beautiful green trees, exotic colorful flowers, and crystal-clear fountains and streams. He could still recall the sweet scent of the blue roses, the crackling of the flames used to prepare the savory meats, and even the bitter taste of the wine that his mentor had offered him and which had turned him off from alcohol for a good long while.

It had been a fun party and had certainly made him want to serve the queen more than ever.

But the garden below looked almost nothing like the one that Hal had attended five years ago.

The fresh grass had mostly withered away, leaving hardened, cracked dirt that reminded Hal of the skin of a corpse. The stench of blood and rotting flesh filled Hal's nostrils, a sharp contrast to the refreshing floral scents that had once dominated the beautiful space.

Yet it was the ritual occurring below that frightened and disgusted him the most.

A massive circle had been carved into the earth. The symbol was foreign to Hal, but his instincts told him it was demonic. It was stained with dried blood, likely from the sacrificed dragons.

Surrounding the circle was a variety of hooded demons who reminded Hal heavily of the Defacer. There also seemed to be a few human mages among them. He saw none of the castle's normal guards or servants, though he did spot a few hulking demons standing guard at the entrances to the garden.

What truly caught his attention, however, was poor Keershan. The smaller-than-average dragon lay on top of a wagon of some sort, strapped down with thick chains.

Not that the chains seemed necessary. Hal could see deep welts across Keershan's scales. He was in pain, breathing with obvious effort on his part.

"There he is," said Tremas in a low voice.

Startled, Hal looked to his left to see Tremas kneeling beside him. Old Snow knelt to his right, a disturbed expression on the former king's face as he gazed down at the garden below.

"Yes," Hal said. His hand rested on the hilt of his sword. "We need to save him now. No one knows I've escaped yet, and there don't appear to be a lot of guards or demons below. If we act now—"

"We'll get killed horribly, and the Nameless One will rise again without any opposition," said Tremas sardonically. "I forgot how much you Dragon Riders love to play the hero."

Hal glared at Tremas but then felt a comforting hand on his shoulder.

"Tremas has a point," Old Snow said. "It's not as safe as it looks."

"What do you mean?" Hal said.

"Tell me what you see."

Hal looked at the garden again. He did not see anything new at first until he spotted movement in the plants outside of the circle.

The shaking was subtle at first, but then something emerged from the bushes. With sleek black scales and sharp teeth, the creature resembled a horrific mixture between a dragon and a dog. Just watching it move made Hal's stomach churn.

It wasn't the only one. About a dozen more of the unnatural beasts came into the open, prowling the perimeter. None of the other demons paid them much attention, although Hal didn't see how they could possibly ignore such creatures.

"Hellhounds," Tremas said without waiting for Hal to ask. "A special breed of demon that possesses the body of a dog and mutates it into something straight out of the dark well."

"Are they more dangerous than the average demon?" asked Hal.

"It is said that one bite and they can suck your soul from your body," Tremas said. She grimaced. "Though it's their affinity with fire that really bothers me. For obvious reasons."

Hal looked down at the hellhounds patrolling the garden. "Their teeth might be a problem, but—"

"It's not just them," Old Snow said. He gestured at the demons below. "It's all of them. We need to carefully plan our next moves."

"We don't have time to carefully—"

Hal did not get to finish his sentence because he heard an uproar rise up from the garden below. Thinking they might have been spotted, Hal pulled his sword halfway from its sheath before looking down.

A set of double doors on the other end of the garden had been opened by the burly demonic guards. Queen Bariwa walked through. From a distance, she looked even worse than she had a few days ago. Her skin was grayer and tighter, and the dark veins stood out sharply against her decaying flesh. She still held herself with authority, although Hal thought she looked like a dead woman walking. A communication necklace hung off her neck.

She did not enter alone. The Dark Priest walked beside her, arms folded together, head bowed. By contrast to Queen Bariwa, the Dark Priest looked more alive, for want of a better term. Perhaps he was feeding on her.

What really stood out to Hal, however, was that it was just the two of them. Given how this was obviously a 'momentous' occasion, Hal would have expected to see Queen Bariwa's whole court with her. Yet it was just the two of them, walking side by side almost like a married couple.

"Where are the rest?" Hal whispered.

Old Snow shook his head. "Either dead or not allowed in the castle. Before my exile, I found out that most of the Nobility didn't support Marial. I assume she didn't want to invite those that might not support her plan."

Queen Bariwa approached a dark throne that Hal had not noticed before. It appeared to be made out of twisted, dead branches, held together by some sort of slimy black tar-like substance. She sat on it without any issue. The Dark Priest quietly took up his position beside her while the rest of the demons gathered around the circle, kneeling or bowing as they did so.

Queen Bariwa looked over them with something resembling contempt in her eyes. "Brothers and sisters of the shadows, it is with great pleasure that I announce that today is the day long whispered of in the darkness, spoken of by the Nameless One himself. This Day of Shadows, this Resurrection Day, will end one era and begin another, greater era, one where we demons will rule and all others will bow to our absolute authority."

The demons cheered on Queen Bariwa with their unnatural roars and grunts. The hellhounds pawed at the ground eagerly, clapping their sharp jaws together in a gruesome approximation of a clap.

More worrying to Hal was how Queen Bariwa referred to *herself* as a demon. Based on the worried expressions of Old Snow and Tremas, that comment had not slipped past them, either.

Queen Bariwa raised her scepter and pointed it at the barely conscious Keershan. "Many dragons have been sacrificed over the past months. But this one, in particular, has been a thorn in our side."

This prompted a series of angry hisses and snarls. Some of the demons clearly wanted to rend Keershan limb from limb already, but they showed remarkable restraint in staying put. The Dark Priest drew a jagged black dagger from the folds of his robes. Demonic lettering engraved in the blade glowed a sickly green.

"Bring him here," said Queen Bariwa, waving her scepter toward Keershan. "Once the dragon has been set in the center of the circle, we can begin the final sacrifice. And within the next half hour, the Nameless One himself will finally rise again."

Cheers erupted while a dozen of the brutes grabbed the ropes connected to Keershan's wooden platform and started dragging it toward the circle. Though their movement was slow, it was steady, and Hal knew it would not be long before Keershan was in the center.

"We need to move," Hal gripped the hilt of his sword. "Now. If we don't—"

"What?" said Tremas sharply. "They'll kill your dragon? We still don't have a plan. If we jump in now, we'll just get all of us killed."

"But this is why we're here," Hal said, gesturing furiously. "If we don't act now, not only will Keershan die, but the Nameless One will rise."

Tremas shook her head. "Perhaps instead of jumping in, we create a distraction. Though the vegetation below is very dead, I think I could potentially make it—"

Twang.

An arrow shot past Hal's face toward Queen Bariwa below. The arrow flew straight and true, unnoticed by everyone below, at least until Queen Bariwa looked up …

And was shot straight in the forehead.

Chapter Thirty-One

ANIJA WAS DYING, AND THERE WAS NOTHING SHE COULD do about it.

General Tikos's shadow tendril had dug itself deeply into her stomach. It felt like someone had stuck a piece of burning metal into her skin. She saw blood leaking out, felt her heart pumping more furiously than ever, but it all seemed so distant.

Just want to sleep. Anija's eyelids felt heavier than stone. *Sleep …*

Through her eyelashes, Anija saw General Tikos's grinning face. "Yes, Dragon Rider. Sleep the eternal sleep. Awaken no more."

That sounded like a good idea to Anija. Her instincts tried to keep her awake, but she didn't care. Each second added another ounce to her eyelids, until she could barely keep them open at all.

Sleep. Anija finally closed her eyes. *Sleep …*

Anija!

Rialo's voice roared with the force of an erupting volcano. What felt like a powerful wave of heat washed over Anija's soul, searing away the sleepiness.

Anija! Rialo screamed again, her voice even louder than before. *Don't fall. Don't sleep. Don't. Let. Him. Kill. You.*

Anija's eyes snapped open and saw General Tikos standing above her. His triumphant grin was quickly replaced by a frown.

"What?" said General Tikos. "You are awake."

Anija grinned. "And you, my friend, are dead."

Drawing upon the dragonfire inside her, Anija didn't channel it through one specific body part or weapon like she was used to doing.

No, Anija channeled it through her whole body. She had no intention of letting him live.

An explosive, fiery force blasted out of her body in one go, completely incinerating the shadowy tendrils clinging to her.

General Tikos—who was right next to Anija—took the brunt of it. The flames consumed his form in a flash. He screamed as he staggered backward, dropping Anija.

The general was frantically trying to put out the dragonfire covering his body, but it was clear that all his efforts were in vain. The fire simply wouldn't go out. In fact, the harder he tried to put out the fire, the hotter it burned.

"What—?" said General Tikos. "This can't …"

He glared at Anija through the flames. His skin was melting, giving him a truly ghoulish look.

He reached out one hand toward Anija, but then Surrels rode up on a horse and, yelling at the top of his lungs, beheaded General Tikos with one swift strike of his sword.

General Tikos's flaming head flew into the air. It spun end over end before hitting the dirt with a rather anticlimactic *clunk*. His body continued to burn, the stench of melting flesh filling the air, though the dragonfire was dying down now that its target was no longer alive.

Surrels's horse galloped toward her, Surrels himself grinning like a maniac.

"Did you see that?" he said as his horse came to a stop. He swung his sword around. "I can't believe I actually took out one of the four generals. And he was probably the strongest of them all."

Anija rolled her eyes. "It was a team effort, or did you forget who set him on fire first?"

"Regardless, it was amazing," Surrels said. His eyes darted to Anija's stomach and then widened. "Are you okay?"

Anija looked down and realized that she wasn't.

Her stomach wound was still very much open. She wasn't quite sure why the pain didn't hurt as badly as it could. Maybe it was the adrenaline flowing through her, or maybe it had to do with drawing upon Rialo's strength through her bond. Either way, she knew that, pain or no pain, she needed to get healed and fast.

Unfortunately, Anija did not see any of their healers nearby. Though General Tikos might be dead, his men apparently had yet to notice, as they continued to hack and slash their way through the Mysterians. The Mysterians, to their credit, continued to fight back, though it meant there was no one to help Anija other than Surrels.

Gritting her teeth, Anija tried to sit up but found that she couldn't. Lying down again, she said, "Forget about me. Go and help the others. I'll take care of myself."

Surrels snorted. "You Dragon Riders are all the same. Why not let your friends actually help you for once instead of this whole self-sacrificing martyr act?"

Surrels jumped off of his horse and knelt beside Anija. He pulled something out of his bag and pressed it against her wound.

Initially, the pressure made Anija's stomach hurt worse, but then a refreshing, cooling sensation swept away the pain. In seconds, it was gone entirely and Surrels removed his hand, revealing Anija's mended skin.

"There you go," Surrels said, rising to his feet. He held out a hand toward her. "Now come on. We have a war to win, don't we?"

Astonished, Anija allowed Surrels to help her to her feet. "I didn't know you were a healer."

"I'm not," Surrels said. He raised his left hand and opened it. "This, however, is."

The object in Surrels's hand was a pretty white flower that Anija had never seen before. It had a faint, fading glow.

"What is that?" Anija said.

"The Life Flower, of course."

Anija's eyebrows shot up into her hair. "The same one that healed you back in the Depths?"

Surrels shook his head. "Its descendant, actually. I took the original one with me after Hal healed me with it, planted it here in the Tops, and have been nurturing it in my little garden ever since."

Anija suddenly understood why the knees on Surrels's pants always looked unusually muddy now. "You have a whole garden of those things? And you didn't tell us?"

Surrels held up a finger. "When I said 'little' garden, I mean *tiny*. It is literally just one Life Flower at a time. And furthermore, it takes months just to grow one. I plucked it before the bonding ceremony today to have it on hand in case of emergencies and am glad I did."

Anija nodded. "Didn't realize you were a gardener."

Surrels's smile became melancholy, and he looked at the Life Flower in his hand. "I didn't, either, until recently. I'm still remembering things."

Anija, not understanding that cryptic remark, was about to ask Surrels about it until Rialo roared in her head again.

Startled, Anija looked to her left in time to see Rialo rushing toward her. The black dragon's scales looked a bit scratched and she was obviously bleeding in several places, but Anija saw no sign of the other slaves she'd been fighting.

"Rialo!" Anija said, a joyful smile crossing her lips. "You're alive!"

Rialo staggered before her, breathing hard. "Yes, but we are losing the battle."

Anija's eyes widened. "Losing? What do you mean?"

Rialo jerked her head toward Mysteria. Anija and Surrels both looked in that direction, and Anija felt her heart fail her.

Enemy earth mages formed stone bridges to let other soldiers cross the village's impromptu moat. Although the Mysterian earth mages did their best to crush the bridges before any enemy soldiers crossed, they weren't quick enough to destroy all of them, and there was now a minority of Malarsan soldiers clashing with Mysterian warriors just outside the village walls.

Worse than that, however, was the pod of slaves making their way over. Though fire mages did their best to distract or slow down the slaves, it was clear that the Mysterians weren't enough. The other Dragon Riders were all stuck in their own battles with other slaves, which left almost no one to stop the slave pod from reaching the village itself.

"They still outnumber us considerably, even with their leader dead," Surrels said. "Not to mention they are also better trained than us."

"It's the slaves," said Rialo breathlessly. She grimaced due to pain in her left leg that Anija could also feel. "Even for dragons, they are an almost unstoppable threat. Because they are controlled by humans, they don't react to pain the way normal dragons do. They will keep going as long as their controllers tell them to."

"Then obviously, we need to find and kill whoever is controlling the slaves," Anija said. "Where are they?"

Surrels threw his arms up in the air. "I have no idea. I've been running all around the battlefield trying to support our troops, and I haven't seen anyone wearing any sort of relic. They might not even be here for all we know."

"No," Rialo growled. "All relics have a distance at which they work. If the relic-holders were in, say, the capital, they wouldn't be able to control the slaves here in the Tops. So they must be somewhere nearby."

Anija nodded. "Right. Rialo, you and I will take to the skies and see if we can find those relic-holders. Surrels—"

"I know. I'll resume leading the troops. Good luck."

With that, Surrels hopped back onto his horse and raced into battle again. He joined a group of Mysterian soldiers nearby locked in combat with a battalion of Malarsan soldiers, swinging his sword while letting loose a battle cry that sent a shiver even down Anija's spine.

Then Anija climbed onto Rialo's back, and the dragon immediately took off into the air. The cold spring air blew through Anija's hair as they climbed higher and higher, until they could see the battlefield as a whole.

It looked even messier from above than on the ground. Hundreds of bodies from combatants on both sides covered the floor. The ground itself was full of jagged holes created by the magical blasts of the mages. War cries, screams of terror, steel clashing against steel, and dragon roars rose up from below in some kind of terrible battle music.

But Anija focused intently on searching for the relic-holders, using Rialo's superior eyesight to improve her own. Dragons had sight similar to that of eagles and other birds, allowing her to view the combatants below almost as clearly as if she was standing right there with them.

There!

Near the back of the Malarsan Army stood a group of close to thirty soldiers. Clad with various forms of jewelry, they all wore similar looks of concentration on their faces. They were surrounded by a loose ring of mages and, unlike the other soldiers, staying put right where they were.

Those must be the relic-holders, Rialo said. *Fry them?*

Anija grinned. *Fry them.*

With a roar, Rialo shot toward the group. Arrows went up from the soldiers protecting them, but the arrows couldn't go high enough to hit Rialo, who flew over them with amazing speed.

Once they got close enough, Rialo opened her mouth and unleashed a massive fireball. Oddly, none of the relic-holders even seemed to notice, keeping their eyes closed and their faces scrunched up in concentration.

The reason for that became clear when Rialo's fireball slammed into an invisible moulash barrier that briefly appeared around the soldiers before fading.

Anija scowled, but then the barrier suddenly glowed again. It launched a fireball back at them, forcing Rialo to bank all the way to the right to avoid getting hit.

"It absorbs dragonfire?" Rialo said as they flew away. "I've never heard of human magic that can do that."

"Fralia would probably know how to disable it, but since she's not here, we're pretty much on our own."

"Killing the mages is our best bet," said Rialo. She glanced north. "But we better be fast. The slaves are getting closer."

Rialo was correct. The slave pod had reached the moat now, although for some reason they seemed a bit confused about how to get around it. It reminded Anija of how puppet-like the slaves were. Although they could be dangerous, they were still humans clumsily controlling bodies that were not their own.

Even so, Anija knew there was nothing to stop the slaves from burning the village to the ground from a distance.

"All right," Anija said. "Let's turn this ship around and—"

A massive black fireball nearly burned her other ear off, flying past her head and singeing her hair. Startled, Anija looked over her shoulder.

A demonic-looking black dragon—similar to the one that Fralia had reported attacking her during her trip to the Glacians—had appeared out of nowhere. It flew after Anija and Rialo with deadly speed, black fire already starting to form inside its mouth.

"Damn it," said Rialo, lurching to the right again to avoid another black fireball from it. "That thing is trying to drive us away from the relic-holders."

Anija grimaced. It was a tricky situation. Between the magical barrier and the demonic dragon, Anija didn't see how they could save the village in time.

But maybe I'm looking at this wrong. Maybe we can kill two birds with one very, very large stone.

"Turn back to the relic-holders!" Anija yelled at Rialo. "I've got a crazy idea that will probably get us killed!"

Rialo grinned. "Those are my favorite plans. Hang on!"

Rialo spiraled through the air with Anija hanging on as tightly as she could. Another black fireball swept past them while the demonic dragon soared past before turning again, hissing.

But Anija paid attention only to the relic-holders

below, apparently content to let the demonic dragon take out Anija.

Their funeral, she thought with a grin.

Anija felt Rialo rumble in agreement.

Getting closer, Anija thought as Rialo flapped her wings. *Closer, closer, closer …*

Anija was not calculating the distance between them and the relic-holders, but the distance between them and the angry demonic dragon behind them. It shrieked in triumph as it neared. It had even stopped shooting fireballs at them, perhaps thinking its teeth and claws would be enough once they were in range.

Anija kept counting down the seconds in her head.

Five …

The demonic dragon roared and spat another fireball at them, though this one flew wildly and seemed more like a warning shot than anything.

Four …

Below, some of the mages defending the relic-holders looked up. A few raised their hands, either to cast spells or reinforce the barrier protecting their allies, but Anija doubted any of them expected her real plan, either.

Three …

They were so close to the enemy force now that Anija could see the intense looks of concentration on their faces.

Two …

Out of the corner of her eye, Anija saw one of the slaves finally cross the moat, red-hot fire building in its throat.

One!

Rialo flapped her wings *hard*.

That sudden gust of wind sent them both flying upward …

Directly above the unwary demonic dragon, which flew too fast to alter its trajectory.

Rialo cut her flight and dropped on *top* of the monster. It thrashed in Rialo's hold, but she was stronger and kept flying toward the relic-holders.

Anija saw shock in the eyes of the mages below. Some raised their hands to reinforce the barrier, now finally catching on.

Too late.

At the last possible second, Rialo released the demonic dragon, sending it hurtling through the air. No longer even remotely in control of its trajectory anymore, it smashed into the magical barrier with the force of a powerful explosion.

The magical barrier grew as bright as a star for the briefest of seconds.

Then it shattered into pieces. The impact of the demonic dragon's crash utterly crushed all of the relic-holders while the shock waves knocked down the surrounding mages and even caused much of the nearby army to stumble.

Anija and Rialo were flying away from the site of the crash.

That was the most foolhardy 'plan' I've ever been a part of, said Rialo.

Anija patted Rialo on the back of the neck, adrenaline rushing through her veins even faster than the dragon they just threw. *Lighten up, buttercup. It worked. See?*

The slaves, no longer under the control of the relic-holders, were now shaking their heads in confusion. Even the village defenders were not sure how to react.

But Anija knew.

They had effectively destroyed the enemy's most potent weapon and turned the tide of the war entirely.

And for the first time since the start of the battle, Anija thought they might actually win this.

That was, until a column of shadow erupted from the Forgotten Temple, driving all other thoughts from her mind.

Chapter Thirty-Two

FRALIA RUSHED THROUGH THE BROKEN STREETS OF Mysteria. Everyone else was either on the battlefield or on the walls.

Which is exactly why I'm sure Shalla is at the Forgotten Temple. Fralia ran, her heart beating rapidly. *No one to stop her from doing whatever she's trying to do.*

The Forgotten Temple soon loomed up ahead. It was an ominous-looking building already, but the darkening sky behind it—despite it being the middle of the day—made it look even more foreboding.

She rushed up to the front doors, which had clearly been forced open, and stopped inside, panting hard and scanning the interior of the abandoned structure.

Not too long ago, Hal had killed a demon inside the Forgotten Temple. There still a hole in the ceiling created by the dragonfire he had used.

A beam of sunlight poured out from the hole onto

Shalla and Mizromi at the altar. Mizromi lay on his stomach, eyes closed.

Shalla stood next to Mizromi's head on top of a stool. In her hands was a long, sharp-looking black blade, streaks of red running up and down its shaft.

"Shalla!" Fralia shouted. "What are you doing?"

Shalla looked up. The crimson light from the spear in her hand reflected off of her glasses, giving her eyes a decidedly unnatural reddish tinge. "Hello, father-killer."

"Father-killer?" Fralia repeated. "What are you talking about?"

Shalla pointed the odd-looking spear at Fralia. "You know exactly what I'm talking about. You murdered General Kolass in cold blood three months ago."

Fralia blinked, suddenly understanding what Shalla meant. "But I *didn't* kill my father. It was a demon that did it because Father saw the light and was going to join us if he didn't kill him."

"Lies," Shalla said, her voice slightly cracking. "You didn't attend his funeral. You didn't see his body. You didn't see your siblings cry. You ran away to the dragons in Dragon Valley, hoping they'd harbor you and your rebellious friends."

"Is that what Queen Bariwa told you?" Fralia said. "Because all of *that* is a lie. Aside from me not attending the funeral, though as a wanted criminal, it's not like I could."

"Shut up," Shalla snapped, her hands shaking. "Do you know how many years I served your father? Working as his best and most trusted assistant. Even though I am terrible at combat, your father always treated me with the same respect and dignity that he treated his own soldiers. He even invited me to your family dinners multiple times, treating me as if I was one of his kids."

Fralia remembered the many times that Shalla would come to their mansion in the capital.

"So when your father died , I was devastated," said Shalla. Her voice dropped almost to a whisper. "But more than that, I was angry. I wanted to avenge him. I didn't want his death to be in vain. I couldn't stand the idea that his killer was out there somewhere, still alive, unpunished for her crimes. It ate at me until I couldn't even sleep. So I went to Queen Bariwa and asked for permission to kill you myself."

Fralia frowned. "But she didn't quite grant you that request, did she?"

"Not exactly," Shalla looked down at the unconscious Mizromi at her feet. "She gave me a more important job: Infiltrate the Dragon Riders, analyze your weaknesses, and send them back to her in preparation for this day. I'm no Dark Tiger, after all. I'm a secretary."

Fralia eyed Shalla's weapon carefully, mentally trying to calculate how quickly she could cast a wind spell. "So you're the reason we were unprepared."

"Yes. But that isn't the only job Queen Bariwa gave me. She also gave me the most important role in this entire war: Aiding her in resurrecting the Nameless One himself."

Fralia gasped. "But his body is still at the capital. Right?"

Shalla smiled coldly. "How inefficient would that be from the Dragon Riders' perspective? Putting his body in *one* place and one place alone, where the demons would be able to retrieve it easily?"

Fralia instantly put two and two together in her mind. "By the gods' names, you don't mean …"

"Yes," said Shalla. "Half of the Nameless One's corpse was brought to the most desolate place in the kingdom."

Fralia's breath caught. "The Desolate Tops."

"Did you not know who the Forgotten Temple was once dedicated to?"

Another stab of horror struck Fralia's heart. "The Nameless One?"

"Exactly. A long time ago, the Forgotten Temple was once taken over by his followers. Here, a variety of horrific crimes and sacrifices were committed, or so I've been told. The original Dragon Riders thought it would be fitting to bury half of his remains here to mock the Nameless One and his followers, for there was nothing he could do to stop them."

Fralia gulped. "All this time, his body has been here …"

Shalla's glasses shone with the red light from her spear. "Yes. And for the Day of Shadows to happen, someone needed to be here in the Forgotten Temple to make a dragon sacrifice at around the same time as back in Castle Lamor. Even as we speak, Keershan the dragon is being prepared as a sacrifice in the name of the Nameless One."

"Keershan's still alive?" Fralia said in disbelief. "But I thought that he, Hal, and Old Snow are dead."

"I don't know about Halar or Old Snow," said Shalla,

"but Keershan, at least, is still alive. Though I doubt he'll live until the end of this hour. Nor can you save him."

Fralia balled her hands into fists. "But I can stop you, right? Sounds like the resurrection ritual requires two sacrifices. If I disrupt your sacrifice, then I can stop the Nameless One from coming back, at least."

Shalla's eyes narrowed. "You could, but you assume that I am going to *let* you disrupt it."

Hissing came from all around Fralia. From out of the shadows slithered pale-white serpents with blood-red eyes. Easily reaching ten feet in length with massive flaps behind their heads that made them look bigger than they were, the snakes looked at her hungrily.

"Did you think I would have come here alone?" asked Shalla. "Queen Bariwa put several demons under my control."

Fralia noticed how the serpents—about six in all—formed a circle around her.

"Shalla, Father wouldn't want you to do this. He'd be so upset."

"General Jeniq also worked toward the resurrection of the Nameless One," said Shalla quietly. "Did you know that? I didn't, not until I approached Queen Bariwa and she informed me. She told me that if I truly wanted to honor General Jeniq's legacy, that I would help bring the Nameless One back."

Fralia's eyes widened in horror. "Queen Bariwa lied to you. Father utterly renounced the demons before his death. I should know. He told me."

"He *told* you, huh?" said Shalla sharply. "Was that before or *after* you killed him in cold blood?"

Frustrated, Fralia said, "How many times do I have to tell you that I *didn't* kill him?"

"I don't know," said Shalla. "How many times can you tell a lie before someone believes it?"

This was going nowhere. Shalla was clearly either too emotional or enthralled with the demons to care about the truth. It wasn't like Fralia had all the time in the world to argue with her, either. Though Shalla had yet to finish off Mizromi, Fralia suspected it wouldn't be long before Shalla did.

"How come Mizromi did not know? When you two bonded, didn't Mizromi read your mind and find out what you're actually like?"

Shalla, still gripping the spear tightly in both hands, said, "Before coming out here, I was given extensive training in preparing my mind against intrusion. Mizromi just thought that he was going to honor the memory of his brother. It never occurred to him that he'd soon be joining his brother in the next life, if such a thing even exists for dragons, that is."

Fralia bit her lower lip. She didn't know how Shalla would make sure to time her sacrifice with the sacrifice in the capital correctly. At least, she didn't know until she noticed the communication necklace on her neck.

That must be how she's staying in contact with the queen. Although it must be a very powerful communication necklace if it can span the distance between here and the capital.

Of course, that was pretty useless to Fralia. The demonic serpents were her biggest obstacle. So long as they continued to circle her, Fralia couldn't act without inciting them. Heck, she suspected that the serpents wouldn't even wait for her to attack. Their tongues poked in and out of their mouths, dead red eyes glaring at her as if she was a particularly tasty meal they couldn't wait to start digging into.

And I can't count on any help from the outside, either. Fralia listened to the sounds of battle in the distance. *Everyone is too preoccupied with the Malarsan Army. I am entirely on my own.*

It seemed like Fralia's only option was clear: Stop Shalla.

Even at the cost of her own life.

"Shalla," Fralia said, her voice lower than normal. "I am going to give you one last chance to drop the spear, step away from Mizromi, and order your demons to leave."

Shalla shook her head. "You know I can't do that, Fralia. I loved your father. His death will not be in vain."

With that, Shalla yelled and drove her spear directly into Mizromi's skull.

Shadows pulsed and groaned, and the entire chamber grew icy. Even the serpents themselves paused.

They haven't forgotten me, Fralia thought with horror. *They're anticipating what is coming next.*

A pillar of pure shadow erupted from Mizromi's skull and shot toward the ceiling. The column of darkness made every hair on Fralia's arms stand on end.

And she realized they had just lost.

Chapter Thirty-Three

EVERY EYE IN THE COURTYARD WAS ON QUEEN BARIWA'S corpse.

The demons were taken aback. Hell, even Hal was shocked. Old Snow, by contrast, looked perfectly at ease. He continued to hold his now empty bow pointed at the spot where Queen Bariwa had been standing mere seconds ago.

The queen's body looked rather pathetic now, lying in a bundle of robes on the ground.

As if a spell had been lifted, the Dark Priest's eyes flicked up to Hal and the others.

"We were supposed to wait," Tremas hissed, her fingers sharpening into dagger-like sticks.

Keershan, get ready.

Okay, Hal, Keershan replied in a voice that was still too weak for Hal's liking.

Dark laughter broke from the Dark Priest. It echoed off the walls of the Courtyard and escaped into the night sky, filling Hal with anxiety as he rose with Old Snow.

"Killing the woman you once called your wife, your beloved? That is a joke even the Nameless One would find amusing."

Old Snow glared at the Dark Priest. "That wasn't Marial. The woman I loved died a long time ago."

"What human nonsense," said the Dark Priest. He gestured at Queen Bariwa's body. "This was indeed your ex-wife. Unlike many humans, she simply had the wisdom to accept that she could not stop the Nameless One's return and wisely chose to work with us rather than against us."

"You played with Marial's ambition, using it against her," Old Snow said, his voice firm. "To act as if she was ever in her right mind is perhaps the worst lie you have told so far, demon."

A sickening chuckling sound suddenly broke the air. It did not come from the Dark Priest, however, or any of the other demons. It seemed to come from everywhere at once, and Hal could not locate its source.

"The Dark Priest hasn't lied, Rikas," said a familiar female voice. "He has spoken the truth."

That was when Hal realized that the chuckling sound came from Queen Bariwa's body.

And then Queen Bariwa slowly rose to her feet. She rose like a puppet picked up by its strings, her movements at once fluid yet unnatural.

She stood tall and proud, the arrow still lodged firmly in her forehead, dark blood running in rivulets down the sides of her face. Her eyes were pools of blackness now.

For the first time, Old Snow looked shaken. "Marial? How—?"

Queen Bariwa chuckled. She reached up and yanked the arrow out of her forehead. Blood flowed more freely down her forehead until the wound magically healed itself, leaving a jagged, hideous scar where the arrow had once been embedded.

Tossing the arrow aside, Queen Bariwa said, "That arrow might have killed me as recently as a week ago. But I've since sold my soul to the Nameless One for true immortality and power. The transformation I have been undergoing since the day I first contacted the demons is nearly complete."

"Nearly?" Hal repeated. "What do you mean by 'nearly'?"

Queen Bariwa turned her gaze to Hal, which made him shudder, as it felt a bit like staring into a bottomless, murky lake that you could not see the bottom of. "The transformation will not be entirely complete until the Nameless One himself arises. Once he returns, he will grant me true immortality, the kind that people richer and stronger than me have sought for millennia. I shall live forever and never taste death."

"Wrong, Marial," Old Snow said. "Your lust for power has blinded you to the reality of what you are working with. You have been manipulated for ten years and will be tossed aside the very second you are no longer useful to the Nameless One's schemes."

Queen Bariwa gazed upon Old Snow coldly. "You would know a thing or two about throwing away those who aren't useful to you, wouldn't you, Rikas? Tanan and Galaro certainly would."

Hal frowned. "Who?"

"Do you think that you and Kolass's daughter are the first? A decade ago, my ex-husband recruited another Relic Hunter, Tanan, and her mage bodyguard Galaro on a similar quest to find the Final Relic and defeat me."

Hal glanced at Old Snow. "He never mentioned them."

Queen Bariwa spread her arms. "That's because their fate doesn't make him look very good, does it, Rikas? They died horribly, unprepared for the true power of the demonic. Old Snow escaped with the relic you once wore."

The Dark Priest lifted a clawed hand. "I killed them personally."

Hal bit his lower lip. He glanced at Tremas, noticing that she did not look surprised or even deny it. It was possible that Tremas simply hadn't known about it, but he sensed that Tremas likely *had* known about it and simply wasn't responding for some reason.

Maybe she wanted to let Old Snow defend himself. The former king of Malarsan still wasn't looking at Hal. Nor was he saying anything. He just kept his bow trained on Queen Bariwa, despite knowing how useless his arrows were by now. It was as if he was trying to avoid the truth himself.

But Hal never accepted evasion. "Old man, is what they said true?"

Old Snow finally lowered his bow. When he looked at Hal, it was with pained eyes. "Yes. Every word."

Queen Bariwa chuckled. "How I love the pain in your face and words, Rikas. It fills my dark heart with such cheer, watching your carefully constructed lies fall apart. The fallout will be delicious."

Hal ignored Queen Bariwa, keeping his gaze fixed firmly on Old Snow. "Why didn't you ever mention Tanan and Galaro to us? Why did you hide them?"

Old Snow looked at his feet, clearly in shame. "Because I was scared. Because I didn't want to scare you off. And because I was—am—ashamed of that failure."

Hal didn't quite know how to feel about that. Though he was aware that he and Fralia had not been the first to visit the Desolate Tops in search of the Forgotten Temple, he had assumed that he and Fralia had been the first to successfully find and use the relic. It had never occurred to him that Old Snow may have recruited others before him, although it made a lot of sense when he thought about it.

But does it make a lot of sense to hide it from us? Hal gripped the leather handle of his sword tightly. *And would either of us have accepted Old Snow's offer if we'd known that he'd already tried it once and failed?*

"A failure it was," said Queen Bariwa, her voice cracking the surrounding darkness. "Yet you still haven't learned from it, Rikas. It would seem that age doesn't always bring wisdom. Or perhaps living in isolation for ten years has degenerated your once quick mind. It has certainly taken away your good looks."

Hal bit his lower lip again. Deciding that he didn't have time to feel angry with Old Snow, Hal drew his sword and pointed it at Queen Bariwa. "Regardless of what Old Snow did and didn't tell us, I am here right here, right now, in this place. Even if he lied, I still have a duty to stop you from sacrificing my friend Keershan, if nothing else."

Queen Bariwa hardly looked phased by Hal's sword. "You may try, but know this: The hour is near. In minutes, we will sacrifice the life of your dragon, and bring about the end of everything as we know it. A new age of darkness will cover the land, and the Nameless One shall grant all his loyal subjects immortality."

Hal scowled. Raising his sword, Hal said, "If you think for even a moment that I'll let you do that, then *you* are the delusional one here, Bariwa."

Queen Bariwa chuckled. "And if you think I will even let you attempt to stop me, then human foolishness truly knows no bounds."

Crack.

The balcony shattered. Hal, Old Snow, and Tremas plunged through the broken floor. They landed on the hard-packed dirt of the Courtyard.

Hal tried to rise to his feet, only for shadowy tendrils to rise out of the earth and form a dome around them. Desperate, Hal rushed over to the bars of the dome and slashed at them, though his sword just harmlessly bounced off as if they were made of unbreakable steel.

"Stay right there, human," said Queen Bariwa, her eyes glinting with madness. "And count yourself lucky. For it is not every day that you get a front-row seat to the resurrection of the Nameless One himself."

Hal could only watch helplessly as the demons resumed pulling Keershan's wooden wagon into the center of the circle. He tried to call upon the dragonfire within him but found that it wouldn't come. He could still feel the heat inside him, but it was a low, burning sensation, more like embers.

Why? Why can't I use my dragonfire? Is it because Keershan is—?

Hal didn't want to think about that: That Keershan was dying.

Queen Bariwa, meanwhile, made her way over to the center. She carried a wickedly sharp blood-red dagger in her hands that looked almost like a living thing itself. She stopped at Keershan's side, looking quite small compared to the runt dragon, though infinitely more powerful.

"No!" Hal screamed. "Stop! If you touch Keershan—"

One of the tendrils slapped Hal in the face suddenly. It felt a bit like getting slapped in the face with a frozen whip, causing Hal to cry out in pain and grab his burning cheek.

Then Hal heard a scream of pure pain and terror, felt awful pain in his shoulder, and looked again, only to wish he hadn't.

Queen Bariwa had driven the knife into Keershan's shoulder. Red dragon blood poured from Keershan's shoulder onto the ground below, rapidly filling what appeared to be a small hole dug out expressly for that purpose.

A second later, a column of shadow and darkness erupted from within the hole. It obscured both Queen Bariwa and Keershan, the wind from it sending the Dark Priest's robes fluttering. Many of the demons were sent stumbling or staggering from the impact of the blast while others took cover where they could.

Looking up, Hal saw the column of shadow collide with a similar column in the skies overhead. He did not know where the second column had come from, but he hardly cared.

All he knew was that they had lost.

Chapter Thirty-Four

THE SHADOWY COLUMNS SLAMMED INTO EACH OTHER with enough force to nearly deafen Hal. White lightning bolts crackled, tornado-like winds suddenly kicked up, and it felt as if life itself was screaming in pure agony at the horror that had been unleashed on the world.

Hal, for his part, felt Keershan's pain and agony as clearly as if it was his own. He also felt an unnatural evil shiver in the air, like evil itself had taken the form of some noxious gas that left him queasy and sick. He struggled to remain standing, but it was a Herculean task.

Hearing some *thuds* behind him, Hal glanced over his shoulder. Both Old Snow and Tremas had fallen. They were not dead—at least from what Hal could see—but they looked drained, as if having lost their ability to stand.

That was when Hal realized: This was not the place for ordinary humans, or even tree spirits.

The Courtyard had turned into a perfect storm of evil. And he was right in the middle of it.

In the next instant, the columns slowly dissipated, revealing a new figure standing in the ritual circle.

Towering well above all others in the Courtyard, it had a vaguely humanoid shape, covered in thick black fur. Bat-like wings ending in razor-sharp tips extended from its back. Horns curled from its forehead while its massive chest heaved in and out, muscles rippling along its arms and legs.

Its face looked like that of a goat mixed with a bat. Fangs extended from its mouth while devilish red eyes gazed out from a skull-like face. A long, forked tail trailed from its behind, covered in red spikes that reminded Hal of crystallized blood.

Absolute silence had fallen over the Courtyard. Then the hellhounds bowed, along with all of the other demons. Queen Bariwa looked on with pride while the Dark Priest wore a reverent expression.

The Dark Priest strode forward, slowly at first, and then quickly. He stopped in front of the entity and, kneeling before it, said, "My Lord. Welcome back to the mortal realm."

With a sudden jerk in his stomach, Hal knew exactly not just *what* he was looking at, but *who*.

The Nameless One—the Demon God, slain ages ago by the original Dragon Riders—had returned.

An awful sound, like bone being pierced by steel, filled the air, along with the roars of beasts and clattering of teeth. The unnatural sounds came from the bowing demons, who were making noises that might have been their version of chants.

And although Hal could not understand the demonic tongue, he could understand the meaning quite well: The demons were praising the Nameless One with a hymn.

Against his will, the 'hymn' brought to mind images of intense pain, suffering, and death in Hal's mind. He saw hordes of demons washing over the kingdom, eating and slaughtering and killing freely. He felt human blood on his hands and the unsteady sensation of walking across a field of freshly killed corpses, looking for their next kill. He sensed complete and utter despair as humans and dragons alike fled for safety.

But there would be no safety from the demons now that the Nameless One was alive.

No one and nowhere would be safe.

Then the Nameless One held up a hand, instantly silencing the opera of fear. The demons ceased their singing, clearly listening closely for their god's next words.

The Nameless One, however, did not speak right away. Instead, he looked at the palms of his hands, as if surprised to see he had them at all.

"It has been ages since I last felt the winds of the physical world," said the Nameless One. He reached up and touched his ears. "Since I heard through mortal ears the chants and hymns of my followers. It is gratifying, and in some ways, I missed it."

The Nameless One's voice was like broken glass being rubbed against skin. It even *felt* a bit like that, making Hal shiver just listening to him speak.

The Nameless One lowered his hands, his gaze

shifting around the Courtyard, perhaps taking in the appearance of his followers.

But then his eyes fell on Hal , and Hal suddenly saw burning wrath in the demon god's eyes. Though Hal did his best not to show fear, he found it difficult, especially now that he was face-to-face with the Nameless One himself.

The Nameless One took a step toward Hal, sharp claws extending from the tips of his fingers, but he didn't get far.

Queen Bariwa suddenly appeared in front of the Nameless One, who stopped and looked down at her with annoyance clear on his demonic features.

"Who are you?" the Nameless One demanded.

"Queen Marial Bariwa. I am the human who helped bring you back to this world."

"Bariwa," said the Dark Priest, who had risen to his feet, in a warning tone. "His Darkness does not—"

The Nameless One raised a hand, never taking his eyes off Queen Bariwa. "Let the human woman speak, my priest. Her audacity impresses me."

Queen Bariwa flashed the Dark Priest a triumphant smirk before putting on a more penitent face toward the Nameless One. "Thank you, Your Darkness, for allowing me to speak. All that I ask is that, having successfully resurrected you, you keep your end of the promised bargain and grant me the immortality I so desire."

The Nameless One raised an eyebrow. "Quite an audacious request. Are you certain that is what you want?"

Queen Bariwa fell to her knees, clasping her hands

together. "More than anything, O mighty Nameless One. This old body of mine doesn't have many years left. It won't be long before the Mother of Time calls me back to her bosom. I would like to delay that meeting forever."

The Nameless One appeared to be seriously considering her request. "I forgot how bold you humans can be. I also do not think you know what you ask."

Queen Bariwa smirked. "Trust me, Your Darkness, I know *exactly* what I want. An indecisive monarch cannot effectively lead a kingdom, after all."

The Nameless One seemed to ponder that statement for a second. "True. But a hasty monarch will only lead her kingdom to ruin."

The Nameless One grabbed Queen Bariwa's face. She began screeching, but his palm muffled her.

Her body began to glow intermittently with a strange bluish-white color. With each surge, the queen struggled less, until, with one final flash of light, her body went limp.

The second her body hit the dirt, it collapsed into dust. Her skull remained intact only to be crushed a moment later by the Nameless One's hoofed foot, shattering into pieces, her crown and communication necklace flying away.

The Nameless One sighed in satisfaction. "I forgot how good human souls taste."

Hal's heart beat rapidly. He hadn't known that the Nameless One could eat souls. And as much as he hated Queen Bariwa for all of the evil things she'd done, he wasn't sure he would have wished such a horrible fate upon her.

I have *to stop him.* Hal rose to his feet, gripping his sword with both hands. *There's no one else.*

"Attack me only if you wish to perish, Dragon Rider," said the Nameless One without even looking up at Hal.

Hal froze. "How—?"

The Nameless One looked up at Hal with interest. "I know your kind, Rider, for I spent the better part of five centuries battling your predecessors."

Hal's eyes widened. "Five centuries? How long did the conflict between the Dragon Riders and the demons last?"

"It was mostly on and off," the Nameless One said. "At times, they would attack me and mine, attempting to eradicate us. We would return the favor, but it wasn't until centuries later that your kind finally defeated me and my followers. Thus, I know you are thinking of killing me right now, which would be a *very* bad move on your part."

Hal's eyes narrowed. "Oh, yeah? Why?"

The Nameless One stepped aside. "Mostly because of your dragon, who looks like he has seen better days."

Keershan looked awful. His golden scales had faded considerably, giving him a deathly appearance. His eyes were closed, and he looked as if he had been dried out overnight. He was so thin now that he was practically a skeleton and looked quite dead, for all intents and purposes.

"Keershan …" Hal said.

The Nameless One smirked. "You Dragon Riders are infinitely weaker without your pet dragons. Yet even if your faithful Steed were still with us, you wouldn't be able to stop me."

Hal scowled. "Then why haven't you killed me yet? I'm practically defenseless."

The Nameless One tapped his chin in interest. "Because I have taken an interest in you, young Rider. You came out of nowhere. You have no pedigree to speak of, no special background or relations. You aren't even a descendant of the original Riders. And yet somehow, you have almost singlehandedly restored the Dragon Rider Corps that I thought I had wiped out ages ago."

Hal pursed his lips. "Ask anyone. They'll tell you what a hard worker I am. Even when I'm thrust into situations I didn't choose."

The Nameless One spread his arms. "But that is the thing: Who thrust you into this situation?"

Hal tilted his head to the side, not certain where the Nameless One was going with this. "If you mean who told me about this stuff, then I guess Old Snow. If not for him, I might have made different choices."

The Nameless One shook his head. "Rikas is not who I am referring to. Rikas, at best, bumbled his way into the plans laid by someone else."

"Someone else?" Hal said. "Who are you talking about? Are you saying that everything that's happened— from the day I killed the Defacer until now—has all been a part of some other person's plan?"

"Not a person, exactly," said the Nameless One. His eyes flickered to the skies above. "But a being. Or perhaps beings would be more appropriate."

Hal shook his head. "I still have no idea what you're talking about."

The Nameless One sighed. "Tell me, Rider, who in the world would have enough power to oppose me? Who do you think could come close to matching me, beings whose might even I cannot deny? Who rules this world, in other words?"

It took Hal a moment to understand the implications behind the Nameless One's words, but once he did, he was stunned. "You mean the gods?"

The Nameless One nodded. "Yes. I was afraid I was going to have to spell it out to you. Perhaps you humans are not so hopelessly idiotic after all."

Hal frowned. The gods of Malarsan were an enigmatic bunch. While Hal had gone to temples and festivals devoted to them, in truth, he'd never been particularly pious. He had been a Relic Hunter, after all, not a priest. "Why do you think the gods are behind my successes?"

"Because they are the ones who created the *original* Dragon Riders, of course," said the Nameless One. He placed a hand on his chest. "And I was once one of them, before I decided to go my own way."

Hal gasped. "The gods created us? And you were once one of them? How—?"

"That is a long story," said the Nameless One. "One for another time. All you need to understand is that you aren't the first mortal to have been used by my siblings for their own agenda. It seems they are still very much up to their old tricks."

Those two revelations sent Hal's mind spinning as he

tried to absorb the information. He wasn't sure whether to believe or disbelieve the Nameless One. He half-wished that the Nameless One would just tell him the full story already.

On the other hand, does knowing the Nameless One's origin change anything? No, it does not. He still needs to be stopped.

With that decision made, Hal rushed toward the Nameless One, screaming at the top of his lungs. He fully expected the demons to try to stop him, though oddly, none of them did. Even the Dark Priest merely watched as Hal drew closer and closer to the Nameless One, as if this was some kind of show put on for his amusement.

But Hal was in too deep now. Once he got close enough, he swung his sword at the Nameless One's neck, aiming to take his head off …

Only for his sword to strike the Nameless One's neck and shatter into a million pieces.

Metallic shards flew everywhere, including a few that put cuts in his cheeks and face. Hal's whole body reverberated from the impact of his sword against the Nameless One, like hitting a solid brick wall rather than a living creature.

The Nameless One, to put it simply, did not look impressed.

Before Hal could do anything else, the Nameless One grabbed him by his neck with one hand and lifted him off his feet. Startled, Hal hit the hilt of his now broken sword against the Nameless One's forearm, although that attack was even more useless than his first one.

The Nameless One tightened his grip on Hal's neck,

driving the air out of his lungs and making him gasp for breath.

"Do not worry," said the Nameless One coldly. "I won't break your neck or strangle you, if that is what you fear. No, I am too *hungry* to let you die that way. I will devour your soul bit by bit, until there is nothing left. And then the world shall know the true meaning of fear."

Then Hal felt his soul being drawn from his body.

Chapter Thirty-Five

"What the hell is that?" Anija stared at the massive column of shadow. "Did the enemy sneak inside while we weren't looking or something?"

"Possibly. I think we will need to deal with that later. Look."

Anija followed Rialo's gaze.

The Malarsan Army still outnumbered the Mysterians by a considerable amount. Even worse, they were fighting like wild animals, as if their recent losses had just made them more motivated to fight to the bitter end. Anija saw one brute carrying twin broadswords take down four Mysterian soldiers all by himself.

"What—?" Anija said, looking around wildly. "Why aren't we winning? We took down their leader and their slaves. They should be begging for mercy."

Rialo shook her head. "Winning a war isn't that simple, Anija. If there's one thing I've learned from fighting your fellow humans, it is that the Malarsan Army is surprisingly resilient. In General Tikos's absence, his captains and lieutenants have taken over."

Anija frowned. She didn't want to agree with Rialo but had to admit that she had a point. She could even spot a few enemy soldiers who looked like officers barking orders to their men or leading their soldiers into battle against her fellow Mysterians. It appeared that the enemy still had more experience and better tactics than them, and Anija didn't like it.

"So what do we do about them, then?" Anija said. "Get back down there and fight with everyone else?"

"It's our only option at this point," said Rialo. "And besides, our odds of winning are a lot higher now that we've almost crippled the enemy army. It's just that 'almost' crippled is not quite the same thing as *actually* crippling."

Anija blew out her breath in annoyance, but before she could tell Rialo to dive, she noticed movement on the horizon beyond the walls of the village. Looking up, Anija felt her heart grow cold.

Coming from the back side of the village was another troop of Malarsan soldiers and mages. It appeared to be much smaller than the group at the front, but the soldiers were in a fresher condition.

Rialo growled. "Damn it. Must be backup. Or maybe they were coming up from behind through the secret path to Giant's Foot. Would explain why we didn't see them until now."

"And the back side of the village is completely unprotected," Anija said in dawning realization. "Crap."

"Change of plans," said Rialo. "Stop the second army. You can't win a war on two fronts."

Anija nodded. She wished she could call some of the other Dragon Riders, but everyone was too far away, and they didn't have time to plan anything.

The wind tore through Anija's hair as they soared past the Forgotten Temple.

A series of explosions suddenly rocked the second army, scattering their men and killing dozens by the score. Shocked, Anija reined in Rialo, who hovered in the sky, flapping her wings rapidly to remain stationary.

The second army was in chaos. Mages were throwing elemental blasts left and right while soldiers drew their weapons or desperately tried to get their spooked horses under control.

Another series of explosions erupted with massive spikes of ice, skewering soldiers in the immediate area while sending those nearby flying. A few of them even froze the soldiers outright, turning them into statues made of flesh and ice, before being shattered by yet another blast.

"Soldiers and mages of Malarsan!" cried an earth mage near the front of the army, who, based on his patched eye and medals, seemed to be the leader of this particular force. "Do not panic! We will not let the Dragon Riders' tricks prevent us from razing their town to the ground and putting an end to their—"

Anija never got to hear him finish his sentence before he, too, exploded.

"This is definitely not one of *our* tricks," Anija said to Rialo. "So what's going on?"

Rialo looked up at the sky above the army. "We are not the only ones in the air."

Anija peered, borrowing Rialo's enhanced dragon vision to increase the distance that her own eyes could see.

That was when she noticed tiny round objects—resembling ice balls, probably about the size of a watermelon—being dropped seemingly from thin air. Wherever the spheres fell, the huge ice spikes from before would appear, killing more enemy soldiers and mages and prompting more frenzied infighting among the enemy.

Anija furrowed her eyebrows. "Someone is attacking them. But who—?"

It seemed like Anija and Rialo were not the only ones to notice the mysterious attackers. A handful of air mages, standing slightly apart from the rest of the mob that was once an army, gazed into the air. They raised their hands, perhaps planning to blow their invisible enemy out of the sky, only for a stream of steaming hot water to launch out of nowhere and bathe them. Screams of agony escaped from the air mages as they were burned to death, collapsing under the stress of the attack, getting trampled by their former colleagues, who evidently did not even notice them.

"The hell?" Anija said. She looked at the sky again. "The gods?"

That was when a loud, booming voice tore through the air. "Soldiers and mages of the Malarsan Army! His Coldness, Emperor Kryo Kardia, has declared war on the Kingdom of Malarsan and has thrown in His support for the Dragon Riders! Let His icy terror freeze your blood and shatter whatever is left of your nonexistent bravery!"

Anija could not believe her ears. "Is that Dedeket's voice?"

"Sounds like it," said Rialo. She squinted her eyes. "But I still don't see him anywhere."

As if in answer, the air above the Malarsan Army shimmered, revealing six very unusual vehicles.

Half a dozen massive balloons hovered in two columns above the Malarsan Army. The balloons themselves were painted with an icy hand gripping a hammer, which Anija recognized as the emblem of the Glaci Empire. The bottom carriages—which had to be at least as long as Rialo—would occasionally drop more of those strange ice explosions onto the army below.

Dedeket's booming voice, combined with the sudden appearance of the balloons, seemed to sap what little courage remained in the invading Malarsans. They immediately broke with some attempting to retreat the way they came, some trying to shoot down the balloons, and some—probably the stupid ones—continuing to try to reach the village, as if under the impression that they would be safe there.

None survived.

As the carnage below continued to intensify, Anija did not know how to feel, other than confused. "Are those balloons?"

"Zeppelins," came Dedeket's voice. He was standing in a nearby basket under a smaller balloon, seemingly without a care in the world. Four other warrior Glacians were with him.

"Excuse me?" called Anija. "Did you sneeze?"

Dedeket gave Anija an amused look. "No. Zeppelin is simply the proper name for the pride and joy of the Glaci Empire's Air Navy. How else do you think we have been able to effectively conquer so many countries? Air warfare is still rather underdeveloped, even in a country like Malarsan where dragons can take to the skies at any moment."

Rialo's eyes glanced toward the zeppelins. "Hmm. Those don't look particularly sturdy to me. My claws could probably rip through them."

Dedeket chuckled. "You can try it if you wish. Just don't come crying back to me if it turns out to be more painful than you imagined."

Anija wasn't quite sure what Dedeket was getting at, but since she had bigger problems to worry about, she said, "When did you guys get here? I thought you wouldn't arrive for another week."

Dedeket gave Anija a proud look. "One of the tenants of the Glaci Empire is that we are always early. If we say we will be there in two weeks, you can expect us in one. Although I must say we picked an excellent time to come. I assume the Malarsans also decided to copy our punctuality and attack early."

Anija nodded. She had once again underestimated the Glaci Empire. Not only had they arrived early, but their zeppelins—although Anija still thought that war balloons was a better term—were an absolutely devastating weapon. Six zeppelins alone were utterly decimating an army about half the size of the Malarsan Army with little to no resistance.

Imagine what an entire fleet of those machines could do in times of war, Rialo said mentally.

Makes me glad the Glacians are on our *side,* Anija agreed.

Rialo rumbled. *For now.*

With that comforting thought out of the way, Anija looked at Dedeket again. "Where's Jinka? Is she safe?"

"She's currently back home with her mother." Dedeket sighed. "I promised to bring back a dragon scale as a present for her, however. You wouldn't happen to have a few spares, would you?"

"Maybe later," Anija said. She glanced at the shadowy column rising out of the Forgotten Temple. "For now, I think we have more pressing issues to deal with."

"I assume your mages are not responsible for that?"

"Probably not," Anija said. "So if you and your friends can keep the bad guys at bay, we're—"

A loud *boom* suddenly interrupted Anija. The sound came from the battlefield behind the village. More specifically, it came from one of the zeppelins, which was on fire.

The zeppelin tilted and turned in the air, but there was no stopping its descent toward the ground below. Dozens of demonic bats emerged from within, shooting up into the sky to attack the remaining zeppelins with frenzied screams.

The other Glacian zeppelins switched targets from the remnants of the second army to the creatures. Odd-looking cannons emerged from the carriages, firing streams of ice and fire.

Anija gripped Rialo's reins tightly. "If you need help—"

Dedeket waved a hand dismissively. "Please. Glacian zeppelins alone took down the entire Sky Kingdom of the flock by themselves. I think we can handle a few demons. Deal with your own problems."

Anija had no idea what this 'Sky Kingdom' was but decided not to argue further.

Instead, Anija directed Rialo toward the Forgotten Temple, hoping to stop whatever was going on inside it before it was too late.

Chapter Thirty-Six

THE BURST OF ENERGY FROM SHALLA'S SACRIFICE SENT A powerful wave that knocked Fralia off her feet.

Shalla stood above the now dead Mizromi, cackling like a witch. Her glasses reflected the light from the energy pulsing up through the shadow column, giving her an otherworldly look that made Fralia shiver.

"It's done!" Shalla screamed in pure joy. "He has risen again! The Nameless One has returned and no one can stop him!"

Fralia did not know for sure if Shalla was correct, although she did feel a sudden shift in the energy of the world, as if something distinctly unnatural had just happened.

But Fralia put aside those feelings to struggle to her feet. She would worry about the Nameless One later. For now, she needed to stop Shalla.

Raising her hands again, Fralia suddenly heard a hissing sound and looked to her left in time to see the open fanged mouth of one of the demonic serpents lunging at her. Fralia immediately blasted it in the mouth, sending the demon flying away from her into a nearby wall.

That demon was far from the only one to have recovered, however. The other demonic serpents, seemingly having gained a second wind, surged toward Fralia, jaws snapping wildly. It took all of Fralia's magical skills just to keep them at bay, blasting them away with concentrated airbursts, but they never stayed down for long and Fralia knew it wouldn't be long before they overwhelmed her and got through.

Need to get closer to Shalla. I might not be able to stop whatever she just unleashed, but I can at least stop her.

That was when a crazy idea occurred to her. It was the sort of insane idea she normally associated with Hal or Anija, the daredevils on the council, but given how their crazy schemes always seemed to work out one way or another, she decided to give it a shot.

Gathering her moulash, Fralia thrust her hands down and jumped, unleashing a powerful blast that sent her flying through the air. Flying was not possible except for the strongest air mages. But Fralia had studied the magic of flying back in the academy and so knew a bit about the basics.

Which helped her crash into Shalla.

The two women went tumbling down onto the altar. Fralia grabbed at Shalla's necklace, attempting to remove it, but Shalla caught Fralia's wrist with surprising strength and yanked it away.

Then Shalla slammed her elbow into Fralia's face,

making her head spin, and a second later Fralia found herself pinned underneath Shalla, who held her wrists down.

Shalla's normally pristine hair was now messy, partially covering her face. It did nothing to hide the absolute insanity in her eyes, which gleamed with a faint red hue that made Fralia feel sick.

"You still struggle," said Shalla in a harsh voice, "despite knowing that you have lost."

"Because I know Father would never want you to do this."

Slap.

Fralia's head spun from the impact of Shalla's hand. She was honestly surprised by how hard Shalla could hit. The mousy-looking assistant certainly didn't look that strong.

"Don't you dare mention General Kolass, murderer," Shalla snarled. "Even if he was your father. I loved him more than anyone else, and you took him away from me!"

Fralia stared into Shalla's eyes defiantly. "No, I didn't."

Shalla screamed. She picked up a piece of rock nearby that might have once been a part of the ceiling and raised it over her head.

But then a loud dragon roar filled the Forgotten Temple.

Anija and Rialo stood in the entrance. Both looked like they'd been through hell and back. The demonic serpents turned their attention toward the two, snapping their jaws.

"You know," Anija said, scratching her chin, "I don't really know what is going on here, but between the snakes, the big shadow, and what looks like attempted murder, I don't like it. Do you, Rialo?"

"Nope," Rialo agreed. "Let's fix it."

"Snakes!" Shalla screamed. "Attack!"

The demonic serpents obliged, hurtling themselves toward Anija and Rialo with frightening speed. Fralia wanted to scream at Anija and Rialo to look out, but as it turned out, she was warning the wrong people.

She should have warned the demons.

Rialo opened her mouth and spewed what looked like a river of fire, consuming the snakes in an instant. The demons' cries vanished as their ghostly pale forms disappeared.

That was Fralia's moment to strike.

She shoved Shalla off her. Rising to her feet, Fralia thrust her hand forward, sending a wind blast that knocked the rock out of Shalla's hand. "Don't move. Or I'll do a lot worse than disarm you."

Shalla looked at Fralia defiantly. Her glasses, cracked heavily now, hung off her face crookedly, though she did not seem to care. "Kill me, then."

Fralia balled her hand into a fist. She drew away the air from Shalla's lungs, causing her to gasp and reach out before collapsing onto the floor.

Fralia scowled. "I didn't kill my father. And I am not going to kill you."

She unclenched her fist, returning Shalla's air.

The sound of heavy footsteps behind her made Fralia look over her shoulder. Anija and Rialo were approaching the altar, walking over the ash-covered floor of the Forgotten Temple. It took Fralia a moment to realize that those were the ashes of the serpent demons, which had clearly been incinerated by Rialo's flames.

"Fralia, are you okay?" asked Anija as she and Rialo approached. She glanced at Shalla. "Is she dead?"

Fralia shook her head. "No. Unconscious. I took her air from her lungs. She'll recover eventually."

"Shalla's fate concerns me far less than what happened to my uncle," said Rialo, staring at Mizromi's corpse. "Is he—?"

Fralia bowed her head. "He's dead. Shalla sacrificed him to bring back the Nameless One. I tried to stop her, but I wasn't fast enough."

"The Nameless One?" Anija repeated. She looked up at the shadow column rising through the ceiling. "Does that mean he's back?"

Fralia shrugged. "Shalla seemed to think so, but I don't know for sure."

"We must stop him," said Rialo, glaring at the shadow column rising from Mizromi's head. "For Mizromi's sake and the sake of the kingdom itself."

"But how?" asked Anija, folding her arms in front of her chest, gazing at the shadow column with a troubled expression. "The Nameless One is all the way back in the castle, right? No way we can travel that far. Even if we did, I'm not sure we can kill him."

Anija raised a lot of good points, Fralia thought, points that she did not immediately have good responses to. She knew how important it was to stop the Nameless

One, but if he really had returned, then there wasn't much they could do about it.

And in that case, it doesn't matter if we defeat the Malarsan Army or not, Fralia observed. *If the Nameless One is back, then we failed. Totally.*

Just before Fralia could give in to despair, however, she saw something flicker in the shadow column. She stepped forward and peered more closely.

At first, she simply saw the strange shadowy-purple darkness that rose up into the sky. But the longer she stared, the clearer the image appeared. Two figures.

Fralia gasped. "Hal!"

That was who Fralia saw in the image. Hal was being held by his neck by a monstrous demon she had never seen before. The demon looked bigger and stronger than any other demon that Fralia had witnessed before, save for the necrodragon, making her realize that she was staring at the Nameless One himself.

"You see Hal in there?" Anija said in disbelief. "Are you sure?"

"Y-Yes," Fralia said, her voice faltering somewhat in disbelief. "It's him. He's being killed by the Nameless One."

Rialo growled. "Then we must go to his aid."

"I don't think we can," Fralia said, shaking her head. "Like Anija said, he's too far away for us to help directly."

"But we have to help him *somehow*, don't we?" Anija said. "I'm not a fan of standing around feeling powerless if I can avoid it."

Fralia frowned. She wanted to help Hal, too, but she

didn't see how. It seemed like all they could do was watch as the Nameless One finished off Hal in a gruesome display of strength and power.

Then Fralia noticed Hal's relic hanging from Anija's belt and how Hal himself was not wearing it. She recalled something Old Snow had told her not long ago, about how a Rider's relic always returned to them no matter where they might be.

Without even asking Anija for permission, Fralia yanked the relic off of her belt and threw it into the image before her. The relic spun until it vanished. The column briefly shone gold before returning to its original dark color.

"Fralia!" Anija said indignantly. "The hell did you do that for? That was Hal's relic!"

"I know," Fralia said, holding up her hands. "But I think Hal needs it far, far more than we do."

"Do you think it will be transported to him somehow through the shadow column?" asked Rialo doubtfully.

Fralia shrugged. "Maybe. I just have a feeling. That's all."

Please let it work. Fralia gazed at the image of Hal and the Nameless One in the column. *Do it, Hal. For the Dragon Riders, for Malarsan, for the dragons and for me.*

Chapter Thirty-Seven

IF HAL HAD HAD THE TIME, HE WOULD HAVE FOUND THE sensation of losing his soul unique.

It wasn't strictly *physical* pain he felt, aside from the discomfort of being held up by his neck by the Nameless One.

No. It felt as if his very self was being ripped apart piece by piece. His memories, his thoughts, his hopes and fears, his personality, his sense of self was being eaten away like a fine garment exposed to a hoard of hungry moths.

Even worse, Hal could feel the Nameless One enjoying eating him. It was part sadistic pleasure at killing one of his hated enemies, part enjoying a good meal he hadn't eaten in a very long time.

Indeed, that was probably why Hal had not yet died. The Nameless One was taking his time, and Hal was going to be conscious for every damn second of it.

Naturally, Hal tried to resist, but having never faced an attack on his soul, he wasn't quite sure how to stop it. Physically, he was no match for the Nameless One, and he didn't have the mental power to fight back, either.

Do not fight. The Nameless One's cold voice swept through his mind, like a cold front after a hot summer day. *Feel the pain, the despair. Know your loss, and know that you never stood a chance against me, even in death …*

It was hard to argue with those words. They sounded so calm, so logical. Resisting did indeed seem pointless. Perhaps giving in to the despair and letting nonexistence take him would be preferable to the seemingly endless torment of having his soul devoured by the Nameless One …

No.

That was not Hal's voice, yet the word reverberated in his skull—in his very soul—as if he himself had said it. Familiar warmth began to fill his body. It wasn't enough to completely counterattack the Nameless One's coldness, but it was enough to give him space to think. He could feel the gnawing icy teeth of the Nameless One on the outside, but the pain was easier to ignore.

Keershan? Hal thought, his mental voice sounding weak even to him. *Is that you?*

Yes, Keershan said, who did not sound much stronger than Hal. *I'm still here. Sorry I didn't reach out to you sooner.*

But I thought you were dead, Hal said in shock. *Didn't Queen Bariwa sacrifice you to resurrect the Nameless One?*

Yes and no, Keershan said. *As it turns out, only my 'dragon energy'—that is, the special power that gives me my abilities—was really needed to finish the ritual. The easiest way to gain access to that energy is by killing the dragon in question, but it is possible to get it without killing a dragon. I believe it is our bond that is keeping me alive. Just as you can draw on my power for yourself, so I can cling to you when I need to. Maybe give us time to think.*

Hal felt the Nameless One's growing pressure against his mind. He didn't know if the Nameless One had realized they were talking yet or not, but he suspected the Nameless One would find out eventually. *We need to stop him. And we can only do that by working together.*

I agree, but we're both so weak, Keershan said. *He can crush us so easily. His power really is beyond anything I've seen before.*

Hal's mind moved quickly. He still didn't quite know what to do, but he knew they had to do *something.* He forced himself to think, to consider everything they'd done up until now, for any hints—any at all—that could help them not merely escape, but put an end to the Nameless One once and for all.

Then it occurred to him. The scene in the crafters' workshop of him and Keershan fighting the Nameless One …

The Final Relic? Keershan questioned doubtfully. *We don't have it. We don't even have the part you had.*

Hal felt the Nameless One's oppressive coldness slam into the bubble of warmth they had created around themselves. *There's no time. Keershan, I need your power. All of it.*

All of it?

Do you trust me or do you not?

I trust you.

Then give it to me. Now!

Even before Hal finished his sentence, he felt heat rush into his soul, dragonfire that burned hotter than any furnace or sun. The heat not merely reinforced the bubble protecting them, but even caused it to expand, to push against the Nameless One's icy influence.

And for the first time ever, Hal felt the Nameless One's surprise.

Opening his eyes in the real world, Hal saw the Nameless One staring at Hal with disbelief in his red eyes.

"You are getting warm," said the Nameless One. "Almost too warm."

Hal narrowed his eyes. He grabbed the Nameless One's forearm and channeled Keershan's dragonfire through both of his hands at once.

Red-hot dragonfire exploded from Hal's palms, enveloping the Nameless One's forearm. The Nameless One roared, dropping Hal to the ground at the same time.

Hal hit the ground at a roll and rushed toward Keershan, whose dying body lay not far away. Hal wrapped both of his arms around Keershan and felt another jolt of power go through him.

Angry hisses and roars suddenly filled the air, which was when Hal became aware that all of the assembled demons were now staring at him with unbridled rage. Even the Dark Priest was making guttural growls that sounded nothing like any human language, red eyes glowing with absolute wrath.

As for the Nameless One, he turned to face Hal and Keershan, still clutching his burned arm. Yet even as Hal watched, he saw the skin on the Nameless One's arm already mending and repairing itself, leaving no sign of the flames that Hal had used on him.

When Hal looked into the Nameless One's eyes, he saw complete and utter wrath.

"I have forgotten what physical pain feels like," said the Nameless One. He gripped his forearm tightly. "But now I remember why I did not like it."

Hal glared defiantly at the Nameless One. "If you didn't want to feel pain, maybe you should have stayed dead. The dead can't feel pain, after all."

The Nameless One chuckled. "True. Which you can confirm for me once I kill you and your pet."

"You seem pretty confident in yourself," Hal said. "How do you know we don't have a trick up our sleeve?"

The Nameless One spread his arms wide. "Look at yourself, Rider. A weak human and his half-dead pet dragon—and not even a fully-grown dragon at that— against a god and his loyal followers. You got in a lucky shot before, but it will take more than a single lucky shot to finish me. And you are not nearly that lucky."

Hal bit his lower lip. He knew that the Nameless One had a point. His odds of success were low, but he was willing to fight. No matter what.

And then something launched out of the shadowy column and landed with a *thunk* on the ground right in front of Hal.

The object's sudden appearance drew the eyes of every single being in the Courtyard to it. Even the

Nameless One stared down at it with confusion in his eyes.

Because it was Hal's relic, smoking slightly, but still very much in one piece.

Hal didn't question where it came from or how it got here.

He didn't even hesitate.

He just grabbed his relic and, in one smooth motion, placed it on his head and did the straps.

As soon as Hal secured the relic, he felt his and Keershan's bond strengthen. More warmth flowed through him, giving his joints strength they'd never felt before.

But it was not just a one-way street. Hal shared some of his strength and vitality with Keershan, channeling it through their bond, deliberately seeking to do to Keershan what Keershan had done to him.

It was working. The wounds on Keershan's body began to close up. Cracked scales repaired themselves, gashes closed, and blood was cleaned away. He even started to smell better, too, like he'd just taken a refreshing bath in cool, clean water.

Keershan's eyes snapped open, full of new vitality, and even glowing. The dragon rose to his feet, causing Hal to step back from him.

"Keershan …" Hal said, tears in his eyes. "It worked."

Keershan smiled at him. "It did. But it's not over yet."

Hal knew what Keershan meant. Their bond was now stronger than ever, so he climbed onto Keershan's back. Now that they were physically touching, Hal felt even more power—pure light—traveling up and down their bond, unlike anything he'd felt before. Their bodies even began to glow with white light, causing the watching demons to hiss and cover their eyes or turn away to protect their vision.

The Nameless One eyed Hal and Keershan with a mixture of trepidation and humor. "So you have managed to heal yourself. You are still as weak as ever."

Hal looked the Nameless One straight in the eyes without any fear or hesitation. "We are *not* weak."

With that pronouncement, the light radiating from Hal and Keershan's bodies exploded. Hal found himself and Keershan encased in pure illumination, which obscured everything from view. He could hear, however, the agonizing cries of pain from the nearby demons and even heard the Nameless One himself curse in an ancient language he did not understand.

But Hal didn't care. He just felt the warmth and purity of the light washing over them. Armor—made of gold and crystal—formed along his body, covering him from head to toe. In his right hand, a sword with a golden hilt and crystallized blade appeared from the light, shining as bright as the sun.

With a yell, Hal raised the sword into the air, causing the light surrounding them to dim, though not vanish entirely.

Hal could now see the Courtyard again. Most of the demons had retreated at the sight of Hal and Keershan's new armor and weapons. Even the Dark Priest had left the ritual circle, fear covering every inch of his demonic face.

The Nameless One took a very small, almost imperceptible step backward.

"Never in my ancient life have I sensed this sort of power," said the Nameless One. "No, not since my brothers and sisters kicked me out of the heavens."

Hal looked at Keershan. Like himself, Keershan was also clad in gold and crystal armor. He even looked a little bigger, as if he'd somehow grown as well.

Gazing up at the Nameless One again, Hal pointed his sword at him. "This is the power of the Final Relic, Nameless One. The power that I had this entire time, yet didn't even know until now."

"Impossible," said the Nameless One. "The Final Relic was hidden under the Castle near my body."

Hal shook his head. "That was a lie. In reality, the Final Relic—the *whole* Final Relic, helmet and armor and all—was with me the whole time, right on my head."

Hal gestured at his relic. "When Old Snow fled Castle Lamor, he took the Final Relic with him. He pretended it was not the Final Relic, but only to protect it from your followers or people who wanted it for its power alone. He was just waiting for the right moment, the right people to give it to. And Keershan and I are the right people."

The Nameless One sneered. "So what? Even if you have the Final Relic, your power is still nothing compared to mine. I am a god."

"*Were* a god," Keershan corrected. "If you were a god now, you wouldn't even be in this situation. You wouldn't be able to be killed."

The Nameless One's hands balled into fists. "Mortal

arrogance never ceases to amaze me. Despite everything you have seen, you still think you can fight me."

Hal raised his sword. "We don't just *think* we can fight you, Nameless One. We *know* we can."

With that, Keershan suddenly spread his wings and launched toward the Nameless One. The Nameless One raised his hand, summoning a wall of pure shadow in front of him.

Such a wall might have stopped them before.

But the Nameless One *still* didn't know their full power.

White fire blazed into existence along Hal's blade and Keershan's claws. With a roar, Keershan tore through the wall with ease, revealing the shocked face of the Nameless One.

And with a yell of his own, Hal stabbed his sword straight through the Nameless One's heart.

The Nameless One screamed as Hal's sword embedded itself in his chest, tearing through his flesh. Black blood flowed onto Hal's hand, but he thrust the sword in deeper and deeper until it pierced the other side.

Then, drawing on Keershan's dragon strength, Hal lifted the demon's body over his head. The Nameless One gasped, his eyes locked onto Hal's.

"If you think this is the end …" the Nameless One coughed. "You have no idea how foolish you are …"

Hal simply gazed into the Nameless One's eyes and said one word.

"Burn."

The sword erupted into a column of white flame that

completely incinerated the Nameless One. He didn't even get a chance to scream as the fire grew bigger and brighter until Hal could feel him no longer.

Then Hal cut off the flames, staring into the night sky, the stars shimmering with hope.

Chapter Thirty-Eight

ASHES FROM THE NAMELESS ONE'S BODY SLOWLY descended on Hal like black snow. The ashes burned wherever they touched, but the energy flowing through his body eased the pain.

"We did it," Keershan said in a voice that did not entirely hide the disbelief in his words. "He's dead. The Nameless One is gone. For good."

Hal agreed. He didn't quite know how he knew that, but on a deep, instinctive level, Hal knew that Keershan spoke the truth. The shadow column had vanished as well, providing another hint of the Nameless One's demise.

Then Hal looked around the Courtyard at the other demons. Most appeared to be dead already. The hell-hounds, in particular, seemed to be struggling to maintain their physical forms, hacking and coughing. Shrieks of terror escaped the lips of the guards as their physical forms disintegrated into piles of ash.

"Why are they all dying?"

Keershan wore a thoughtful expression. "I once read something that said that demons can only exist in the physical plane on two conditions. One is that the person who summoned them stays alive. The other is if the Nameless One wills them into existence."

"And with both Queen Bariwa and the Nameless One dead, then that means there's no one to keep the demons alive anymore," Hal said in realization. He smiled. "We really *did* do it."

"Don't count your chickens just yet," said a familiar demonic voice behind them, "to use a human term."

Hal and Keershan turned.

The Dark Priest stood underneath the balcony, two long blades in his hands. The blades glowed with dark energy and were pointed at where Old Snow lay at his feet. The Dark Priest's eyes were twitching with madness.

"You're still alive," Hal said in disgust. "You know you can't win."

"I know," said the Dark Priest. Pieces of his skin were starting to chip off. He raised his sword. "But I can at least take your mentor with me."

The Dark Priest raised his sword and plunged it into Old Snow's chest …

Only for Tremas' hand to come out of nowhere and catch his wrist.

The Dark Priest cried out in pain, looking at Tremas, who stood next to him. She looked stronger than before, her wood-like skin a soft green color while her eyes glowed as blue as water.

"Cursed tree spirit," the Dark Priest spat, "this isn't your war. You have no business being here."

Tremas cocked her head to the side. "On the contrary, you made this my war as soon as you brought back your vile god. We tree spirits recall how the Nameless One attempted to burn down our forests the first time he was alive. We do not want that to happen again."

Tremas raised the Dark Priest overhead, extra tree limbs grabbing him. The Dark Priest fought violently against her grasp.

"Struggle all you like," said Tremas. "But without your god to protect you, you are nothing more than a pale shade ready to be wiped out by soft candlelight."

Green energy began pulsing up Tremas' limbs into the Dark Priest's body. He struggled, but it was no use.

Before Hal's startled eyes, the Dark Priest shrank more and more, until soon he was no longer visible. Tremas brought her hand close to her chest, her extra arms retracting into her body.

"What did you just do to him?" asked Keershan in horror.

Tremas shot them a rather eerie smile. "I turned him into a seed. He will make an excellent addition to my garden, although I doubt he will grow very big."

Hal made a mental note to never mess with a tree spirit.

Old Snow sat up, a dazed look on his face. "Is it over?" His eyes fell on Hal and Keershan and a big smile spread across his lips. "I knew it. I knew you could do it."

"You knew that we'd find the entire Final Relic," Hal

said. He gestured at the armor on his body. "Because we had it the entire time."

Old Snow nodded, a satisfied smile on his lips. "Yes. For a while there, I worried that you might not realize it."

"Why didn't you just tell us from the start?" asked Keershan. "That would have saved us a lot of heartache and headaches."

Old Snow slowly rose to his feet with help from Tremas. "Because I wasn't entirely sure myself. I could have been wrong, and I didn't want to raise your hopes if that was the case."

Hal perhaps should have been annoyed with Old Snow, but in truth, he wasn't. He was just happy that they were alive.

"What do we do now?" asked Keershan. He glanced over his shoulder. "If Queen Bariwa is dead, then who will lead the kingdom in her absence?"

Old Snow walked over to the pile of dust that had once been Queen Bariwa and picked up her crown. Turning it over in his hands, Old Snow said, "I should. I was once the king of Malarsan, after all. I am sure that most of the people and the Nobles will accept me as their new ruler."

"Most?" Hal questioned.

Old Snow glanced over his shoulder at Hal with a serious expression. "Some—perhaps many—were loyal to Marial. Still, I think I should be able to win them over, especially once I explain everything that happened."

Hal noted a hint of doubt in Old Snow's voice but did not press the subject. He trusted that Old Snow knew politics better than him.

"We should contact the other Dragon Riders and Steeds," Keershan said. "Tell them that we won."

Hal nodded. "Old Snow, will you come with us?"

Old Snow shook his head. "Not yet. I need to stay here and get everything in order. With Marial's demise, there is a lot of work to be done."

"Back to the Dark Forest for me," Tremas added. She bounced the tiny black seed in her hand. "With the demons gone, I have no further reason to be here. But I do wish you good luck with the reconstruction process. I suspect you will need it."

Hal sighed, thinking about his father and everything that had happened recently.

I hope I did you proud, Father. I avenged you and saved the kingdom. And, most importantly, I saved Mom.

Chapter Thirty-Nine

A MONTH LATER, HAL SAT AT THE HEAD OF THE COUNCIL table in the Forgotten Temple, the helmet of the Final Relic resting in his lap.

To his left sat Fralia, who wore nice new green robes that indicated her new status as an archmage. To his right sat Anija, clad in shiny new armor that made her look like a true warrior. Surrels, also wearing new armor, sat across from Hal alongside Old Snow and Wilme. And Rialo and Keershan sat not far away.

"Reports from the council?" Hal said. Due to their busy schedules, it felt like they had not met in forever.

Old Snow spoke first. "I have made great progress in winning over the Nobles to my side. Most have already agreed to recognize my kingship, although I am still in negotiations with many of them. Only a handful continue to oppose my rule, though they are rather loud."

"What about the rest of the kingdom?" asked Surrels. "Any rebellions needing to be put down?"

"No. Marial was a brutal ruler who wasn't very popular anyway. The people seem to prefer me already. It helps that I gave Marial a public funeral and have not given her supporters any reason to hate me."

Hal nodded. He had attended the funeral along with the other council members, despite his hatred of Queen Bariwa. It was necessary for political purposes that the new leaders of Malarsan showed up and paid her their respects, or so Old Snow said. It helped that the council had agreed not to reveal the truth behind Queen Bariwa's death, blaming it on the Dark Tigers, with her will specifying Old Snow as her proper successor.

Then Hal looked at Fralia. "How are the mages?"

"All of the major guilds and the academy itself support Old Snow's regime," Fralia replied. "Oh, and Emperor Kryo Kardia has sent aid to Malarsan to help with the rebuilding process with promise of even more to come in the next six months. He is also intending to visit the kingdom at some point too."

That was good to hear. Hal had been worried about how their alliance with the Glaci Empire would go once Queen Bariwa was out of the picture. Thus far, Emperor Kryo Kardia had respected the kingdom's sovereignty.

Not thrilled about that visit, though. But hopefully Old Snow will be able to handle him.

"Militarily, I am happy to announce that I am now the new general of the Malarsan Army," Surrels said. He sat up and brushed off his new armor. "General Mokoa has been imprisoned for her war crimes, and I am currently in the process of selecting three new Generals to aid in the rebuilding of the military."

"What about the Black Soldiers?" asked Fralia.

Surrels frowned deeply. "I've disbanded them entirely. I am also working with mages to have them restore the memories of the Black Soldiers who want to remember. Including myself."

Hal was tempted to ask Surrels if he remembered his family yet but sensed that Surrels was still working on it.

Changing the subject, Hal said, "Good to hear. But how is the army working with the Dragon Rider Corps? Any issues?"

"Not so far," Anija gestured at Wilme. "We've bonded over three dozen new pairs in the last month alone and are thinking of opening a Dragon Rider school soon. Right here in the Tops, though not sure when or where exactly. We're still ironing out the details."

"But it *is* coming," Wilme said. "It's just that finding qualified teachers is hard."

Hal nodded. "I'm more than happy to help teach the next generation of Dragon Riders."

"Yes, I know," said Wilme. "It does help that we retrieved the lost relics that Hanok the demon had stolen before the Battle of the Tops last month."

"Where did you guys find them?" Surrels asked.

"In a cave not too far from the village," Anija explained. "We think he put them there until he could take them back to Castle Lamor, which obviously didn't happen."

"We also have access to the other hundreds of relics that Queen Bariwa had yet to use," Wilme said.

"Reports on the Clawfoots?"

"We are in the process of moving back to Dragon Valley," said Rialo. "I anticipate we will finish moving all of the refugees back home in about three months, not counting the ones who choose to bond with humans and become their Steeds. We have also freed all of the slaves and given their relics to the Dragon Riders to use to make *willing* Steeds, instead of brainwashed ones."

That was a relief. Hal had been slightly worried about how the dragons would feel about having been temporarily enslaved by the Malarsans. It sounded like they weren't as upset as he'd feared. He knew that giving Dragon Valley back to the Clawfoot Clan would help and hoped that it would lead to closer alliances in the future.

"And I can confirm that the History Hunters are pretty happy about their new jobs of preserving whatever remaining historical knowledge we can find," Keershan added. "Already we've recovered quite a bit about the pre-Fall Dragon Riders, and I am confident we will keep finding more."

That was even better to hear. With the Relic Hunter Corps no longer necessary for stealing relics, Hal had decided to retool the organization into a group dedicated to finding and preserving Malarsan's ancient history, renaming it the History Hunter Guild. Technically speaking, both he and Keershan were in charge of it, though in practice, Keershan did more of the day-to-day work due to his unique interest in ancient history.

"The only issue is that Jaspus escaped during the Battle of the Tops," Rialo said with a sour expression on her face. "He may have fled the kingdom to avoid getting imprisoned for betraying the clan."

"But we're keeping an eye out for him," Keershan said. "So if Jaspus does show up again, we'll make sure he gets what he deserves."

"All of these reports sound very good," Hal said, clapping his hands together. "Any demonic sightings?"

"None whatsoever," Surrels said.

"Knowing how sneaky those demon bastards are, I wouldn't put it past any survivors to try something." Anija added.

"Let them," Hal said confidently. "With the Malarsans and Clawfoots united as one, even the Nameless One couldn't stop us now."

"What about you, Hal?" asked Old Snow. "Do *you* have anything to report?"

"Just that I am in the process of rebuilding Lamb's Hand, though I don't expect to finish for a long time."

Surrels whistled. "Rebuilding an ash town. Never thought I'd see anyone try that."

Hal shrugged. "Now that the Dragon War is over, I'd say we've entered a new era in Malarsan history. If humans and dragons can be friends, then we can easily rebuild. Plus, my mother doesn't want to live anywhere else."

Hal genuinely believed in that idea. Now that they controlled Malarsan, Hal fully intended to rebuild the kingdom, and the best place to start with, in his opinion, was the long-abandoned ash towns. Already, he'd received a lot of applications from people all over the kingdom willing to move to these rebuilt towns, hoping to make a new life for themselves and their families. Even more surprisingly, people were willing to work and provide their skills and knowledge to bring these towns back to life.

Which is good, because it's going to take real work to make these places habitable for humans again. It's what dad would have wanted.

That was true. After several long discussions with his mother—who was currently living in a tent in Lamb's Hand despite Hal telling her she could live in Mysteria or even the capital if she wanted—Hal realized that his late father would want him to do this. He even planned to rename Lamb's Hand to Jamas Town in honor of his deceased father.

Pushing that thought out of his mind for now, Hal looked around the table at the other council members again. "Has everyone finished giving their reports?"

Everyone nodded at that, prompting Hal to say, "All right, everyone. We have a kingdom to rebuild. Let's get to it."

Grab the next book in The Lost Riders: Dragon Uprising.

The Nameless One has been defeated. Now they must rebuild.

Having defeated the Nameless One, Hal and the others have gone their separate ways to help with the rebuilding effort.

Not all are pleased with what has come to pass.

When allies become enemies, all must choose a side —even dragons.

War has come, and this time both sides fight with the power of the riders.

Series by Jasper Alden

The Lost Riders

Made in United States
Troutdale, OR
04/19/2024

19293416R00202